David Shepherd ... Lancaster. He w... and at ...
After University, he was a probation... ...
West Lothian and a student at the Episcopal Theological
College in Edinburgh. He was Chaplain of St Paul's
Cathedral, Dundee and Anglican Chaplain
in the University of Dundee.
He is now Rector of St Mary Magdalene's
Church in Dundee.

Eleven detective novels have now been published.
In chronological order, they are:

WHO KILLED SOPHIE JACK?
MURDER WITHIN TENT
A MISHAP IN MAJORCA
A CHRISTMAS CRACKER
A PROSPECT OF RYE
SLAUGHTER AT THE POLLS
MURDER ON THE MALLAIG EXPRESS
BURIED IN BAPTISM
THE BURNS SUPPER MURDER
FROZEN IN NICE
THE PUDDLEDUCK AFFAIR

Copies are available from:

**Meadowside Publications
14 Albany Terrace,
Dundee DD3 6HR
Telephone: 01382 223510**

THE PUDDLEDUCK AFFAIR

A DETECTIVE NOVEL
BY
DAVID SHEPHERD

MEADOWSIDE PUBLICATIONS
DUNDEE
2012

Meadowside Publications
14 Albany Terrace, Dundee DD3 6HR

© *Meadowside Publications 2012*

Printed by
Robertson Printers,
Forfar

The characters portrayed in this novel are all imaginary and bear no intended resemblance to any person alive or dead.

ISBN 978-0-9574915-0-2

All rights reserved.

No reproduction, copy or transmission of this publication may be made without written permission. No paragraph of this publication may be reproduced, copied or transmitted save under the terms of any licence permitting limited copying issued by the Copyright Licensing Agency, 33-34 Alfred Place, London WC1E 7PA

Meadowside Crime
is a © imprint of
Meadowside Publications,
Dundee

Contents

1. Smoke Gets In Your Eyes 7
2. Slow Train 9
3. A Dead Duck? 13
4. Keep The Homes Fires Burning 16
5. The *Railway Inn* 24
6. Brief Encounter 37
7. A Treasurer's Lot 47
8. A Ticket to Ride? 51
9. The Rottweilers Pounce 59
10. The Runaway Train 63
11. Fire Below 67
12. *In Vino Veritas* 75
13. Go Gently Into That Dark Night 83
14. We're Watching You! 88
15. Sunday Lunch 92
16. Dicing With Death 97
17. A Marked Man 103
18. Battered But Not Beaten 108
19. Ladies' Day 111
20. The Enemy Within 123
21. The Welsh Letter 128
22. A Broken Reed 133
23. A Silent Witness? 138
24. The Unwanted Guest 141
25. All Creatures Great And Small 146
26. Friend Or Foe? 150
27. A Quantum Of Wickedness 154
28. The Green Goddess 170
29. Pandora's Box 177
30. Dead Men Tell No Tales 183
31. Red For Danger 189
32. A Bullet Train? 193
33. Ladies Of The Night 204
34. Daybreak Express 212

35. On Guard!	223
36. Bush Telegraph	228
37. Hot Mail	233
38. Morning Glory	238
39. *Veniente Occurite Morbo*	246
40. No Whistle-blowers Here	257
41. Tunnel Vision	260
42. The Last Victim	271

*The story is set on the Pwddldwc Railway
on the west coast of Wales,
between April and June 1990.*

1: Smoke Gets In Your Eyes

It was over coffee that Detective-Inspector Raynes received an unexpected invitation.

He was a guest of the Grasshallows Rotary Club at their March meeting. Knowing that the Rotary met at *The Green Man*, he had anticipated a fine lunch before he delivered his talk on "The Perils of Policing". But the lunch had been a poor one – the wine cheap and nasty. Come to that, his speech had not been that much better. But at least the coffee was good. And as his host poured him a second cup, he said:

"I hear that you're a bit of a railway buff, Inspector?"

"I don't admit to it."

Tom Hayward smiled.

"I heard you talking to Harry Dugdale about the old station in Grasshallows."

Raynes nodded

"Yes. I was pointing out that picture in the passageway. I used to look at it every day when I was staying here. Such a fine building. It's a great shame it was ever pulled down. I was wondering if it could be rebuilt . . . And whether someone could buy up an old LNER L1 and a couple of carriages. It could be quite a tourist attraction."

Tom smiled more broadly.

"No one but a railway buff would ever have heard of an old LNER L1. Nor that they used to operate on our local line."

Raynes admitted that he had read O.S. Nock's famous book on the branch lines of England.

"But why read the book when you can do the real thing?"

Tom looked at their fellow diners to make sure no one was listening. He spoke with his hand to his mouth in case there were any lip-readers present.

"I'm actually a member of the Puddleduck Railway Preservation Society."

"Never heard of it," said Raynes.

"It's in Wales. I go there most weekends during the

summer. I'm a fireman. I find it highly therapeutic."

Raynes was amazed that the proprietor and publisher of the *Grasshallows Echo* should admit to such a humble occupation.

A distant look came into the older man's eyes.

"We've just restored our third locomotive. A little saddle tank: *Lady Ermintrude*. She's a real beauty."

"That must have cost you a packet!"

"Well, she wasn't cheap. But we received many generous donations. It's really quite a successful little business. We made a profit of £8000 last year – even after re-laying half a mile of track. Of course, the chaps give their labour free."

"A labour of love?" murmured Raynes.

"Very much so," said Mr Hayward. "Of course, there are quite a few ladies involved. Wives of members. Daughters. Even the odd widow. They look after the souvenir shop and the tea rooms. There's plenty for them to do."

The Inspector sipped his coffee thoughtfully.

"Might be right up your street?"

"Mine?"

"Come over for the weekend and make yourself useful. You could help in the ticket office or man one of the stations."

Raynes' spirits lifted. So long as he wasn't being asked to push a wheelbarrow, shovel ballast or clean out a firebox, he might just be interested.

"I think I could manage that."

"Well, find yourself a free weekend and I'll take you over. I stay with a Mrs Williams. Wonderful woman! Superb cook! It's worth going there just for the food."

It was an invitation which touched Raynes' heart at a vulnerable point. He had a sudden vision of beef stews, roast duck, syrup puddings. After such a disappointing lunch, a weekend in Wales had an almost mystic charm. He felt an irresistible urge to return to that boyhood world of Hornby Dublo – and the Fat Controller.

Raynes smiled a conspiratorial smile as if he was sharing some disreputable secret.

"I'll look at my diary and let you know."

"You'll enjoy every minute," said Mr Hayward, glad that his fish had risen to the bait. Of course he had his own reasons for inviting the Inspector to join him for a weekend in Wales. But he would not say anything until the Inspector had seen the "Puddleduck" for himself.

2: *Slow Train*

It was on Friday 27th April, two weeks after Easter, that Raynes joined Tom Hayward for his weekend in Wales. They left Grasshallows in the early afternoon and motored westwards for several hours. During the journey, the Inspector was given a brief history of the Pwddldwc Railway.

Like most of the small lines in Wales, it had been built to carry slates down from the quarries to the coast. It had been very busy during the Victorian era but, in the face of two world wars and years of severe depression, trade had declined, the quarries were closed and the line abandoned.

After the Second World War, the revival of the Tal-y-llyn and Ffestiniog lines had shown what could be done to create a first class tourist attraction. But the Puddleduck had seemed an almost hopeless proposition. There was no rolling stock, no locomotives, very little track and not much public interest. Ramblers were the only visitors who made their way up the deserted track.

A new generation of enthusiasts decided to try their hand. Fortunately, they had the backing of a wealthy Birmingham businessman – Walter Greenaway – later Sir Walter. He put up sufficient cash to buy the land and used his professional contacts to obtain sleepers and chunks of rail. There was no need of ballast. The deserted quarries were filled with heaps of stone chips. Sir Walter paid for lorries to transport all this stuff down to Pwddldwc.

Fortunately, the bridges along the line had been solidly built and were still in good condition. But every yard of track had to be dug up and relaid. There were 1760 sleepers to every mile of track and initially fewer than twelve volunteers. Not surprisingly, the locals greeted them with some derision, doubting whether their enthusiasm would last.

They hired two horses – Glyndwr and Dolgellau (Glyn and Dolly) to tow the flat-bed trucks that carried their tools and equipment up the valley. But once they had reached the first milestone, they felt an irresistible urge to purchase a locomotive and make it feel more like a real railway.

The enthusiasts were unwilling to approach Sir Walter for any more money, so a public appeal was launched to buy a Beyer Peacock 2-4-0. Several of the enthusiasts increased the mortgages on their homes; others dipped into their savings. Five hundred and forty eight members of the general public joined the Pwddldwc Railway Preservation Society and the number of active volunteers increased to forty-three. Sir Walter chipped in £50,000; and, with great excitement, the locomotive was delivered to the station yard and housed in a wooden shed.

Of course, everyone wanted to see the little engine make its maiden run. A couple of tons of coal were delivered. The tanks were filled by hosepipe from a single tap – a long job – especially when it was discovered that one of the tanks was leaking. There was much oiling of bearings and polishing of brass. Even when the locomotive was ready to be fired up, it took several hours to raise enough steam. A slow procession accompanied the train up the track and then back to the station yard. It was clear that they still had much to learn.

Everyone wanted to try their hand in the cab – either as fireman or driver. Inevitably, on one sad afternoon, someone managed to derail the locomotive, which then toppled over on to its side. A crane had to be hired to put *Sir Walter* back on the track – but the local farmer refused to allow the crane to cross his land.

There followed some hard bargaining whilst the engine lay pathetically on its side. It was a desperate moment; but, happily, the Birmingham businessman had deep pockets and the farmer was duly compensated for the damage done to his crops. Thereafter, the Society was very careful who was allowed to drive the train. Such an incident must never happen again.

Gradually, the line advanced up the valley and reached its first natural halt – the ruined castle. It was not much of a castle but the ley lines converging on it were said to be very significant. In time, the castle became less of a ruin and now featured a small cafe. The time had come to carry a few passengers.

Valuable experience had been built up on *Sir Walter* and there was a pressing need for a couple of carriages. The supply of genuinely vintage carriages had long since dried up, so two replicas were built by a job creation scheme in Sunderland and brought over to Wales by road. The carriages were duly attached to the locomotive, a bottle of champagne was burst over the front buffers and, on the last Saturday of June 1972, the line carried its first paying passengers. It was said that the ticket machine had been stolen from Manchester City Transport!

Work continued on the track – soon extended to the spectacular Pistylloed o Idris (The Gushers of Idris). On the way there, the volunteers faced an appalling attack of midges; sheep invaded the line; and the winter rains washed away part of the embankment. But nothing seemed to dampen their enthusiasm. Every weekend, the volunteers poured into the village, often bringing their families with them. Some of them stayed in the local B & Bs; others were in the caravan park; a few brave souls camped out in the fields. The money spent in the local shops was a welcome boost to the rural economy.

By the time they had reached the village at the head of the valley, the railway was attracting almost five hundred visitors every weekend. This put a heavy demand on the Society's resources and it was recognized that a second locomotive and more carriages would have to be bought. To raise enough money for these improvements, the Society decided to become a publicly limited company and issued two million

10p shares which were rapidly snapped up.

At almost the same moment, Sir Walter died, leaving the Society half a million pounds in his will. The will was contested by his nephew who resented the family inheritance being squandered on such childish fantasies; but the case was successfully defended by one of the Society's members, who was an experienced barrister. The nephew had retired with a bloody nose – or, more precisely, a large legal bill. The legacy had helped to pay for major alterations to the station building at Pwddldwc, a signal box and more carriages. In gratitude, the second locomotive was named *Lady Sylvia* after Sir Walter's wife.

By the summer of 1982, there were six trains up and down the valley every Saturday and Sunday. Two of the stations were fully staffed; the other two had such helpers as were available.

The preparation of an effective duty roster was now one of the most vital parts of the railway organization, making sure the railway had a full complement of drivers, firemen, guards, signalmen, ticket collectors, tea ladies, cleaners and maintenance staff. For, in the background, people were still restoring old trucks and carriages, keeping an eye on the track and the station buildings. As Tom Hayward had said, they were now preparing *Lady Ermintrude* for her first run.

"When I'm not being a fireman, I look after the souvenir shop," Tom explained. "We sell books and postcards, tea towels and mugs, toys and pictures. Posters go very well. You'd be amazed how much people spend on such things. Two-thirds of our income comes from sales – not tickets. I also do most of their printing at the *Echo*."

"How many volunteers have you got?"

"About one hundred and twenty. But we can always do with more. Some of us are getting a bit long in the tooth. We need more young blood – particularly tradesmen, builders, engineers – people who are good with their hands. We've been very lucky so far . . . but we need to look ahead." He paused significantly. "The Society depends on its volunteers. If any of them left, we would be very hard hit; we need to work together as a happy team."

3: A Dead Duck?

The way that Tom Hayward spoke gave Raynes the first indication that perhaps all was not well with the little railway.

"It's not all sweetness and light, then?"

"No. I'm afraid not." The older man sighed deeply. "In fact, to be honest, that's why I wanted you to come over. We've got a bit of a problem and I wondered if you might be able to help."

Raynes said nothing.

"Last year, we had a spot of bother. One of the chaps – a friend of mine – had an accident. Run over . . . Had both legs cut off . . . Fell under a carriage . . . Lost a lot of blood – and died. He wasn't found for a couple of days – and that made it worse. Then the newspapers got hold of it. I don't blame them . . . Just doing their job . . . But it was bad publicity.

"The police, of course, were involved. They asked us lots of questions. The whole thing hung over us like a dark cloud. At the inquest, it was declared: 'death by misadventure.' No one else was involved. But . . ." Tom Hayward paused. " . . . But I can't see how he came to be run over by the carriage. They look pretty; but they weigh about ten tons apiece, People said he'd been drinking – whisky. But I can't believe that. Derek wouldn't be so stupid as to be run over.

"We did all we could for his wife. Sent cards and flowers. Went to the funeral. But she was very upset. Derek was devoted to his family. Two boys and a girl. He was the only breadwinner. I sent her a couple of thousand to tide her over. But she just couldn't accept it . . ."

Tom hesitated.

"Couldn't accept that it was an accident?"

"No. She said that Derek wouldn't do anything stupid like that. She's convinced it was murder. And she believes that one of the Society's members did it. Sadly, she didn't keep her thoughts to herself. Everywhere she goes, she tells people: 'My husband was murdered.'

"After the funeral, we thought we'd seen the last of her. But she's made a point of coming over every weekend – making a complete nuisance of herself! I thought that once the season was over, that'd be the end of it. But no. She turned up at the Annual General Meeting in London – and then, when the new season opened, there she was – back at the railway – making everyone thoroughly uncomfortable. She doesn't actually accuse anyone; but we all feel a sort of collective guilt. It's most unpleasant."

"And what would you like me to do?"

"Talk to her. Listen to her story. See if you think there's any truth in it. If there is, I suppose the case will have to be reopened. But after all this time . . ." Tom Hayward shrugged his shoulders. " . . . the scent will be pretty cold." He paused. "But if you feel she's got the wrong end of the stick, perhaps you could have a word with her. Tell her to lay off. It might be better coming from you – a policeman – a complete stranger. I mean, we're all her friends . . . At least, we were."

Raynes felt a small frisson of disappointment. He'd been looking forward to a happy weekend where he could cast off all his professional worries. A boyish escape. And yet, here he was – invited, it seemed, under false pretences – having to deal with a tiresome woman; solve an unlikely murder already thoroughly raked over by the local police. Expectations being raised – and probably dashed. The weekend completely ruined; going home with a deep sense of frustration.

But he kept his thoughts to himself.

"What was the chap's name?"

"Derek Barclay."

"And his wife?"

"Virginia."

"And how long have you known him?"

"At least ten years. Probably more."

"And what did he do on the railway?"

"He was our builder. A very practical man. He put up the signal box. Built the extension to the tea room. At the time of his death, he was restoring the castle."

"A very useful person?"

"Indeed. He was in the building trade, you see. Ran his own business in Wolverhampton. No trouble laying his hands on the slates, bricks, cement, plastic pipes and all the rest. You name it; he would bring it over. When trade was brisk, you'd never see him. But, come a quiet patch – or a recession, he'd be over here every week. He was a fast worker. Did a power of work for the Society – and only charged for the materials."

"He had plenty of friends?"

"Oh, yes. I don't think he had a single enemy. He had a warm, outgoing nature. Always thinking how he could improve things . . ."

"And was he a heavy drinker?"

"No. He was a man who liked a pint. He'd drink a couple of pints . . . Three at the most."

"But not whisky?"

"No."

"So there might be some truth in her story?"

"Well, I didn't think so – to begin with . . ." Tom took a deep breath. "And I still don't. But you just can't put the matter out of your mind. She's always there. Like a ghost which won't go away."

"It could be a domestic problem."

"I doubt it. They always seemed so happy together. When they were first married, they used to come over most weekends. But when the children were born, we didn't see so much of her. But now we can hardly avoid her."

"Who's looking after the children?"

"Heaven knows! Her mother, I suppose. Or Derek's mother. They're probably as glad of a break – just as much as we are."

Raynes could see no obvious solution to the problem. It looked like a dead end. He asked nervously: "How many people know you've invited me to look into this?"

"No one. I've told two or three of the chaps that I was bringing over a friend from Grasshallows; but I haven't told them you're a policeman. And I certainly haven't told Virginia. I suppose when you start asking questions, they'll realize what you are. But I thought anonymity might give you a flying start."

Raynes shook his head.

"I don't think I shall be flying anywhere. This case has all the hallmarks of a dead duck!"

Tom Hayward smiled.

"A Puddleduck?"

Raynes laughed. "Just so. But I'll do what I can."

4: Keep The Home Fires Burning

As Tom had said, the development of the railway had brought increased prosperity to Pwddldwc and the region round about. Every Friday and Saturday night, from April to September, there would be seventy or eighty volunteers staying in or around the village. Some brought caravans or camper vans; but most of the railway enthusiasts had long since established themselves either in the local hotel or with some friendly natives. Tom Hayward invariably stayed with Mrs Williams at No 14 Chapel Road.

Mrs Williams not only provided bed and breakfast but also a very substantial evening meal. Tonight, it was leek and potato soup, jugged hare, followed by apple crumble and ice cream. Having driven all the way from Grasshallows without a single break, Raynes was glad to tuck in.

"She's very reasonable," said Tom. "She only charges twenty pounds a night; but I always give her an extra tenner."

Raynes assumed that the same amount would be expected from him, even though his bedroom was much smaller than the commodious chamber provided for the publisher.

The Inspector soon discovered that there was an additional attraction at No 14 Chapel Road. Mrs Williams had a beautiful daughter, called Emily. In fact, she had four beautiful daughters but the other three were married and now lived in England. She assumed that when Emily had completed her A levels, she too would fly away.

The evening meal was *en famille* with everyone gathered round the dining room table. Emily opened the bottle of claret which Tom had brought and went round filling the glasses. She handed out the bowls of soup and made sure everyone had a couple of slices of homemade brown bread and rolls of fresh farm butter.

Raynes was very conscious of her dark – very dark – bobbed hair, her smooth creamy skin and her black button eyes. She had a slight figure – a maroon jumper covering small breasts and grey jeans encasing slim hips. He also noticed that she only had eyes for Tom Hayward. She seemed to hang upon his every word and responded with quiet smiles.

"Emily's hoping to do Politics at Grasshallows," Tom explained. "If she gets good enough grades, she'll start in October."

Raynes was tempted to ask where she would be staying in Grasshallows; but he thought better of it. The owner of the *Echo* might already have made special arrangements for her; arrangements which her mother knew nothing about.

"I just hope," he said, "that you won't be bringing any of your firebrand politics over to Grasshallows!" He laughed. "Emily's an ardent member of Plaid Cymru. I'm surprised she can tolerate an Englishman eating at her table – let alone two Englishmen staying in her home."

Emily vouchsafed a minx-like smile.

"My grandmother was Welsh," said Raynes. "She was born in Cardiff, I think."

"That redeems you," said Mrs Williams. "What about another bowl of soup?"

The Inspector declined. He had already feasted his eyes on the large casserole of jugged hare. However, he accepted a second glass of wine.

Mrs Williams proceeded to relate all the latest gossip from

the village. The new minister at the Methodist chapel had been seen drinking whisky at a recent wedding. What was the world coming to when even the Methodist ministers were being led astray?

It was rumoured that Mrs Ifor Davies had left her husband again – this time for good. Surely she wouldn't be stupid enough to go back? It was reported – reliably reported – that he had beaten her – pervert that he was!

The accounts of the local Women's Institute had been found to be irregular. It was suspected that Mrs Thomas had been putting her hand in the till to meet all her household debts. Of course everyone knew her husband was a compulsive drinker who kept her short of money. But that was no excuse!

"And how's the railway going?" asked Tom. "Have they tried out *Lady Ermintrude* yet?"

Mrs Williams looked at Emily. It was to be supposed that she knew more about what was happening at the railway.

"No. I heard she'd got a cracked piston rod. They're forging another."

"What a damned shame! They've been working on her all winter. I hope she'll be ready for the Whitsun weekend."

"And that wretched woman's turned up again. I saw her getting out of her car at Jones the postman."

"Oh dear! Not another weekend of it?"

"Is she still going round making those allegations?"

"Does she ever stop?"

Although Raynes had been fully briefed about Mrs Barclay, Tom Hayward made a point of explaining the situation to the newcomer.

"This is the lady – the wife of a member – who lost her husband last year in a tragic accident . . ."

"But she insists it was murder," said Emily. "She won't hold her tongue. She speaks to all the visitors – anyone who enters the tea room. It's so embarrassing. Instead of asking questions about the railway, everyone talks about her husband. It makes us all look so guilty."

Emily had a fine voice. Each word was clearly enunciated but with a strong – even a commanding – Welsh accent.

For the first time, she spoke directly to Raynes:

"You're bound to meet her, so it's as well to be prepared. She'll give you the whole story – chapter and verse."

Raynes wiped his mouth with his napkin.

"But surely the local police have investigated the matter?"

"To be sure they did," said Mrs Williams, "but the coroner said it was death by misadventure. That should have settled it."

"He was run over by one of the carriages," said Tom.

"Had both his legs chopped off," said Emily – with great emphasis on the word chopped.

Raynes smiled.

"I hope he hadn't done anything to offend the Welsh nationalists?" he said.

Emily gave him a sly look.

But perhaps he had? Perhaps she knew more about Derek's death than most? The Welsh were very adept at sussing out the wickedness of others.

"Emily quite liked him," said Mrs Williams. "Didn't you, love? She used to help him with the painting. Covered herself with emulsion."

Her daughter made no comment. Raynes detected a pink glow of embarrassment on her cheeks. It appeared that Emily had known Derek Barclay rather well. In fact, she seemed to have a penchant for the older man.

Mrs Williams spared her daughter any further embarrassment by serving the jugged hare with its rich, dark, chocolate-coloured sauce. This was not something that appeared on the menus of the restaurants which the Inspector normally visited, so it was a rare gastronomic treat. Raynes reckoned that it must have been at least six years since he had last eaten jugged hare. He wondered whether the local butcher might have a few more in stock so that he could take a couple back to Grasshallows.

To Mrs Williams, he said: "Is it a complicated recipe?"

"Lord, no! It's just a question of preparing it in good time. You need to do it about forty-eight hours in advance. Give it plenty of time to soak through. I cut up the pieces; put them in a large bowl with the onions, carrots, garlic, bacon and herbs. Then I cover it with red wine." Mrs Willliams' eyes twinkled. "I always put in a few drops of plum brandy."

"More than a few drops!" said Emily.

"Well, I won a bottle at the Institute's Christmas Draw. No point leaving it hanging around in a cupboard. Use it – that's what I say! I put in a cupful. I think it makes all the difference. You leave it in the fridge till you're ready. Then you transfer it to a large casserole in the oven. I cook it slowly for about three or four hours."

"And can you buy them locally?"

"Well, this one was a gift. But Spence the butcher normally has a couple hanging up in the shop. Are you thinking of trying your hand?"

"Well, if it's quite straightforward, I can probably manage it."

"The hardest part is skinning it and getting it cut up. Mr Spence does it for me. But if you're thinking of doing it, start with the hind legs."

Raynes decided that skinning a hare was probably beyond him. It was much better to enjoy the finished product. He tackled the rich, dark meat with relish. Like his hostess, he was quite sure the plum brandy made all the difference.

"You'll need all your strength tomorrow," said Tom.

"Are you working on the track?" said Emily.

"No. I believe I'm being put in the ticket office."

"A cushy number!"

The publisher jumped to Raynes' defence.

"I want the Inspector to meet as many people as possible."

The Inspector?

Mrs Williams and her daughter looked up in surprise.

Raynes smiled broadly and looked at Tom who clearly had no idea of what he had just said.

"I think you've dropped a bit of a clanger."

"Me?"

"'Inspector . . .'"

Tom Hayward groaned with embarrassment.

"Oh dear! We weren't going to say anything about it. We were going to keep it secret. But I thought Mr Raynes might be able to investigate Mrs Barclay's allegations and see if there was any truth in them . . . He's an Inspector in the Grasshallows police . . . A very able officer," he added patronizingly. "He managed to find out who murdered our new MP when he was killed last year. A brilliant piece of detection."

Emily looked at Raynes with greater interest.

"Have you solved lots of murders?" she asked.

"Quite a few," said Raynes modestly. "But the trail on this one will have gone completely cold after all this time. What is it – a year?"

"Almost."

Mrs Williams seemed to be both pleased and proud to have a real live police inspector in her house.

"Our local bobby isn't up to much," she confided. "He's only got two 'O' levels. But once he came out of the Army, they put him on a training course – and, suddenly, there he was – out on the beat. No one was more surprised than his mother. She thought he'd never do anything in life."

"He's got three children," said Emily maliciously, "so he must have some talent!"

"Why that poor girl married him, I shall never know. Poor Helen! She could have done better for herself."

"Well," said Raynes, "I'm not going to interfere with the local constabulary; but I shall talk to Mrs Barclay . . ."

"You'll be hard put to avoid her!"

" . . . and I shall look at the events surrounding her husband's death. If I find anything vaguely suspicious, then perhaps I shall make a few suggestions. But for the moment, I shall merely be an interested spectator. I'm not allowed to interfere in the work of another police authority."

Raynes neatly side-stepped the fact that time and again

throughout his professional life, he had crossed swords with other police forces the length and breadth of the country as he second-guessed and challenged their conclusions. In this case, if he found the local police had muffed it, he wouldn't hesitate to put the boot in.

"Some more jugged hare . . . Inspector?"

"Yes, please."

Tom Hayward tried to repair the damage caused by his indiscretion.

"I would be very glad if you could both keep quiet about this. It would be better if as little as possible is said about why the Inspector is here. We don't want to upset anyone; and we certainly don't want to give that woman any further ammunition. But I still want to know why Derek died. I feel I owe it to him."

Mrs Williams assured him: "You can be perfectly sure, Mr Hayward, that neither Emily nor I will say a word. Our lips are sealed."

Her daughter placed a second helping of jugged hare on the Inspector's plate. She had a slightly mocking smile on her lips. Raynes doubted her sincerity.

But if there was any public disclosure – any embarrassment – why should he worry? The blame would fall on Tom. He, Raynes, could always walk away from it. He could imagine some of the railway officials being quite annoyed. "Bringing in the police? Behind everyone's backs? Stirring up another hornets' nest?" Yes, It could cause the publisher quite a lot of trouble.

Fortunately, it seemed that the Williams family had a vested interest in keeping quiet. They would not want to lose such a generous guest; someone who was almost a family friend.

During the dessert, the conversation turned to other matters. The recent death of Dolly – one of the two horses which had done all the donkey work in the early days, carting the sleepers and rails up the valley. Thompson the vet had had to put her down. Dolly had been part of the railway's history.

People were wondering how she might by remembered. Something more than a photograph. Perhaps a brass plaque? Derek would have known what to do.

The other subject which seemed to animate Mrs Williams was the delay in treating cancer patients in that remote part of Wales. Some women had had to wait six months before they were seen by a specialist. They had had to go all the way to Bangor or Caerdydd to get a CTI scan. By the time they were seen, their cancer was often much worse. It was a scandal – and no mistake.

"All the more reason for voting for Daffyd Ellis Thomas at the next election!" said Emily triumphantly. The Welsh people would never get a fair deal until they had achieved full independence.

As she spoke, there was fire in her eyes. Strong passions burnt in that small bosom. Tom Hayward was embarrassed, but Raynes admired her spirit.

The publisher declined an offer of coffee. Apparently, it was his custom to go down to the village pub to meet other members of the railway and discuss with them the latest developments. He intended to introduce the Inspector as a member of the business community in Grasshallows. But whether his anonymity would survive a night in the *Railway Inn* . . . Raynes doubted it.

Tom went upstairs to collect his wallet and empty his bladder. Raynes helped Mrs Williams and her daughter clear the table and carried the plates and glasses through to the kitchen.

When her mother was out of hearing, Emily looked the Inspector squarely in the eye.

"I hate policemen."

"English policemen?"

"Any of them."

"And why's that?"

"They arrested my best friend."

Raynes raised his eyebrows.

"What for?"

"For burning down the cottage of a *saesneg*!" She used the official Welsh word for an Englishman. Doubtless, she could have used some sharper epithet – *mochyn* (pig) or *lleidr* (thief) might have been more abusive. But the way she said *saesneg* left no doubt about her bitter feelings. "They gave him two years," she added.

Raynes wondered if she was expecting him to say: "He deserved it." Instead, he said: "Your three sisters are living in England. I don't suppose anyone'll burn down their homes. It's a great pity you can't show us the same courtesy."

Although the rebuke was delivered in a gentle voice, Emily felt the sting of his words. To cover her frustration, she tore the tablecloth off the table and stormed out of the room, slamming the door behind her.

Raynes watched her go – but sadly. It seemed to be the end of what might have been a beautiful relationship.

But who was he kidding?

She hated him.

5: *The Railway Inn*

By the time Raynes and Tom Hayward had reached the *Railway Inn*, the public bar was full. The atmosphere was noisy – mostly chat and laughter. The Inspector was glad that there was no background music which so often made conversation impossible.

His first impression was that it was very much a family gathering; everyone knew everyone else. Even if some were locals and others belonged to the railway, they had long since become good friends.

The publisher steered his way towards the bar. Raynes was pleased to note that it seemed authentic – not an olde-world makey-up supplied by the brewery. The titles of the beer on the pumps were also unfamiliar. It was obviously an independent establishment.

The worn surface of the bar itself, though lovingly polished over the years, suggested that many a wholesome pint had slid across its mahogany surface. Undoubtedly, the slaters and railwaymen of old would have gathered here on a winter's night to drown their sorrows and complain about their boss. "A mean-fisted git – and no mistake . . ."

Tom interrupted his sentimental thoughts.

"Inspector, what will you have?"

Raynes raised his eyes to heaven.

"You've done it again!"

"What? Oh, no!"

"Just call me Richard – or Dick. Don't think of anything else."

Tom Hayward shook his head.

"Twice in one night!"

Raynes looked around.

"I don't think anyone heard you."

"Anyway, what will you have?"

"A whisky. Neat."

As he spoke, he peered over the shoulders of the crowd milling around the bar, trying to get a closer look at the barmaid – a rather feisty, middle-aged woman in a stunning red dress with an exciting cleavage. She had thick dark hair, flashing black eyes, generously enhanced with black eyeliner. She had gold hoops in her ears and an unbelievable collection of gold rings on her fingers. Raynes fancied there was something of the gipsy in her.

Whilst he was considering her generous features, Raynes suddenly became conscious of someone watching him. A thick-set, rough-looking man, standing behind the bar, wiping his hands on a towel. He had noticed the Inspector's lengthy stare. He seemed faintly amused. Raynes gave him a friendly nod and turned away.

"Here's your whisky."

"Thank you."

Raynes took a sip.

"The lady behind the bar seems quite a character."

"That's Anna. She owns the place."

"And the dark, sinister-looking fellow behind her?"

"Black Bob. Her husband. At least, I think he's her husband. I've never asked . . ."

They moved to a less crowded part of the room.

Tom Hayward's method of introduction was to throw out a name, describe the person's role in the railway, their real occupation and their home-town. He would then engage in a little shop-talk – before moving on to the next person. Raynes found the process daunting.

"Hello, Brian! This is Brian Williamson – our chief engineer. This is a friend of mine from Grasshallows – Richard Raynes. Brian works for British Rail – in Crewe. Looks after their electric locos. No romance . . ."

"None whatsoever."

"Is your wife here this weekend? He has a wife and two daughters . . ."

"No. She's taken the week off to go and see her mother."

"I'm sorry to hear about *Lady E*."

"Yes, it is a pity. But I still think we'll have her up and running by Whitsun."

Brian Wilkinson was given no opportunity to speak to the Inspector. They moved on.

"And here's Bill . . . Bill Naylor. Bill's our chief signalman. The signals are all electrically controlled. But we do our best to disguise the fact."

"Progress!" said Mr Naylor, downing the dark remains of some fluid which might have been Guinness.

"Spoils things a bit," said Tom. "But as you say, we have to move with the times." He smiled. "In real life, Bill's a University lecturer. He has a fantastic railway lay-out at home. Keele, isn't it?"

"Nottingham," said Mr Naylor reprovingly. Even amongst the red-bricks, there was a certain hierarchy!

"And this is his wife. Lydia . . ."

A lady in a lilac cat suit – with deep grey eyes.

"She looks after the souvenir shop at Abernirvana, the upper station."

Mrs Naylor gave Tom a slightly frosty look.

"That last set of postcards you gave us – they're not selling at all well. No one's interested in the carriages. You'll have to get some more done of *Lady Sylvia*. They sell like hot cakes."

"You're only saying that because it shows you posing with an oil can beside the front buffers."

"Must have been taken five years ago," said her husband. "They'd never recognize you today!"

"Well, it's still very popular!" said Lydia defensively. "We've only got half a dozen left."

"I'll run off some more this week," Tom promised.

As they moved away, he murmured: "Compulsive show-off!"

Raynes smiled.

"If you've got it, flaunt it. And she obviously does."

"She's a good saleswoman," Tom conceded. "She knows how to rake in the shekels." He turned to his left. "And so does this one."

A small bald-headed man, wearing a pink bow-tie and sporting a neat military-style moustache.

"Our Treasurer, Dr Campbell. Archie's a doctor in Cheltenham. Spends his time buttering up old ladies and persuading them to leave him their money."

The doctor gave Tom a self-deprecating look but did not deny the truth of his statement.

Raynes was informed that this was the person he would be working with in the ticket office the following morning. He could already sense that Dr Campbell was assessing his potential as a donor. Was he the sort of person who would sign a direct debit to the Society? Would it be covenanted? A cool hundred was probably an acceptable starter.

Well, treasurers had to think about such things.

"How are we doing?" Tom asked. "Is the cash pouring in?"

Dr Campbell gave him a cold, contemptuous stare.

"You know perfectly well that we are always in deficit at this time of year. For the first two months, it's spend, spend, spend . . . Later in the season, we begin to recoup our losses."

He touched his moustache nervously. "But it all depends on the weather. People expect it to rain in Wales – and it does; sometimes for days at a time."

The Treasurer was a born pessimist.

"Well, at least you won't have Derek landing you with huge bills for renovating the castle!"

"That is a distinct benefit," said the doctor. "But *Lady Ermintrude* is already costing us a fortune. How many piston rods does a tank engine need?"

Tom Hayward looked around the bar, seeking more congenial company. His eyes lighted on a tall, burly man with a red, shiny face and jet-black hair.

"You must meet our Padre, Father Morris. He comes from some spiky church in Manchester. His bishop is always glad to see the back of him. That gives him plenty of time to come over here. He adds ballast to our proceedings."

The clergyman laughed, showing a fine set of white teeth.

"What Tom means is that I am the man with the wheelbarrow. I've been hard at it for the last two weeks. It's hot work."

Tom grinned.

"I suppose that's a cue for another pint?"

"Well, I never say no. I'm on the Special. The Puddleduck Special." He looked at Raynes. "It used to be called 'rat's piss'; but they've sold a lot more since they changed its name."

The Inspector took a second sip of his whisky. At least it was good stuff. No chance of hiding its pedigree. Straight from the burns of Scotland; distilled to perfection.

Tom ordered another pint for the Reverend and introduced his guest.

"I'm afraid you won't get much mileage out of my friend, Richard. He's an atheist."

"No one's perfect!" Father Morris laughed. "Perhaps, whilst he's here, he will learn the truth of that famous medieval saying: 'Laborare est orare'. To work is to pray. I do a lot of both."

As they moved deeper into the crowd, Tom Hayward said confidentially: "Father Morris also does the Society's newsletter . . . badly! He's been doing it for the last eight years. I've tried to get it off him; but he hangs on like grim death." He sighed. "Everyone complains about it, but no one wants to hurt his feelings. He's such a hard worker . . . And so is this one . . ."

In the far corner, they came across a young couple who were laughing – and giggling – obviously very happy in each other's company.

"What's the big joke?" asked Tom.

"Graeme's just told me a really naughty verse."

"I got it from Charlie."

"Really. I didn't think he had a sense of humour."

"He got it from one of his Communist chums."

Tom turned to Raynes.

"Charlie's one of our guards. Very left wing. Always goes on about workers' rights; but he never charges us a penny. Not even for expenses."

"Bit of a political nutter – but a hard worker," Graeme said approvingly.

"Better a green flag – than a red one!" said Raynes.

Tom clearly felt it was time to introduce the couple.

"This is Graeme Kennedy – the maestro of the track. Keeps the trains running smoothly. And Joanne – his lovely wife, Joanne . . . " Mr Hayward looked down at her with adoring eyes. "She works with Lydia at the upper station. Joanne runs the restaurant. They fight like cat and dog, but they certainly make a great sales team."

Joanne looked more than a little tipsy. She was hanging on to her husband's arm – more to retain her balance than to show any affection.

"I want an early night," she said.

In the corner, beside a blazing fire, an elderly man in a grey tweed suit was sitting beside a solitary glass of lager and lime. He had just lit up his pipe and the sweet smell of Balkan Sobranie was rising from his briar.

"Evening, James."

"Evening, Tom."

"This is Richard Raynes, a friend of mine from Grasshallows. And most people call this gentleman 'Thompson the Vet'."

The elderly man smiled.

"If they get too personal, the bill goes up!"

He seemed to have a rather droll sense of humour.

Tom said: "I was very sad to hear about Dolly. Mrs Williams was telling us that she had had to be put down."

Tears came into the vet's eyes.

"An old friend. Many years of faithful service. I've treated her for many things in her time. But she couldn't stand; she wouldn't eat and she was almost blind. No quality of life at all. The poor soul is better away."

"The end of an era?"

"Very much so."

Tom Hayward turned aside to choose his next victim. Blocking his way was a barrel-shaped woman with large horn-rimmed spectacles. Her hair was short-cropped, so she looked more like a man than a woman.

"This is Mrs Joyce Packer – our catering manager. She does everything from Welsh rarebit to cordon bleu steaks."

Mrs Packer's eyes twinkled behind her spectacles.

"And is this Inspector Raynes?" she asked. "Your friend from Grasshallows?"

Tom Hayward was embarrassed.

"Who told you he was coming?"

"Well, Anna did. She told us all to mind our Ps and Qs and quickly bury any unsightly skeletons that might be lurking around."

Tom looked apologetic.

"I'm sorry about that. We had hoped to keep his occupation a secret. But, yes; this is Inspector Raynes."

Joyce's eyes narrowed.

"Your name rings a bell."

"The Royal Kidnap case?"

"Yes, that was the one! A brilliant piece of detection. They tried to shoot you, didn't they?"

Raynes nodded.

"You'll find it much quieter down here."

Raynes raised his eyebrows.

"Really? I thought you had a tragic death down here – less than twelve months ago?"

"Don't remind me! I have to live with it every weekend!"

Tom nodded.

"That's why I brought Richard down. It was your idea that we should obtain a second opinion. You said that he should decide whether it was an accident or murder."

"Of course it was my idea! The local policeman is brain-dead. And I can't bear that wretched woman endlessly spreading her poisonous views and upsetting all my customers. If she doesn't go soon, there'll be a second murder – and I will accept full responsibility!"

There would be no easy way of getting away from Mrs Joyce Packer.

Tom Hayward said: "What are you drinking?"

"Tequila Sunrise – a double."

Joyce watched Tom heading off to the bar.

"That got rid of him!"

Raynes laughed.

"I notice," he said, "that you referred to a 'second' murder. Does that mean that you think Derek Barclay was murdered?"

"Most certainly. Derek was very safety-conscious. When he was building our new tea room, he was very particular. Proper scaffolding; everyone wearing safety helmets; careful handling of tools and machinery. He had a young man helping him who was completely the opposite. He sacked him on the spot. Everything had to be done properly. You wouldn't catch him on a dark night, wandering round the railway sidings, waiting for his legs to be chopped off!"

Mrs Packer started coughing. Mr Thompson's tobacco smoke was beginning to get to her.

"Let's move away from that wretched man. I can't bear

people smoking in public places. I tell my customers: 'You can smoke on the platform – but not in here.'"

They moved to another corner of the bar and sat down.

"That's better."

Black Bob arrived with the double Tequila Sunrise.

"Mr Hayward's compliments. Would you like another whisky?"

Mrs Packer croaked maliciously.

"Go on. He can afford it."

"Yes, I will."

Mrs Packer took a sip of her exotic drink.

"Now where was I?"

"You were saying why you thought Derek Barclay was murdered."

"Well, it's quite clear. No sensible person is going to put his legs under a moving carriage. I can't believe Derek would have done anything so stupid." She looked at the Inspector. "It was one carriage – not three – that went over him. There were no grizzly bits on the wheels of the other two carriages! So – one carriage. And no train! If there had been a train, there would have been witnesses. So it must have been some other form of locomotion!"

"A lorry?"

"No. A common or garden tractor. There's plenty of them round here. One Massey Ferguson would shift a ten ton carriage. Probably all three."

Mrs Packer was painting a very compelling picture.

"Derek must have been held down – or tied to the rails. The carriage rolled over him. No one would hear his cries. Steadily, all his blood drained out of him. He died. They removed the ropes tying him down. No evidence. Just a dead body."

"So you support Mrs Barclay?"

"No, I don't. I can't stand her moaning voice. She used to be such a happy girl. So full of life. Always laughing. Derek's death has destroyed her. No doubt about it. She's completely unbearable. None of my staff want to work with her. We need to have the truth – quickly – and so does she."

Raynes said: "You have suggested that two people did it. You said 'they'."

"Well, Derek wouldn't have gone willingly to his own death, would he? He must have been tied up – or drugged. There were no other injuries to his body."

"He wasn't laid across the track?"

"No. Otherwise, he'd have had his head chopped off, wouldn't he?"

Raynes said: "You must have thought this out."

Mrs Packer smiled.

"I read a lot of detective stories . . ."

Tom Hayward appeared.

"I wonder if I might spirit Mr Raynes away? I'd like him to meet Mr and Mrs Jacoby."

Mrs Packer immediately took offence. She had clearly expected to have the Inspector with her for the rest of the evening.

She said aggressively: "I can't compete with the big-wigs. I shall have one more Tequila and go to bed."

Tom asked solicitously: "Are you staying at the inn?"

"Of course I am. Where else do you think I'd go? At my time of life, I need comfort. And good food. I've got a beautiful meal waiting for me upstairs. Fresh salmon and smoked trout with asparagus tips. That'll keep me going!"

Tom did not offer to buy her another drink.

Raynes said: "Thank you very much for all your useful information. Perhaps I could speak to you again?"

"Whenever you like."

Tom Hayward apologized for dragging the Inspector away.

"I thought you'd probably had enough of her."

"No. She seemed remarkably clear-headed. She's obviously given a lot of thought to the matter."

"Well, you've got to meet Simon Jacoby. He's the President of the Society. He drives *Lady Sylvia*. I'm his fireman. His wife is called Arlene. Not as dim as she looks!"

Simon Jacoby was – in the immortal words of the

Cambridge Footlights Revue – "a smooth man". Smooth skin; smartly groomed hair; watchful eyes behind rimless spectacles; a dark-blue pin-stripe suit and slim white hands. The President of the Pwddldwc Railway Preservation Society was a distinguished lawyer; a QC with ambitions to become a High Court judge. His sharp eyes surveyed Raynes in a single glance.

"Good evening, Inspector. I'm glad Tom's brought you over from Grasshallows. We shall greatly value your help. We need to resolve this matter once and for all."

Raynes was equally cordial.

"I've heard a great deal about the railway – and its wonderful history. It would be terrible if its reputation were to be tarnished by innuendo and suspicion."

"Precisely. Have you prepared your line of attack?"

"I was only told about the purpose of my visit this afternoon – on the way over. It came as something of a surprise."

Simon cast a reproachful look at his fireman.

Raynes continued: "I shall have to speak to a number of people to find out who was involved. I need to discover all possible motives. The sands of time will have blotted out many useful pieces of information. Unfortunately, my cover has already been blown. So the investigation will have to be conducted in broad daylight."

"Hopefully, it will not be murder."

"I expect to meet Mrs Barclay some time tomorrow."

"You will, Inspector. You will!"

* * * *

The interview was soon over and Raynes was introduced to Arlene Jacoby.

She was a tall, languid woman who conveyed the unmistakable impression that everything was tiresome and boring.

"Arlene is a French name, isn't it?"

"I believe so."

"William the Conqueror's mistress was called Arlene."

"I didn't know that."

"Do you come down to Wales often?"

"As often as I can." She smiled. "I don't want Simon getting into any kind of trouble."

"What sort of trouble?"

Mrs Jacoby looked round the crowded bar.

"All these nubile young women. The railway seems to attract them." She looked pointedly at Raynes. "And so did Derek."

"Do you think that was the cause of his downfall?"

"Don't you?"

"I've been told about how he died; but not much about his love life."

Mrs Jacoby took a sip of her vodka and pineapple.

"Dashing!" she said. " I think that is the best word to describe him. He would do anything to help a damsel in distress and some of them wished to reward him generously for even the smallest act of kindness. It was difficult to resist so much temptation."

She looked at her glass.

"His death was so sad. He left a lovely wife and three children. I don't know how she'll manage. Simon gave her a lot of legal advice – and paid for the funeral. But there was little more he could do. Her present behaviour irritates him terribly."

Raynes tried to look on the bright side.

"His death may have nothing to do with the railway. There could be some business problem back home. In Wolverhampton, I believe?"

"A dreadful place! I don't know how anyone with any taste could live in the Black Country. You're very lucky to live in Grasshallows. Do you have any family?"

"No. I'm divorced. I have two sons, but I haven't seen them for years."

"How sad for you!"

"They're probably better off without me."

Mrs Jacoby smiled a superior smile.

"Well, there's plenty to choose from round here. All ages; all shapes; all sizes; all tastes. Ex-wives; would-be wives. I call it the Devil's playground."

Raynes decided to steer the conversation into less turbulent waters.

"I believe Mrs Packer is an excellent cook?"

Arlene's face lit up.

"Oh, she is. The railway people don't realize how lucky they are having her here. Her roast duck is delicious. And even her salmon fishcakes with feta cheese are to die for."

Raynes had discovered that Mrs Jacoby's real passion in life was food. She could talk about it for hours. She ended a passionate monologue on fresh truffles by saying: "When I'm down here, I always give Joyce a hand with the serving. It's all I can do to help. But I always make sure Simon gets a healthy breakfast."

* * * *

On the way home, Tom Hayward asked the Inspector if he had discovered anything.

"Not a great deal. I discovered that Mrs Jacoby likes good food and that she always makes sure her husband has a healthy breakfast!"

Tom chuckled.

"She's trying to make sure Simon keeps away from Joanne. He quite fancies her."

"She described this place as the Devil's playground."

"With reason," said Tom. "People seem to abandon all their morals when they come down here. There's something corrupting in the air."

Raynes said: "I didn't have a chance to speak to Anna; but Joyce Packer was quite interesting. She outlined a compelling picture of how Derek might have been murdered. But she said it would have involved two people. He would have been tied down to the track. One to hold him down; the other to do the tying."

"She fancies herself as a sleuth," said Tom. "She reads a lot of Agatha Christie and Ngaio Marsh. Quite a blood-thirsty woman. You should see how she cuts up steaks." He paused. "She married a rich old man. A businessman. No one is still quite sure how he died." He paused again. "She asked Simon to defend her if ever she was prosecuted! Makes you think, doesn't it?"

6: Brief Encounter

Raynes had been well briefed for his inevitable encounter with Virginia Barclay. He had been told that she worked in the tea room and, long before he stopped for a bowl of soup, he had identified her as the tall woman with dark hair in a grey dress who seemed to glide around the building bearing flasks of tea and coffee for the volunteers.

Consuming a bowl of homemade carrot and coriander soup, he watched her emptying rubbish into a black bag; carting off the dirty plates and wiping the tables with almost manic efficiency. He could see that she was moving steadily in his direction. Eventually, her deep, sad eyes met his.

"Are you new round here?"

"It's my first weekend."

"I thought I hadn't seen you before. What are you doing?"

"I'm in the ticket office."

She raised her eyebrows.

"You must have friends in high places."

"I came over from Grasshallows with Tom Hayward."

Raynes could see that this information immediately put him on the side of the angels.

"Oh? Tom's always been a good friend. He was a great help to my husband . . ." She paused significantly. "Did he tell you what happened to Derek?"

"Yes," said Raynes. He saw no point in pleading ignorance.

"It must have been a terrible blow to you and your family."

Mrs Barclay sat down at the Inspector's table and eyed him with dark intensity.

"It wasn't an accident. It was murder."

Raynes did not display any reaction. He calmly broke off a piece of French bread and dipped it in his soup.

"They've been trying to cover it up . . . but I won't let them."

Raynes consumed his bread and wiped his fingers on his napkin.

"When did it happen?"

"Last July. The second weekend, he went missing. He never came home. I thought that perhaps he'd had to do some extra work – but he would have phoned. Then I thought he might have had an accident . . ."

Raynes ventured another mouthful of soup.

" . . . I phoned round several of the other members to see if they knew where he was; but they didn't. They said that the yard had been locked up at about 8.30pm and everyone had gone home. I phoned the police but no accident had been reported. I didn't know what to do."

"Did you know where he was staying?"

"Derek stayed in all sorts of places – wherever he could get a bed. No one seemed to know where he'd been. But he could have been anywhere. Once or twice, he dossed down in a sleeping bag in the castle. He didn't mind roughing it."

"What did you do next?"

"I phoned the police again on Tuesday morning and reported him as a missing person. They instituted enquiries. I believe someone opened up the station and had a look round; but they didn't see him." She paused. "There was no sign of his van, either."

"It wasn't till Friday that they found his body. He was found in the sidings where they keep the carriages. He must have been there since Sunday. That was the last time the carriages were used."

Remembering what Tom had told him, Raynes said: "The

carriages must be quite heavy?"

"The police said they were about ten tons each. He couldn't have moved the carriage on his own. Someone must have run the carriage over him."

"But surely he would have heard the train coming? These things make quite a lot of noise. They don't just creep up on you. He would have had plenty of time to get out of the way."

"You would have thought so."

"But perhaps he was in no condition to move." Thinking of Mrs Packer, he said: "He might have been tied down. Or perhaps he was already dead?"

"That's what I think. And that's what the police thought. But they couldn't prove it one way or the other – because of the time he'd been there. His body was quite decomposed – even in that short time."

Raynes was silent.

Five days. A lot could happen to a body in five days.

"Did you come over to identify him?"

"Yes. Right away. But of course I didn't see his injuries. He looked quite peaceful. As if he was sleeping."

Raynes nodded.

Mrs Barclay continued: "The one strange thing was the whisky. They said he'd been drinking. They found the empty bottle lying beside him. A litre bottle. They said he'd spilt a lot of it over his clothes. But Derek didn't drink whisky. Well, he may have drunk a small glass from time to time. But he would never have drunk even a quarter of a bottle. He was always very careful that way. Frightened of losing his licence. He needed it for his work; and for coming over to the railway each weekend. What Derek really liked was a couple of pints of beer. That was enough for him. He liked to keep his mind fresh. That's what he used to say . . ."

"So it was completely out of character?"

"Completely."

"And where was his van found?"

"Up near the castle. That's where he was working. He'd been restoring the tower, making it safe. He's converted one of the old chambers into a cafe. He was very proud of that."

"And where were the keys of the van? In his pocket – or in the van?"

"They were never found."

Raynes finished his soup. He turned to Mrs Barclay.

"Would you like to show me where his body was found?"

A look of gratitude came over Mrs Barclay's face. This was the first time for several weeks that anyone had shown any real interest in her story.

She took the Inspector out of the tea room, along the platform and down the incline to the tracks. The station yard was empty at that moment. *Lady Sylvia* had just taken the 1.45pm up to Abernirvana; *Sir Walter* was due back in forty minutes.

Raynes took a closer look at the lay-out of the station yard. There was a boundary wall about twelve feet high, topped with shards of glass – illegal but effective. There were many sidings for carriages and trucks. The locomotives were stored in a large grey shed. Across from the main platform, there was a long blue metal shed which ran parallel to the sidings and housed the engineering department.

They crossed the main track and headed for the siding where there were three spare carriages. It was the siding nearest to the boundary wall. Virginia led the Inspector round to the far side of the carriages.

"It was here."

"Are these carriages always here?"

"They're the spares. The oldest stock. They're only used at the height of the season."

"No one would see anything from the main platform?"

"No."

Raynes looked at the wheels and the couplings between the first and second carriages.

"Just here?"

"That's what they said."

The Inspector looked at the heavy iron frames of the carriages. Ten tons seemed about right. Their weight would

Pwddldwc Train Station

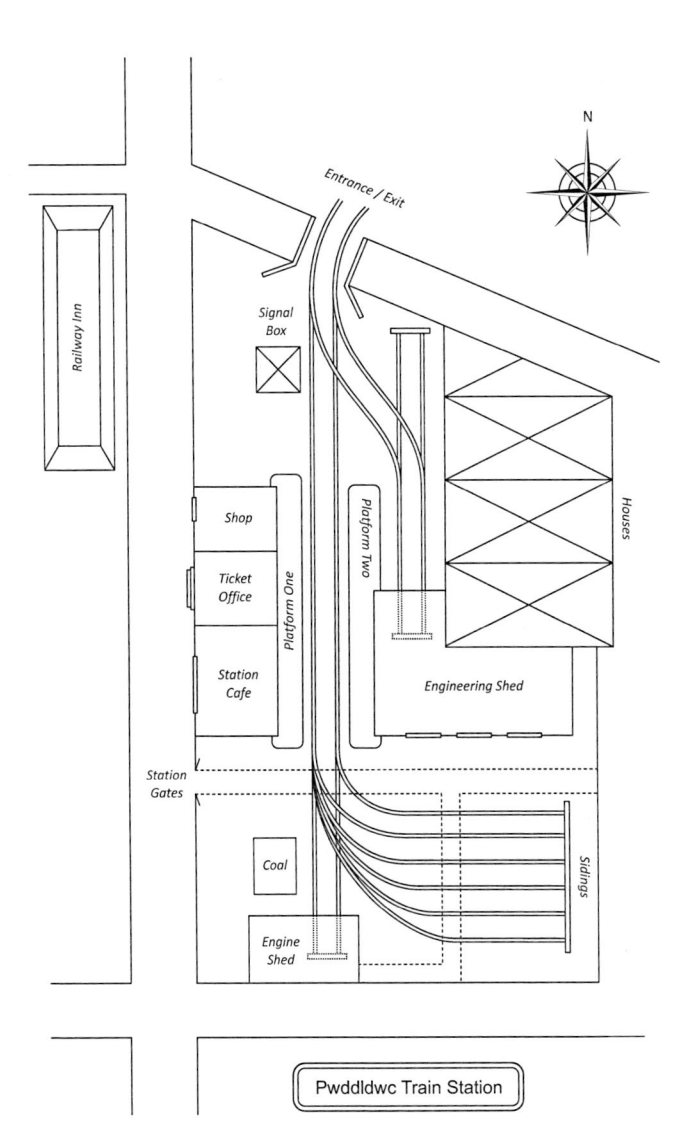

Ian Christie

carve up a body lying on the track. But it might be easier cutting off a person's legs rather than crunching through a torso.

"How tall was your husband?"

"About five foot eight."

Mrs Barclay could guess what Raynes was thinking. The body would have been well hidden. Very few people would venture into this corner of the railway yard. The carriages could have been shunted into the adjoining sidings without anyone noticing the legs or the body on the far side. The carriages had a low clearance over the track. The two locomotives would bring their carriages back to the sidings. They would be uncoupled and would return to the main platform before heading for the grey railway shed. The gates to the main road would have been locked. Everyone would have gone home. It was quite a lonely place.

Raynes walked round the three carriages and looked across the other empty sidings to the blue engineering shed. There was a concrete roadway leading from the main gates along the longest side of the shed. The roller doors were partially raised and he could see machinery, lathes, work benches, bags of sand and cement.

Mrs Barclay followed his eyes.

"That's all Derek's stuff. They're still using it. He brought it all over from Wolverhampton in his van."

"How often did he come over?"

"When he was busy on a project, he'd come over every weekend. But, other times, he might be back home for six weeks or more. He did most of his work out of season. In the spring or in the autumn – not when the place was crowded."

"Had he finished restoring the castle?"

"No. He still had a lot to do. He's made the walls safe. But he felt that a lot more could still be done to make it a first-class tourist attraction." She paused. "Of course, some people didn't approve of what he was doing. They felt it should be left as a ruin. The local landowner was particularly nasty. He tried to block the planning applications. But Derek thought that the castle was an important feature. It gave the Railway a touch of class."

She smiled sadly.

Raynes returned to the lay-out of the station yard.

"A train would have to come a long way before it reached this siding, wouldn't it?" He pointed a finger. "It would come off the main track there . . . then there's two sidings for the trucks and that yellow thing . . ."

"That's the maintenance diesel."

"Well, it would have to pass two more sets of points before it reached these three carriages. That ought to have given him plenty of warning."

Raynes looked again at the metal couplings.

"Were they attached?"

"I don't know."

"Could he have been doing anything to the carriages?"

"I shouldn't think so. He was mostly engaged in building projects . . . like extending the tea room or building the signal box. Or even that . . ." She waved a hand at the engineering shed. "He'd tackle anything."

Mrs Barclay sighed.

"It was his last weekend. He'd done all he was going to do to the castle. He was planning to be off till September. We were supposed to be going on holiday to Majorca at the end of the month."

Raynes was reminded of Derek's other life in Wolverhampton.

"How many of a family do you have?"

"Three. A boy of five – very like his father. A girl of three and a new baby – born in April last year."

Raynes asked the obvious question: "How do you manage to get away each weekend?"

"My mother looks after the children."

"Is she quite happy about that?"

Mrs Barclay looked surprised at his question.

"Of course she is. She shares my view . . ."

" . . . That Derek was murdered?"

"Yes. And that those who killed him should be punished."
"You're quite determined?"
"Utterly."

Raynes admired her determination. But he realized how difficult her task was – a year on – with all the evidence long since obliterated; the police enquiry inconclusive; the coroner's report dismissive. People wanting to move on . . . to forget . . . Hoping she would go away. He could see it from both sides.

Mrs Barclay looked at the Inspector. She found his presence reassuring. He asked the right sort of questions.

"Are you some sort of detective?" she asked.

"Yes," said Raynes shortly. "But I have no power to interfere in this case. Tom invited me to come over and see the situation for myself."

"And what do you think?"

Raynes took a long time before he replied.

"It will be very difficult to re-open the case. Almost impossible, I should think. There is so little evidence to go on. I'm sure they've checked the fingerprints . . . and everything. I don't know any members of the Society except Tom. I've never been in this part of Wales before. But . . ." He paused. ". . . as an ordinary member of the British public, I cannot see how a man of his experience on the railway came to have his legs chopped off in a siding. How he came to be drinking huge quantities of whisky. His van up at the castle – his body down here. Unless . . . his body was brought down here . . . and set up to look like an accident."

Mrs Barclay's eyes lit up.

"You agree with me?"

"I'm afraid so."

"Oh, thank you!"

Virginia flung herself into Raynes' arms, buried her head in his shoulder and burst into tears.

The Inspector was taken completely by surprise. To start with, he was embarrassed – but then he realized that no one on the station could see them. He also realized how important it must be to her that someone believed her story. After all the dead ends, the rejections, the continuing doubts, it must be a tremendous relief to receive some professional support – even from a complete stranger.

He put his arm round her shoulders. They seemed so thin – too fragile to carry the burden she was carrying. Raynes was conscious that she was still a young woman, in her early thirties, who might be very attractive if she was not so overcome with grief and despair.

He held her for several minutes; then they broke apart.

"Have you a handkerchief?"

Raynes nodded.

She wiped her eyes.

"I'm sorry. I couldn't help it. It's just . . ."

"I understand," said Raynes. "It must be very hard believing what you do and being completely unable to do anything about it."

"They all think I'm bats."

"They probably do."

Raynes felt that was an understatement.

"It's just . . . I can't let it rest. There's something inside me, driving me on . . . Do you believe in spiritualism?"

"No," said Raynes.

"It feels as if Derek's there, crying out for justice – and I can't do what he wants me to do. I know, if it was him, he wouldn't let the matter drop. He'd insist on getting to the bottom of it. I can't let it rest."

She wrapped the Inspector's handkerchief tightly round her hand. He could imagine the violent feelings that were crashing around inside her. The passion to find out the truth about her husband's death. If he had been her, he would have felt precisely the same. But he couldn't make her any false promises.

He said: "I cannot give you any hope. No encouragement whatsoever. But I can tell you that I will give this case my fullest attention. I will need your help – and the help of many other people – to find out what happened. I need to gain people's confidence – so that they will speak to me. I need to look closely at the Railway and its members. At this moment, I know hardly anyone. So this will take time.

"If it is murder, then someone here – or in the village – must know something. I need one clue. One lead. One memory. If I get that, I may be able to do something – but I cannot make you any false promises."

Mrs Barclay was beginning to look more hopeful.

"Derek will help you!"

The suggestion jarred.

Raynes continued: "I must ask you not to say any more about Derek's death. If you have anything to say, say it to me. Let the railway people get on with their job. Don't talk! Listen! Whilst you go on about your husband's death, no one will speak to you. They'll shun you. But we need information. Once you shut up, they'll start talking and then we may pick up something of value. One lead could be enough."

His words gave Virginia Barclay renewed confidence. She began to see a way out of the nightmare.

"You definitely believe he was murdered?"

Raynes looked into her deep, dark eyes.

"I can see no alternative."

Virginia gave him another desperate hug. To his surprise, the Inspector quite enjoyed it. Together, they walked back to the station.

7: *A Treasurer's Lot*

When Raynes returned to the ticket office, his colleague looked at him with a wry smile.

"I hear you've met the widow from hell?"

"News travels fast."

"It does. But when people see the two of you heading for the sidings, they know what you're in for."

The Inspector smiled affably.

"The matter is still very fresh in her mind."

Dr Campbell scowled.

"Most of us are trying to forget it - and so should she. We have a very good record where accidents are concerned."

"She doesn't think it was an accident."

"Well, that's what the coroner said - and I believe him. I agree it was a horrible death. But those carriages are heavier than you think. If they run over you, you're quite likely to lose a couple of legs. And if there's no one around to phone for an ambulance, you're not going to survive. That's for sure."

Raynes decided to change the subject.

"Did you like Derek?"

"No."

Raynes said nothing so that Dr Campbell felt obliged to explain: "He was a very good tradesman. He did a power of work for the railway. He never took a penny for any of his labour; but the cost of materials was quite staggering." He paused. "Don't misunderstand me. I'm not suggesting that he cheated us in any way. He didn't. But those bills came in at very inconvenient moments. Just before the railway opened in April – or at the beginning of July. It completely upset the cash flow – just when we were needing it for other things. And he expected us to pay on the dot."

Dr Campbell flicked through a handful of return tickets.

"Of course, that was the way he conducted his business back in Birmingham. He paid his suppliers for the cement, wood, steel beams, pipes and slates. And he expected us to pay equally promptly. But when you get a bill for £4000 and you've only got a few hundred in the kitty, it can really throw you."

"You had a few rows?"

Dr Campbell smiled grimly.

"Quite a few. But it was no use complaining. He had all the members of the Railway eating out of his hand. They loved all the things he was doing. I warned him about the castle project. 'I know you want to rebuild that castle,' I said, 'but I'm not going to give you a penny.' But what did he do? He built a cafe in the ruin. Put in all mod cons – electricity, water pipes, a full-scale kitchen. Then he installed a set of toilets in the dungeon. Everyone thinks it's wonderful; but I'm still paying the bill!"

"Still?"

"I've still got £2000 to pay Mrs Barclay; and she'll get it when I have it – and not before! They're also spending a fortune on that new locomotive . . ."

"*Lady Ermintrude?*"

"Bloody stupid name! Simon Jacoby should have known better."

Raynes could understand the pressures that weighed on the Treasurer. Even though the little railway was an undoubted success and an immense tourist attraction, it could be a complete nightmare to someone who had to pay the bills. A new tea room, a new locomotive – or even a ton of coal – could prove a headache for the Treasurer.

Raynes looked at Dr Campbell in a more friendly fashion.

"Was that the only reason why you disliked Derek Barclay?"

"No. That was not the only reason."

Their discussion was interrupted by a group of healthy young men all bearing huge rucksacks.

"Eight returns to the castle."

Raynes punched out the tickets.

"Are they valid for Sunday?"

"Yes. Whenever you come back."

Archie Campbell intervened: "Are you planning to camp near the castle?"

"No. Further up the hill."

"Better have a word with the local farmer. Just let him know where you're camping. You'll find him at Castle Farm – not far from the station."

As they moved off, the Treasurer said: "They won't get much joy from the farmer. He's always frightened of campers setting fire to his woods. They're more likely to go away with a thick ear!"

Raynes returned to the original subject of their

conversation.

"You were saying why you disliked Derek Barclay . . ."

Archie Campbell sighed.

"You're a man of the world, Inspector. You must have come across a lot of immoral people in your time. Derek was utterly promiscuous. He had a lovely wife – sparkling, kind, the mother of his three children. But he was consistently unfaithful to her. He couldn't keep his hands off other women – and they couldn't keep their hands off him.

"Now, what might pass unnoticed in a big city like Birmingham is immediately picked up in a small village. They're very devout people round here. Even if they don't go to the chapel, they expect people to behave. When the Methodist minister drank a glass of whisky at a wedding, everyone was up in arms. The fact that a member of the Society was having affairs with local women caused a lot of anger. It also brought the railway into disrepute.

"We're outsiders. We come from all parts of the country. But we depend on the locals to provide us with beds, food, car-parking, people to clean the carriages, a neighbourhood watch team to stop people pinching our copper cable or vandalizing our rolling stock. They're glad to help. But if the villagers start feeling we're people with loose morals, wife-swapping and fornicating, we'll soon find them putting up the shutters. And we would be the ones to suffer."

"Do you think Derek brought the Railway into disrepute?"

"Undoubtedly."

"Did you do anything about it?"

Dr Campbell looked awkward at having to answer that question. Eventually, he said: "I spoke to Simon Jacoby about it. He was aware of the problem. I spoke to Brian Williamson – you met him last night. But then I discovered that his wife was one of Derek's victims . . ."

"Did they do anything?"

"They said they would. But nothing happened. Derek continued in his merry way right up to the time of the accident." Dr Campbell looked aggressively at the Inspector.

"And it was an accident!"

Raynes said nothing.

"No one murdered him!"

"You didn't speak to him yourself?"

"Not about that. He wouldn't have taken it from me."

"Why not?"

The doctor flushed angrily.

"Because he thought I was a self-righteous prig!" He scowled at the crowd of people pouring into the booking hall and heading towards the counter. "And perhaps I am."

8: A Ticket To Ride?

The 3.15pm train did not seem to have attracted all that many passengers. Only fifty-two tickets had been sold; but as Dr Campbell had said, the return train – the last one of the day – would be packed.

Raynes was suddenly conscious of Emily standing beside him. He had not heard her entering the ticket office. Today, she was wearing an old grey jumper with the same grey jeans.

"Job's over," she said. "Time to come out and play."

Raynes counted up his money and put it in the drawer.

"There's nothing else you can do here."

The Inspector looked anxiously at his colleague.

"The girl's right. You've done your bit for the day. Go and enjoy the beauties of the Puddleduck!"

Raynes looked at his watch.

"We've still got two minutes. Do I need a ticket?"

Emily sniffed contemptuously.

"Staff go free."

"Are you staff?"

"When they need me."

She led the way out on to the platform and stepped into a small half-open guard's van that was attached to the rear of the train. There were low bench-type seats surrounding a large metal wheel.

"Emergency brake," she said. "They'll need it on the way down."

A young man was wandering up and down the platform, bearing a furled green flag. His face was not improved by the presence of a large silver whistle in his mouth.

"That's Charlie. Communist agitator. Doesn't wash. But he's a very keen guard."

The engine gave a muted toot which seemed to suggest that the driver was ready to move off. Charlie blew a strident note on his whistle, waved his flag and the engine responded with a high-pitched shriek.

Charlie leapt into the open van, rolled up his flag and drew out a bottle of beer from his large black bag.

"Hot work!" he said.

Raynes sat back, feeling very content.

The little train set out on its short journey with a monstrous outpouring of smoke, which seemed to engulf the entire locomotive. There was a furious chugging as the wheels started to turn. After a sudden jerk, the carriages began to glide past the platform and the dripping leather sleeve of the water tower. It passed over a miniature railway crossing with people leaning over the gates and waving to the passengers. Then out past a series of stone walls and fences as the line skirted the final houses of the village.

The furious chugging diminished into a more purposeful sound as the train began to gather speed. An overhead bridge came as a nasty shock; thick grey smoke enveloped them – but soon they were out in the open countryside, passing the first milestone, where *Sir Walter* had once come to grief.

The terrain was quite flat at this point and the train made good progress towards a small wooded hill where Raynes could see the jagged walls of a ruined castle. The locomotive confidently rattled along the single line track – such a familiar sight that the cows and sheep grazing in nearby fields did not even raise their heads.

As the wooded slopes came closer, the beat of the engine became slower. There was a sighing, hissing sound as the speed was reduced. The Inspector guessed that the driver was hoping that the momentum of the train would carry it the full length of the platform without any need to apply the brakes. And so it turned out. There was a cheerful clatter as *Sir Walter* negotiated the points at the western end of the station and rolled to a halt at platform one of Caercraig.

Emily rose to her feet.

"D'you want to see the castle?"

"What about the train?"

"It has to wait for the down train to pass. Probably another ten minutes. The driver'll let us know."

They climbed out of the van and crossed the second line. A steep path led them up to the postern gate of the castle.

It was quite a small building, with a cobbled courtyard and the remains of a tower, about forty feet high. To their left, a square chamber had been converted into a cafe.

Emily said: "There's time for an ice cream. A Magnum would be nice."

"Two Magnums, please."

Ice creams in hand, they walked round the courtyard. There wasn't much to see. At the foot of the tower, there was a large notice: "Danger! Do not climb these steps." And beside the cafe, a second staircase descended into the bowels of the earth – with another notice: "Toilets closed." Raynes supposed that, now Derek Barclay was dead, the castle would probably remain a ruin.

Emily waved her ice cream in the direction of the cafe.

"I painted those walls."

"Is that where you were covered with emulsion?"

She smiled.

"I saw you pick up on that."

"You were quite fond of Derek?"

"He was quite fond of me. We always had a cuddle after we'd had our sandwiches . . . And in the van going home."

"Was he a ladies' man?"

Emily shrugged her shoulders.

"He was a very attractive person. You couldn't help liking

him. He put his arm round you; said nice things. Before you knew where you were, you were kissing and cuddling. He was very gentle. He didn't force himself on you."

"Do you think he might have done the same thing to other women?"

Emily grinned.

"Probably. But he wouldn't have hurt them."

"Their husbands – or boyfriends – might have a different opinion."

"You're looking for motives."

"Of course I am. Even your boyfriend might have objected."

"I wouldn't have told him."

"Perhaps other ladies also kept it dark?"

"Perhaps they did. But it's difficult to keep things secret round here. People always talk. They add feet and legs to a story. I suppose it would be easy for someone to get jealous."

Raynes looked at Emily. She had an old head on young shoulders. She could be very useful.

"Do you think you might be able to draw up a list of all the ladies who might have had . . . a cuddle with Derek?"

Emily laughed.

"It would be quite a long list."

"Well, if you're going to become an investigative journalist, it might be a useful exercise."

"Useful to you."

"Very."

"How much is it worth to you?"

Raynes was surprised at the sudden mercenary turn the conversation had taken.

"One hundred pounds," he said generously.

"Double it."

Emily's eyes showed that she was not joking. She would make a very shrewd businesswoman. The Inspector reckoned that the price was not unreasonable. Her information could save him a lot of time.

"O.K. Two hundred pounds. But it must be a proper list.

Genuine people – plus local rumours. Delivered to my office in Grasshallows some time in the next two weeks."

"Done!"

They shook hands on the deal.

In the distance, there was the screech of a whistle. *Lady Sylvia* was fast approaching the station.

"We have to get back."

They walked down the hill and climbed back into their train. They watched the down train pulling into platform two. The fireman looked out of the cab and waved a black hand. His face was black, too. Raynes didn't recognize him, but Emily did.

"That's Tom," she said. "I must go and give him a kiss."

Raynes watched her climb on to the footplate and raise her face for a kiss.

"Are you doing all right?"

She bent forward as if she was looking at the pressure gauge.

"He's asked me for a list of all Derek's women."

"That'd be useful."

"He thinks it might be a jealous lover."

"No harm in finding out."

Emily grinned mischievously.

"I'm charging him two hundred pounds."

Tom Hayward laughed.

"He can afford it."

Emily returned to her own train.

"I thought he might be jealous seeing us together."

Raynes wiped a black smudge off her cheek.

"You seem to prefer the older men."

"They're richer."

After a petulant blast, *Sir Walter* set out on the next stage of their journey. They seemed to have lost Charlie. Perhaps he was on the footplate – or, better still – he might have been left entombed in the castle dungeon.

"Be careful you don't lean out," said Emily. "You may get a small cinder in your eye. It can be quite painful."

It was tempting to lean out. The train was curling up through woodland carpeted with bluebells. The incline was now steeper and the little engine was working hard as it climbed the two mile gradient to the Gushers of Idris.

"Are you married?" asked Emily.

"No," said Raynes. "Divorced. Twice."

It was a question women always seemed to ask. An act of global positioning to see how the land lay with an unknown male. Was he available or not? What was the level of competition? Was there a wife or a partner lurking in the background? Was he worth all the effort? It amused Raynes that, even at the tender age of seventeen or eighteen, Emily should ask him that question. He hoped that his reply would be suitably discouraging.

"Are you engaged?"

"No. Nor likely to be. By the time Marc comes out, I shall be in Grasshallows . . ."

" . . . Enjoying yourself?"

"Of course."

"Is Tom going to provide you with accommodation?"

"He's going to pay for it." A merry smile played on her lips. "He's going to give me a job as a part-time reporter. That should help to cover my costs."

"Is Tom married?"

Raynes felt he should have known the answer to that question; but Tom had never mentioned it.

However Emily was fully conversant with the publisher's private life. "His wife left him two years ago. He's quite lonely."

"But he's not divorced yet?"

"Does it matter?"

"Not really."

"I think it's more profitable being a mistress!"

Raynes shook his head.

"You are really a most unscrupulous young woman."

"Have you ever met a Welsh girl who wasn't?"

"I don't think I've ever met any Welsh girls."

"Poor you."

The train had now entered a long, stone gully. You could brush your hands against the walls on both sides. The steady chugging had ceased. Once again, the locomotive was coasting into the next station. Before it did so, it rattled over a high bridge spanning a deep ravine which gave them a tantalizing glimpse of a spectacular waterfall. The station itself seemed to have been carved out of rock. On the western side, the platform was protected by a massive outcrop of granite.

"You should have brought your camera," said Emily. "You could have got a nice photograph of me posing beside the waterfall."

"Do we have time to go and see it?"

"Of course. This is where the train takes on water." It takes about five minutes to fill her up."

Most of the passengers descended from their carriages and went down the concrete steps beside the bridge. This took them along the edge of the ravine so that they could look down into the deep pool into which the waterfall plunged about one hundred feet below. Most of the passengers were busy taking photos.

"Most impressive!" said Raynes.

"It's even more impressive when you know how it's done," said Emily enigmatically. "Derek built it. It was one of his brainwaves. In summer, there used to be only a trickle of water. But Derek put in a pump. That ensures a constant flow. The water in the pool is pumped back to the top of the waterfall."

She spoke quietly so that none of the other passengers would hear. "When the last train comes down, the pump is switched off. It's one of the guard's jobs. Clever, isn't it?"

"Very."

They were rapidly summoned back to the train. *Sir Walter* was anxious to cover the final four miles of track, which were mostly downhill.

Charlie had also reappeared and was counting the numbers

to make sure no one had fallen into the ravine. He waved his flag and jumped back into the van.

"Where did you get to?

"I was shovelling coal. Old Gordon's getting a bit past it. I was giving him a hand. We don't want another death on the railway."

"How long has he been working on the Puddleduck?"

"Over twenty years."

There was an appreciative silence at such dedication.

The little train seemed to be working its way round the side of a large mountain. Once they had cleared the woods, there were spectacular views to their left – including a large lake.

The locomotive gave a friendly toot and began to slow down. There were men on the track – including Father Morris.

Emily explained.

"That used to be the entrance to the slate quarry. It was quite an eyesore. You could see the empty shell for miles. Now they're blocking it off – building an embankment, planting trees, so it doesn't look quite so horrible. We've even had a grant from the Government."

Raynes said mischievously: "You didn't refuse English taxpayers' money?"

Emily smiled.

"We never refuse anybody's money! Besides, it was probably our own money – recycled. Lord knows, we've paid enough taxes to fund it!"

Father Morris waved to them.

"We'll be joining you on the way back! Keep a few seats for us."

Round the final corner of the mountain, they could at last see the little village which lay at the head of the line. It had originally been a small mining village; but many of the terraced houses had been cleared away; others had been restored and a large number of holiday cottages covered the hillside. It seemed quite a prosperous little place.

Emily looked at the Inspector.

"This is where Marc burnt down a *saesneg* holiday home."

Raynes was sarcastic.

"Just one?"

Emily's lips were cold and hard.

"That's all he admitted to."

Charlie was drawn into the conversation.

"They knew he'd done more than eight – but they couldn't prove it! He was lucky to get only two years; but I suppose he'll be out by Christmas."

Raynes said: "I take it that you are not a nationalist?"

"No way!" said Charlie. "My family's Labour through and through. My dad used to help Michael Foot at each General Election. He got huge majorities every time."

"But you're a Communist," said Emily.

"Doesn't stop me working for the benefit of the people of Wales. At least we don't burn down people's houses! We need these rich people to pay their taxes so we can help all those poor families in the mining villages which have lost their pits. Yes, I'm a Communist – and proud of it!"

Emily said nothing.

The train swung past a small signal box and pulled in alongside a platform filled with tubs of flowers and brightly painted seats. It was a splendid example of Victorian railway architecture – lovingly restored. There was a strong smell of coffee coming from somewhere. The station sign said "Abernirvana". For railway enthusiasts and other weary travellers, this was a foretaste of heaven itself.

9: *The Rottweilers Pounce!*

Like ancient Gaul, the upper station was divided into two parts. One was a restaurant-cum-tearoom, finished in Art Deco style with the furnishings to match. The other was a flourishing souvenir shop, selling everything connected with railways – books, magazines, postcards, tea towels, train sets, the complete works of Rev W.V. Awdry and reproduction posters from the great days of the GWR and the LNER.

Raynes visited the shop. He was looking for the postcard of Lydia Naylor brandishing an oil can in front of *Lady Sylvia*, which apparently had a certain rarity value – with only six left.

He discovered that the lady in the lilac cat-suit, with the alluring grey eyes, was not only a "compulsive show-off", but also a liar. There were at least eighty copies of the postcard available. It was also prominently displayed. The Inspector bought two copies – one for himself and the other for Dr Stewart, who had recently prepared him for the Burns Supper in Glenmoidart. He thought it might cheer up the police surgeon when he was doing a post mortem.

The girl behind the counter tried to interest him in a Welsh doll, a golden box of cream toffees and an illustrated history of the Puddleduck Railway; but he managed to resist temptation and save his credit card for the tea room. He was feeling hungry – and time was short. *Sir Walter* was due to leave in twenty minutes. He ordered a cheese omelette with a glass of chilled orange juice.

The waitresses were dressed in traditional Welsh costume. Long black skirts with white blouses, red pinafores and black shawls. No pointed hats – but white lace caps. He was observing this pleasant scene when he was approached from two different directions by two very purposeful ladies whom he had met the night before. They sat down on either side. He was unable to escape.

Linda Naylor was the first to speak.

"I didn't know you were a police inspector . . ."

" . . . we thought you were just a new volunteer Tom had brought over."

"Miss Williams has spilled the beans?"

"No. My husband has phoned – from the signal box – to say that you were speaking to that dreadful woman . . ."

" . . . Not just speaking! But kissing and hugging her!"

Raynes tried to look shocked.

"There may have been some hugging – but there was certainly no kissing!"

"And why was she hugging you? She hardly knows you."

Raynes smiled cautiously.

"She was grateful that I took her views seriously. That I was willing to listen to her." He added: "I don't know how your husband could see all that from the signal box."

"There are cameras everywhere."

"Well, it's a pity they weren't working on the night Derek died. We might have discovered how he was killed."

"He was run over."

"No, he wasn't. Those carriages were parked at the back of the siding. They were the oldest stock. I'm told that they are only used at the height of the holiday season. There was no train in the vicinity. He was run over by one carriage – not three. You tell me how that could happen – by accident!"

Raynes had decided that the best means of defence was attack.

"The police said it was an accident . . ."

" . . . And so did the coroner."

"Were you at the inquest?"

"No."

Linda had the look of one who would never be seen dead in a coroner's court.

Raynes continued: "Mrs Barclay has every reason to believe that her husband was murdered."

"She blames us . . ."

" . . . She accuses us of killing him!"

"She may be right."

Joanne picked up a knife from the table.

Raynes said quietly: "Please put it down. I'm still waiting for my omelette."

"You're not getting anything to eat. You're going straight back on the train. Tom will take you home tonight. Otherwise . . ."

She continued to wave the knife in a menacing fashion.

"Are you threatening me?"

"Yes."

"We want you to go."

Raynes looked round the tea room to see if he might have

any support. Any witnesses. But the room had emptied and the waitresses had disappeared. He decided that he was unlikely to see his cheese omelette.

In a more conciliatory voice he said: "Will you please tell me why everyone is so sensitive about Derek's death?" He looked at the two women. "He seems to have been a very popular man; very hard-working. He certainly did a power of work for the Railway." He looked round the tea room. "I imagine he had a big hand in restoring this place . . . Why should anyone want to kill him?"

"No one killed him!" said Lydia emphatically.

"That's our point!"

Raynes continued: "The only thing that I have learnt about Derek is that he could be . . . over-friendly with the ladies. Only too happy to have a kiss and a cuddle when the opportunity arose. Someone's husband – or partner – might have objected. I don't think you could deny that possibility."

Lydia said: "You shouldn't believe anything that slimy little bitch says!"

Raynes assumed that she was referring to Emily.

"Did you say 'bitch'?"

"Witch!" said Joanne. "She was one of his groupies."

"And so were her sisters!"

Raynes looked at the two fierce women beside him. They were potentially well-armed with Art Deco knives and forks, a silver-plated salt cellar and a pepper pot.

He smiled a gentle smile.

"I am sure neither of your husbands had any reason to seek revenge."

Lydia eyed the Inspector coldly.

"None whatsoever."

Raynes looked at Joanne.

"Never in a month of Sundays!

Raynes had not the slightest doubt that both women were lying.

"So," he said, "if the case is re-opened, it won't affect you."

Lydia said: "The case will not be re-opened."

"The police handled it perfectly," said Joanne.

"Well, there we are."

All passion spent!

Most conveniently, at that very moment, *Sir Walter* signalled that the train was ready to depart.

Raynes looked at the two women.

"Will you allow me to catch my train?"

They nodded.

"But," said Lydia, "if you do not leave tonight, you will be forcibly removed – by the police. Graeme has spoken to them. They know what to do."

Raynes rose to his feet.

He looked down at them.

"I think you both have something to hide. I shall be interested to see what it is."

10: The Runaway Train

Raynes walked along the platform to the guard's van, thankful that he had been allowed to leave the restaurant without being attacked.

As he stepped into the van, Emily said: "I thought we'd lost you."

Raynes said coldly: "I'm sure you were well aware I was in the tea room – waiting for an omelette which never arrived."

"They've been very busy."

Raynes said: "I also think you told one of them I was here. They descended on me like a pair of wolves. I was threatened with a knife."

Emily said nothing.

The Inspector looked at her.

"Joanne and Lydia do not seem to have a very high opinion of you. One of them claimed you were a witch; the other said that you were one of 'Derek's groupies'."

Emily blushed.

"I told you what I felt about Derek."

Raynes nodded.

"You have been very honest with me and I respect that. But these women have something to hide."

Emily looked round to make sure no one was listening. (The engine itself was making an immense amount of noise.)

She said: "You're quite right. Both of them had affairs with Derek – but their husbands know nothing about it. It was several years ago. Joanne had just come back from her honeymoon. Derek said they were like animals – gagging for it."

Charlie blew his whistle and waved his flag. As he jumped back into the moving vehicle, he said: "We've got to pick up the Reverend and his lads. It's going to be quite a squeeze."

As they slowly rolled out of the top station with a full train of passengers, Raynes pulled his two postcards out of his inner pocket.

"Lydia!"

Raynes laughed.

"Greasing the wheels of justice! I thought it might add a bit of glamour to my police files."

Emily look surprised.

"Are you keeping a record of all you've been told."

"Of course."

* * * *

Father Morris and his team could not have chosen a worse place to join the train. *Sir Walter* had taken full advantage of the falling gradient from Abernirvana and had picked up quite a bit of speed; but the extra passengers were waiting at the side of the track just where the little train was preparing to climb up the twisting line to the Gushers of Idris.

Father Morris climbed into the guard's van and sat beside the Inspector.

"You're ten minutes late!"

"Too many people trying to get on. What happens if the train can't make it?"

"We all have to get out and push! We've done it once or twice." He looked at Raynes' anxious face. "Don't worry! She'll make it."

It was certainly a bit of a struggle. There was an immense amount of energy being expended for a very small return. The train moved – but very slowly. It crawled up the hill – at less than walking pace. The pressure gauge began to rise. Old Gordon shovelled in more coal. People crossed their fingers and hoped she would make it. Others prayed; and their prayers were answered. *Sir Walter* finally passed the summit and everyone relaxed. The little train had made it.

To take everyone's mind off the train, Father Morris was busy pointing out places of interest along the line. He had written an article about Lake Nirvana in the Society's newsletter – quite a boring article – but it occupied everyone's attention for a few vital minutes.

"Of course, this is the home of the Cadwaller family. They own all the land round here – including the lake and its fishing rights. They don't mind the railways running across their land; but, boy, do they object to us restoring the castle! They claim it is theirs. And with some justification. Their home is just a stone's throw away from the station car park.

"They didn't mind people going up to look at the castle, but when we started building, they caused us a lot of trouble. They went to court; took out injunctions; tried to organize a public petition." He laughed. "They didn't get much support locally. They'd been charging their tenants high rents for years. This was a perfect opportunity for the peasants to hit back.

"So they took their grievance to court – in fact, they took it as far as the Court of Appeal – but they got their socks roasted! It was all great fun. Fortunately, it didn't cost the Railway a penny. Our Chairman, Mr Jacoby, is a brilliant lawyer. He made mincemeat of Sir David Cadwaller. But they took it out on the chap who was working on the castle. They slashed his tyres; they covered his van with manure; clamped his wheels. Not very nice people. I can tell you this . . ." He looked at Charlie. " . . . If there was a revolution here in Wales, they would be the first to get their heads chopped off! And serve them right!"

Charlie raised his fist.

"Death to the aristocracy!"

Raynes listened to the story without revealing his interest in Derek Barclay. But it gave him food for thought. There were other enemies outside the railway community. They had already attacked him when he was working at the castle. They could have planned his death over many months and then dumped his body in the railway yard in Pwddldwc. Their local influence might have encouraged the authorities to decide that Derek's death was an accident.

The train stopped briefly at the Gushers of Idris to give Charlie time to switch off the waterfall and for *Sir Walter* to take on a little more water. As they passed the ravine, there was nothing to see. It was strange to think that for most of the day water had thundered down into a distant pool.

By now, the little train was coasting happily down the side of the mountain – and Charlie was applying the handbrake wheel to assist in keeping the speed under control and prevent *Sir Walter* racing to her doom.

Raynes had been expecting a major influx of passengers at Caercraig and wondered how they could squeeze them in to an already overcrowded train. But, being aware of this problem on a busy Saturday afternoon, *Lady Sylvia* had already been sent on a pre-emptive mission which had reduced the crowd to a few stragglers who had been up the mountain.

Sir Walter had now fully recovered his breath and the last four miles across the fields were covered at a cracking pace – with many of the younger passengers leaning out of the windows and cheering on the driver.

It had been an exciting journey – and Raynes had almost forgotten his experience in the tea room. But, as he walked down the platform and passed through the booking hall, someone handed him a note. He waited till he was outside the station before he looked at it.

Ignore my wife – and Joanne. They get very worked up

about everything. They were deeply upset by Derek's death. Cannot bear old wounds being re-opened. Good luck in your investigations.

Bill.

It is said that "a soft answer turns away wrath". But it was unlikely that this note would change Raynes' mind. Both women had lied and both they – and their partners – would remain high on his list of suspects.

11: Fire Below

When Raynes returned to No 14 Chapel Road, he discovered that Tom Hayward was having a hot bath. He felt like one himself. He was sure his hair was filled with coal dust and his body liberally coated in ash.

When the two men finally sat down in Mrs Williams' front living room with a welcome glass of gin and tonic, Raynes asked: "Who is the local farmer at Caercraig?"

"Sir David Cadwaller. But he's more than a farmer. He's the local landowner. Owns more than five thousand acres."

"Does he own the castle?"

"No. That's the one thing he doesn't own. A sore point! He thinks he does; but the Society went into all this some years ago. It was owned by a man called Mervyn Hodges who died in 1902. Mervyn was the last in a line of penniless aristocrats. To keep their family going, they'd sold most of their major assets. The castle wasn't worth much; but they had no intention of selling it to the Cadwallers, who had been given most of their land by Henry Tudor – upstarts that they were!

"The Hodges had owned the castle since the time of Edward I; and it was they who allowed it to become a complete ruin. They sold off some of the stonework to the Cadwallers, who probably pinched more than they had paid for. That's where the trouble began. But the remains of the castle were left to the Railway – just to spite the Cadwallers, who have had their eyes on it for four hundred years!"

Tom downed the rest of his gin.

"Why are you so interested?"

"Well, Father Morris told me that Derek had a terrible time with them. They had tried to prevent him restoring the castle. They had taken out writs, petitioned Parliament . . . even sabotaged his car . . . to try and stop his work."

Tom Hayward went over to Mrs Williams' cocktail cabinet and poured himself another gin and tonic.

"Want some more?"

"No thanks."

The publisher sank back into his armchair.

"They did all that – and more. But, as I told you on the way down, the Railway has an excellent lawyer in Simon Jacoby – and he defeated them at every turn. But the real issue was not the castle – but Sir David's wife – Lady Margaret. Derek had an affair with her."

"When?"

"About five years ago. Sir David knew nothing about it. But then she had a son. He thought it was his. His first son – after three daughters. Great celebrations. But then Lady Margaret confessed. A stupid thing to do. The child was disowned – and adopted by persons unknown. Derek's name was never mentioned – but Sir David knew who the father was."

"He threatened to kill him?"

"Yes. But he didn't. He just used every legal obstacle to prevent him restoring the castle."

"He didn't succeed?

"No, he didn't."

"And it cost him a packet?"

"It did."

"And where was Derek's van found?"

Tom Hayward laughed.

"I see what you mean. Derek's van was found in the station car park – just four hundred yards from Castle Farm – Sir David's home!"

Raynes finished his drink.

"I should like to meet this man."
"I don't think you'll get a very warm welcome."

* * * *

For supper, Mrs Williams had prepared a delicious steak pie with traditional shortcrust pastry. As she placed it on the table, she said to the Inspector: "I think you'll be needing this after all your hard work on the railway."

Raynes said modestly: "I think Tom deserves it more than I do. He's been shovelling coal into the fire-box all day whilst I was working in the ticket office. But," he said proudly, "we did sell 260 tickets. Dr Campbell said he thought it was pretty good for a Saturday in April."

Mrs Williams cut the pie crust into four equal portions.

"Did you have anything at lunchtime?"

"I had a bowl of soup and a roll in the cafe." He paused. "I also had a chat with Virginia Barclay."

Mrs Williams' brow darkened.

"That dreadful woman! May God forgive her for all the trouble she's caused us. She should go back to wherever she comes from – and look after her children."

Emily came in with a bowl of garlic potatoes. There were also some French beans.

"Frozen, I'm afraid. Did you manage to get away from her?"

"Yes. But she showed me the place where her husband's body was found."

Mrs Williams carefully lifted out the pastry and laid it to one side. She then scooped out the rich, thick pieces of steak in their dark gravy and put them on the hot plates. She finally re-positioned the quarter pieces of the crust on top of the meat. It was almost a surgical operation.

"Emily! Get the Inspector some wine."

Raynes thought it amusing that, having denied him his omelette and chilled orange juice, she was now being ordered to make sure he had enough wine.

"Did you go up the railway?"

"Yes. Emily took me up to the top station."

"They have a very fine restaurant up there."

Raynes cast an eye at the dark-haired girl who was pouring out the Medoc.

"There wasn't time to get anything to eat. The train was due to leave in less than twenty minutes . . ."

A minx-like smile from her ladyship.

" . . . I spent most of the time looking for a photograph of a lady in a lilac cat suit."

He reached into the inner pocket of his jacket and produced the colourful postcards. He turned to Tom Hayward. "I know she said she had only six left; but there were at least eighty in the shop."

Tom said: "She does tend to exaggerate. I don't take her demands too seriously. But she is right. It is our best-selling postcard."

"Mutton dressed as lamb!" said Emily.

Her mother failed to understand that her daughter was talking about Lydia Naylor. "Don't be ridiculous!" she said. "It's the finest beef steak. Spence the butcher always cuts it up nicely for me."

"It's out of this world!" said Tom.

Mrs Williams gave him a hard look.

"And so is the price. When you think what the farmers get paid for their animals!" She turned to Raynes. "How are your investigations going?"

"Well," said Raynes. "It's early days. I spent six hours in the ticket office. Emily has shown me the railway and all the building work Derek did. I especially liked the waterfall. Last night, at the Inn, I was introduced to about fourteen people connected with the railway – but only two of them spoke to me about Derek's death. I don't even know who found his body."

"It was the Amos sisters."

Raynes looked blank.

"The daughters of Captain Amos . . ."

" . . . Both of them in their seventies."

"They clean the carriages every Friday morning. They won't clean them on the Sabbath because they're devout Jews. And the rest of the village would disapprove of cleaning them on Sunday . . ."

"It would be the height of depravity!" murmured Tom.

Raynes smiled.

"That answers one question. What did they do when they found him?"

"They told Father Morris. He gave him the last rites – a bit late in the day, I should think. But he gave him the benefit of the doubt."

"What was Father Morris doing in the yard?"

"He usually comes down on a Thursday evening. On the Friday morning, he would have been loading up the trucks with ballast and timber. He would then be taking it all up the line to where it would be needed by the volunteers on Saturday and Sunday. The line would be clear on Friday."

"He would be using the maintenance diesel?"

Tom nodded.

"Very useful piece of equipment. Never breaks down."

Raynes absorbed this information. So much so that he almost forgot the steak pie. He very quickly ate three more chunks of the finest steak.

"What time would this have been?"

"Probably about half past eight. Father Morris is an early bird."

"What happened then?"

"Well, the story has gone round the village . . ."

"He sent the Amos sisters off to tell P.C. Roberts . . ."

" . . . Who was having a bath!"

"Father Morris stayed with the corpse."

"After he'd had his bath, P.C. Roberts arrived with his notebook and pencil."

Mrs Williams put her head in her hands.

"That man is useless!"

"The first thing he does is pick up the whisky bottle.

'Empty,' he says. No gloves! His fingerprints all over the bottle. It's a wonder he didn't clean it with his handkerchief!

"Then he turned his attention to the body. 'Dead!' he says. Father Morris says politely: 'That's why we've called you.' P.C. Roberts tried to take his pulse; but the Amos sisters pointed to the brown patch on the ballast. 'All his blood's run out!' 'Run out?' he says. 'Why?' 'Because his legs have been chopped off!'"

"It was a complete farce."

"It had to be pointed out to him that the legs were under the carriage – between the rails. He started to reach under the carriage to pull them out. Father Morris pointed out that it would be easier to move the carriage. 'Well, move it!' he said."

Emily said: "He needed to be told that police detectives would want to see the body exactly as it had been found."

"Finally, he started taking notes . . ."

"And he isn't very bright . . ."

"It was painful . . ."

"An hour it took!"

"'What's his name?'"

"'Derek Barclay.'"

"'How d'you know that?'"

"'He drinks in the pub. He's often bought you a pint!'"

"'How d'you spell Barclay?'"

"Then, of course, he had to go and phone the police in Aberystwyth . . . I don't know what they must think of him."

Raynes said charitably: "I don't suppose he's had to deal with a murder before."

"But he's so stupid!"

The drama of P.C. Roberts examining the body had completely eclipsed the pleasure of eating the steak pie. And there were no seconds.

Mrs Williams and her daughter cleared away the plates.

Raynes looked at Tom.

"So there's no point going to see P.C. Roberts?"

"None whatsoever. His wife is far more intelligent than he

is. A very good woman . . ."

"You must have met some of the other police officers involved in the investigation?"

"I was interviewed twice. They seemed to be mostly interested in what Derek was doing in the railway yard. Was he trying to sabotage the rolling stock? Had he been trying to climb on to the roof of the carriages and fallen? Was he trying to commit suicide? Murder didn't seem to come into it. The empty whisky bottle seemed to convince them that it was a drunken escapade.

"Of course, my real worry was that, if it was decided Derek had committed suicide, Virginia might not be able to claim on his life insurance policy. Some firms are a bit difficult about such things. I think that's why everyone settled on 'death by misadventure'. It seemed to be the kindest solution in the circumstances."

Mrs Williams re-appeared with a large bowl of trifle. With evident pleasure, she introduced it as a 'Methodist Trifle'. "It's got a lot of sherry in it."

Raynes quickly drank the rest of his glass of Medoc – before his taste buds were assaulted by some ferocious Cyprus sherry.

Emily handed round the bowls of trifle.

Mrs Williams said to Tom: "I know it's one of your favourites."

Mr Hayward laughed.

"It's about the only thing that would encourage me to join the Methodists. I am not destined to be a Rechabite!"

Raynes cautiously approached the fruity sponge. He feared it might be 40% proof.

He continued to voice his thoughts on the strange circumstances surrounding Derek's death.

"No one seems to know where he was staying that last weekend. His wife didn't know."

Tom looked up.

"No one knew he was in Pwddldwc. There was no sign of his van. He did no work on the castle. He never appeared in the pub. We all assumed he was back in Wolverhampton."

Raynes looked across the table at Mrs Williams.

"Would he have stayed with Jones the postman?"

"No. That's where his wife stays. They took pity on her. Normally, they wouldn't take anyone."

"Would he have stayed at the *Railway Inn*?"

"Too expensive."

"Really?"

Raynes looked surprised.

"You only saw the public bar last night. At the back, there's quite a good restaurant. And the five bedrooms they have are quite luxurious."

"His wife said that he sometimes slept in the castle in his sleeping bag."

"You could do that in summer – but not in winter."

Mrs Williams said: "I think he often stayed with Ifor and Marion Davies at Penbass farm. They were quite good friends of his."

"She was!" said Emily.

Mrs Williams looked reprovingly at her daughter.

"You shouldn't speak of things you know nothing about."

But, clearly, her daughter did know something.

Mrs Williams continued to search her memory.

"I think he stayed with the Amos sisters. They like to have a man about the place. And, of course, he stayed with Catherine before she took ill. She was a splendid cook. He also stayed with Helen's mother. But that was before she married that wretched policeman and had all those children." She looked at her daughter. "And we mustn't forget he stayed here sometimes. Remember how he brought those huge Easter eggs for all of you." Mrs Williams smiled. "He was a very generous man. He loved children."

Raynes was watching Emily's face whilst her mother was talking. He noticed the flash of anger when her mother rebuked her. He also thought he detected a certain anxiety about what her mother was saying – or about to say.

Did she know where Derek was sleeping that weekend? If

she did, she was saying nothing. She remained silent and continued to eat her trifle. But this was not the moment to cross-examine her. On the previous night, he had seen how angry and hostile she could become. He did not want to endure another scene.

Mrs Williams looked at the Inspector's empty plate.

"A little more trifle?"

12: In Vino Veritas

Inspector Raynes was pleasantly surprised to receive a warm welcome on his second visit to the *Railway Inn*.

Brian Williamson, the Chief Engineer, treated him to a glass of whisky and asked him if he had enjoyed his first day on the Puddleduck. In return, Raynes asked him how *Lady Ermintrude* was progressing.

"Can't do anything until the new piston rod arrives. We hope it'll be here by Friday. Then we'll give her a trial run. Just as far as the castle. No further. There's always a danger of something else going wrong."

A little later, Anna Patterson gave him a knowing look.

"I believe those two harpies set on you this afternoon at the top station?"

"News travels fast."

"Bill Naylor has read the riot act. They won't trouble you any more. They've got bigger fish to fry."

Raynes followed her gaze.

Simon Jacoby was talking to Joanne. His wife, Arlene, who was sitting next to Thompson the vet, was watching his every move.

Raynes said: "It's more like a dating agency than a railway."

Anna laughed.

"I think it's the sea air that gives them an appetite."

Raynes said: "The sea? I haven't seen it yet. Is it far away?"

"Walk two hundred yards down the road and you'll fall into

it! But be careful crossing the main line. The trains don't stop here – so they come up upon you rather fast."

"Has anyone ever been killed?"

"Not while I've been here. We've had more fatalities than they have."

"Derek?"

"A lovely man. He didn't deserve to die."

"Do you think it was murder?"

"I prefer to think of it as an accident. And so do most of them."

"But in your heart of hearts?"

"It's better for business if we put the past behind us."

"I take your point."

Raynes drifted away from the bar and went over to Father Morris, who raised his hands to heaven. "We meet again!"

"I've just been told that you were present when Derek Barclay's body was discovered."

"Yes. I had that sad honour. But it was the ladies who were cleaning the carriages who found him. The Amos sisters – you've probably heard of them. They're devout Jews."

"What time did they find him?"

"Must have been about ten o'clock. They'd cleaned the insides of the twelve main carriages and then moved on to the three reserves."

"Can you describe what you saw?"

"Vividly. He was lying on the far side of the carriage – close to the wall. He was about half way along the first carriage – about level with the second compartment. Just the torso. He looked as if he had fallen backwards. An empty bottle of whisky – 47% proof – had fallen from his left hand. The bottom of his two legs were cut across at an angle. You couldn't see them unless you looked. They were in the middle of the track – under the carriage.

"A large brownish patch of dried blood lay on the ballast. Soaked through – quite a long way. The back wheels of carriage No 1 had run over him. The sheer weight sliced through his legs quite neatly. No mess on the front bogie or on any wheel of carriages two and three. I had a good look at it whilst the sisters went off to tell the police."

"What was his face like?"

"Terribly disfigured. It didn't look like Derek at all. I think the local insect population had done their bit. Exposure to the elements. Loss of blood. I covered his face with my newspaper."

"I'm told that the local police didn't handle the situation very professionally."

"It was farcical. Disastrous. Tragic. All three . . ."

Father Morris looked over Raynes' shoulder.

" . . . Be careful what you say. He's right behind you! In fact, I think he's wanting a few words with you."

Raynes turned.

Here was the figure which had caused such mirth. Tonight, he was in plain clothes.

"Mr Raynes?"

"Yes."

"I'm Constable Roberts. I've been told that you are down here investigating the death of a gentleman who died on the railway last year."

Raynes smiled politely.

"I came down here to work on the railway at the invitation of Mr Hayward. I've spent six hours in the ticket office. I haven't had any time to do any investigating."

"People have told me you've been asking questions."

Raynes was as gentle as possible.

"It's still a free country, Mr Roberts. People are allowed to ask questions. They can still disagree with a coroner's report. I have spoken to Mr Barclay's widow. In fact, she spoke to me. She remains convinced that her husband was murdered."

"Well, he wasn't. It was an accident."

"So I'm told."

P.C. Roberts summoned up as much authority as he could muster as a member of the Welsh Constabulary.

"May I warn you, sir, that any allegation made by you against any person, here present, would lead to serious action being taken against you . . ."

"Oh, bugger off, Roberts!" said Joyce Packer. "Leave the Inspector alone! Remember your position. Mr Raynes has worked for the Royal Family. He's one of the most famous detectives in England."

"I have my job to do, ma'am."

"No, you haven't. You're just an incompetent bungler. You go and tell those who put you up to this to look to their own consciences. Or they could be in serious trouble."

Raynes remained gracious.

"Thank you very much for your advice, Mr Roberts."

He returned to Father Morris.

"I presume the locomotives were all locked away?"

The cleric nodded.

"But not the diesel. It sits out in all weathers."

"I see."

"There are only three keys. One is kept in the safe in the ticket office; Brian Williamson has one; and I have the third."

"So someone could get the key?"

"Only with difficulty. There are ten people who have keys to the station; but only four with keys to the safe."

"Who?"

"Dr Campbell, Simon Jacoby, Bill Naylor and Brian Williamson."

"Would Derek Barclay have had a key to the station?"

"To the station, yes. But not to the safe. Dr Campbell wouldn't have given him a key. He didn't trust him."

"Really?"

Raynes raised his eyebrows.

"For Dr Campbell, the safe is the Ark of the Covenant. The Holy of Holies. Not to be trusted to a mere mortal."

He laughed.

Raynes moved on.

"What about the points? Electric or manual?"

"It's only the signalling that's electric. All the points are manual. You always have to check that no one has touched them before you start moving. Otherwise you could have a derailment. And derailments cost time – and money."

Inspector Raynes thanked Father Morris for all his information and asked if he could offer him a drink.

"A double whisky would be lovely."

Raynes returned to Anna at the bar.

"Two double whiskies, please."

Anna said to the Inspector: " I wonder if you could have a word with Ifor. He's feeling pretty low tonight. His wife's just left him."

"Who is Ifor?"

"A local farmer. He knew Derek extremely well."

"Did he like him?"

"No. He hated him."

"Does he have a tractor?"

"Several. Why do you ask?"

"Joyce Packer said that she thought that the carriages were moved by someone with a tractor."

"Well, this is your chance to ask him."

Ifor Davies was in the snug – a small room just off the bar. He was the only person there – probably because he was in one of his blackest moods and was not very good company.

Having taken the whisky to Father Morris, he ventured into the snug.

"Hello. I'm Richard Raynes. A friend of Tom Hayward. Anna's asked me to have a word with you."

"Get me another Special!"

There were already two empty glasses on the table.

Raynes returned to the bar.

"Can he have another Special?"

"It won't do him any good. You'll probably have to take him home."

She poured out the Special. Raynes took it through.

Ifor seemed surprised.

"She said she wouldn't give me any more. You must have waved a magic wand."

"I did."

"Good for you. You're a good man."

Raynes waited till he had taken his first swig.

"I wanted to ask you about Derek Barclay."

Ifor almost choked on his drink.

"That bastard! Why do you want to talk about him? He's dead. And good riddance to him!"

"You didn't like him?"

"Would you like a man who fornicates with your wife in front of your very eyes?"

"Probably not."

"She had no shame. No shame whatsoever."

"What's your wife's name?"

"Marion. Everyone knows that."

"Anna told me that she's left you."

"Again! This is the eighth time."

"Perhaps she doesn't like living with you?"

"I hit her."

"Well, that's as good a reason as any."

"But I need her."

"On the farm?"

"For everything."

Raynes was feeling mischievous.

"Well, she won't have gone to Derek Barclay!"

"No," said Ifor. "No, she can't. He's in hell. He deserves to be in hell. Coming between a husband and a wife. They won't have it in the village. A fornicating woman should be stoned on her father's doorstep. Except that her father's dead. He was a good man."

"But Derek wasn't?"

"No."

Raynes wondered if there was anything to be got out of this drunk man. Perhaps he could ask a series of provocative questions. If Ifor knew anything, he might blurt it out.

"So you think it was good that Derek was murdered?"

"Very good."

"Did you do it?"

"No." A pause. "But I wanted to do it. Several of us wanted to do it."

"Who?"

Ifor raised a bleary eye.

"I wouldn't tell you that. You're a *saesneg*. You don't share secrets with a *saesneg*!"

"How would you have killed him – if you had got the chance?"

"Crashed into his car. Cut his brake pipes. Electrocuted him."

"How would you have done that?"

"When he was on the scaffolding. I was going to connect up a wire to the mains. The moment he touched the metal, he'd be a goner."

"You might have electrocuted yourself."

"That's what Dr Campbell said."

"Did he know about your plans?"

"We talked about it one night. But he also pointed out that Derek had rubber soles on his boots. That might have saved him."

"Did you mention this plan to your wife?"

"Of course not."

"Why not?"

"She'd have told Derek."

"So you gave up your idea of killing him?"

"No, I did not . . ."

An angry flush spread over his face.

"It's just . . . someone else got there first."

"So there were other plans?"

"Yes. The best one . . ." He emptied his glass. " . . . The best one was to put a gas cylinder in the back of his van and rig it up to a timer and attach . . ."

Ifor had great trouble saying the word "attach".

"Attach it?"

"Yes. Attach it to the ignition. Then, when he turned on the ignition, he'd be blown to Kingdom come . . ."

"I imagine he would." Raynes smiled. "And then everyone would be happy?"

"Everyone."

"That wasn't your idea?"

"No. We got the idea from the IRA. You know – Mountbatten's boat."

"So various plans were being talked about; but someone else did it before you were ready?"

"Yes."

"And you know who it was?"

Ifor looked suspiciously at Raynes. "No, I don't. But if I did, I wouldn't tell you. It's better to leave the dead – dead. What's the point of raking it all up again? The job's done. Well done – and that's enough for me. And that's all I'm saying."

"Was your wife very upset?"

This was very difficult for Ifor to admit.

"Cried for two weeks." The drunk man looked glum. "She accused me of killing him. I said I wished I had. She hit me for that." He rubbed his cheek as if he could still feel the blow. "But I didn't do it. It was too clever for me. The lucky sod got clean away with it. Not even murder. Death by misadventure! I ask you. Even fooled the police and the coroner! You have to take your hat off to him . . ."

"Him?"

"Or her. It could be both of them. I just don't know."

Ifor sat reflectively – staring at his empty glass. Then he looked at the Inspector as if his mind was made up. "He had to be stopped. It's common justice. An eye for an eye and . . . I can't remember the rest."

"A tooth for a tooth?"

"Yes. That's it."

"I'll get you another drink."

"You're a pal."

But perhaps it was too late for another drink? Ifor collapsed over the table with his head in his hands. His empty glass rolled off the table and smashed on the floor.

Anna came rushing in to the snug.

"I think he's collapsed."

"Looks like it. I'd better get a brush before anyone treads on that glass. Would you be willing to help Bob get him home?"

Raynes nodded.

He didn't want to help Ifor home. But what else could he do? Ifor had helped him. It was the least he could do.

13: Go Gently Into That Dark Night

In the event, it took three people to get Ifor into Bob's car. They shoved him into the back seat and Raynes slipped into the passenger seat.

"Is he often like this?"

"Quite often on Sunday nights. He watches "Songs of Praise" and it brings back memories of him singing in the Pwddldwc Male Voice Choir."

"Is there such a thing?"

"There used to be."

"Is that where he met his wife?"

"Afterwards. In the pub. Marion was a sensible lass. Kept her feet on the ground."

"Do you think she'll come back?"

"She always has."

"She must love him."

"She deserves better."

Raynes watched the winding country road heading into the dark hills on the north side of the valley.

"Is it a long way?"

"Three and a half miles."

As they came up to the farm, they noticed that all the lights were on.

"Perhaps she's back?"

"More likely Ifor's left the lights on to scare off the burglars."

But Raynes was right.

Standing in the lighted doorway of the farmhouse was a blonde-haired , middle-aged woman with her arms folded and a resigned look on her face.

"Evening, Marion."

"Is he out cold?"

"Completely."

"He's better that way."

All three of them hauled Ifor out of the car and dragged him into the farmhouse.

"Do you want him taken upstairs?"

"No. Shove him in the kitchen. I'm not staying. I've just come to collect the rest of my clothes. I've discovered that he's put our wedding album in the dustbin."

"Have you rescued it?"

"Yes. Sentimentalist that I am."

She looked at the unknown man standing beside Black Bob.

"Who's he? He's not one of the locals."

"This is Mr Raynes. Inspector Raynes from Grasshallows. Tom Hayward brought him over to work on the railway. He's been trying to find out who killed Derek."

"Bit late for that!"

She held out her hand.

"Welcome to Penbass Farm, Mr Raynes. Would you like a cup of tea? It's all I can offer."

Bob said: "I've got to get back to the pub."

Marion said: "It's all right. I'll bring Mr Raynes back to the inn on my way home."

Bob drove off and Marion put on the kettle.

"So why are you asking questions about Derek?"

"On my way down to Pwddldwc, Mr Hayward told me that several people – including Derek's wife – did not accept the coroner's verdict that his death was an accident. He wanted me to see if there was any truth in the allegation that he had been murdered."

"And is there?"

"I believe so. I have spoken to Mrs Barclay and to Father Morris, who was in the station yard when the body was found. From all that they have said, I am convinced it was not an accident."

Mrs Davies continued to look at the Inspector. He sounded

honest – but could he be trusted?

"And what will you do when you can prove it is murder?"

"I shall ask for the case to be re-opened."

"Mr Roberts won't like that."

"He's already told me to stop my investigations. Certain people don't like it."

"I'm not surprised. One or two people had it in for Derek. Not the ladies; but the men."

Raynes looked at the creature snoring on the sofa.

"Your husband said that he knew several people who were plotting his death."

"Don't listen to him! He doesn't know what he's talking about. He just picks up idle gossip."

"He said he had a plan to electrocute Derek."

"Not he! Coward that he is! He wouldn't dare touch Derek. Derek had knocked him out several times."

"He mentioned Dr Campbell."

"That's more likely. But all of them – it was just talk. Nothing serious. There's only one person who had the motive and the means. But they wouldn't dare arrest him."

"Sir David Cadwaller?"

"Yes. You're on the right track there. He hated Derek. Accused him of trespassing on his land. Threatened him with a double-barrelled shotgun. But Derek seemed to have a guardian angel looking after him."

Raynes smiled.

"Was that you?"

"No. But he was a guardian angel to me. He stopped this brute attacking me. Many a time."

She looked at the Inspector.

"You know, I really feel like pouring this boiling water all over his face. Just to make him feel how much I've suffered."

Raynes tried to defuse the tension.

He shrugged his shoulders.

"No skin off my nose. But I'd rather it was used for a cup of tea."

Marion laughed. At least the stranger had a sense of

humour. She turned back to the cupboard. "Mug or cup?"

"Mug."

"Sugar?

"Two."

She made the tea whilst Raynes speculated on the nature of her relationship with her husband. It seemed totally destructive.

He asked: "Are you intending to come back to the farm?"

"I usually do. But I intend to let him fester for another few weeks. So long as the animals don't suffer."

"Do you love him at all?"

Marion looked at her husband with complete contempt.

"I can't stand him. If I had the courage, I'd kill him." She looked at the Inspector. "I tell you this because you're a stranger and don't belong to these parts. The only reason why I have not left him permanently – or got a divorce – is because this farm would then go to his brother, who is just as much a drunk as he is.

"I've worked on this farm for years. Given it the best years of my life. Endured pain and misery. I am determined to keep it going. Preferably after this rat is dead."

Raynes said quietly: "I admire you for your courage."

But there was no mistaking her feelings; and since the kettle full of boiling water was still close to hand, he decided to divert her attention back to Derek.

"Apart from Sir David Cadwaller, is there anyone else you think might have killed Mr Barclay?"

Marion thought long and hard for several minutes. Then she said: "There is one distant possibility. Just before he died, Derek did say that he thought his wife might be having an affair with someone. He wasn't sure. But it wasn't anyone connected with the railway. He just said it one afternoon when we were together . . . I think it was worrying him."

This was a new line of thought. But if Mrs Barclay had someone else, why would she keep coming down to Pwddldwc? It didn't add up.

Raynes drank his tea – and they continued to stand looking

down on Ifor – this useless piece of human garbage – better dead.

Eventually, Raynes said: "Can you perhaps tell me where you are staying? Or give me a phone number where you can be contacted?

Marion Davies permitted herself a broad smile.

"Is this for professional purposes?

"It is."

"What a pity! I could do with a strong policeman to protect me."

"Your last protector didn't fare too well!"

"You might survive a little longer!"

They ceased joking.

Marion said: "I'm not giving anyone my address or phone number. I am staying with an old school friend whom nobody knows. The last time I went away, a little rat tried to blackmail me. She discovered my address – and said she would tell my husband unless I gave her £100."

"Did you give her the money?"

"Did I hell!"

"And did she tell Ifor?"

"She did – and he came over and made a terrible scene. Dragged me by my hair to the car. Punched me in the face and gave me a bloodied nose. This time, I am keeping my movements to myself."

"Did you get your own back on the little rat?"

"Yes. I shopped her and her boyfriend to the police. He is now in jail. Two can play at that game."

It clearly did not pay to cross Mrs Davies. She was a very tough, determined woman.

Since there was nothing more to do at Penbass farm, Raynes said: "When you're ready, I shall be glad to have a lift back to the pub."

Mrs Davies cheered up.

There was a twinkle in her blue eyes.

"We could always take the scenic route."

"At this time of night?"

"I could show you the stars."

Raynes was delighted at this unexpected invitation.

"If you insist."

As they left the farmhouse, Marion said: "I'll leave the front door open. With a bit of luck, the foxes'll get him!"

14: We're Watching You!

On the following morning, walking down to the station, Tom Hayward asked what he had been doing up at Penbass Farm.

"I waited for you at the *Railway Inn* till eleven o'clock. I couldn't wait any longer."

"At least Mrs Williams left the front door open for me."

"I left it open for you. Didn't want you to undermine your reputation with the locals."

Raynes laughed.

"I was talking to Mrs Davies about her husband."

"Was she at home?"

"She was at the farm when we arrived."

"Nobody knows where she's been staying. Mrs Williams hadn't a clue."

"She's been staying with an old school friend; but she'll soon be back."

"Did Ifor recover consciousness?"

"No. She wanted to pour a kettle of boiling water over him; but I discouraged her."

"You worked your charm on her?"

Raynes smiled at his memories of the previous night.

"No. It was the other way round."

Tom Hayward shook his head.

"You're a dark horse, Inspector. And no mistake!"

* * * *

Sunday was always a busy day on the railway and crowds

began to arrive at the station quite early in the morning. The ticket office opened at 8.30am and the first train left at 9.15am.

Outside the engine shed, *Sir Walter* was already building up a fine head of steam. Coal was being loaded into *Lady Sylvia* who would be taking the second train at 10.45am.

People who were staying on the local caravan site were the first to arrive; but, soon, carloads of visitors began to appear. They were directed down to the seafront where there was plenty of parking space.

Whilst the passengers were milling around, waiting for their train, there was a healthy sale of books and postcards. As Tom had said, more was spent on the merchandise than on the tickets.

Very soon, *Sir Walter* was ready to move. She was brought up to the platform and then reversed into the siding to pick up the first set of carriages. Youthful helpers kept a close watch on the points.

Tom Hayward and Simon Jacoby were enjoying themselves immensely. It was a beautiful spring morning and *Sir Walter* was raring to go. Great billows of smoke blossomed out of the chimney. With a few warning shrieks of the whistle, the long-awaited train rolled into the station.

The booking hall immediately emptied. Everyone was out on the platform taking photographs and sharing in the drama. The leather sleeve from the water tower was being placed in the saddle tank. *Sir Walter* had already been topped up; but huge cascades of Welsh water greatly attracted the enthusiasts.

One or two people were allowed on the footplate; but Tom was busy shovelling more coal into the firebox – so there wasn't much space.

Eighty-two tickets had been sold and everyone was waiting for Charlie to wave his green flag. Charlie was feeling a little under the weather, having eaten a king prawn vindaloo curry the night before. He was still suffering twelve hours later. He wandered up and down the platform, trying to make sure everyone had a seat – but there was still much coming and going.

Brian Williamson came over from the engineering shed to check the gauges and add a final drop of grease to the pistons.

Raynes watched all the excitement from his position at the ticket counter. A few last-minute travellers hurried in to buy tickets, fearful the train would leave without them. Rushing out on to the platform, they realized they still had a couple of minutes spare and dashed back into the booking hall to buy a map or use the toilets.

Charlie blew his whistle and waved his flag; and the small train chugged its way out of the station on its way to Abernirvana.

There was now peace in the ticket office. Time for a coffee before the next influx at about 10.00am.

Raynes decided to use the coffee break to join Bill Naylor in the signal box. He was sitting in front of a very high-tech control system, which not only marked the progress of each train, but also contained a bank of security cameras, covering the two main stations and the two small halts.

The Inspector watched *Sir Walter* approaching the castle and pulling in to the station. The screens switched to events at the upper station – the shop and the restaurant. Tables were being laid and Joanne was directing operations.

Raynes said: "You keep a close eye on your customers."

"It's certainly cut down the shoplifting."

At the touch of a button, the camera focused on the table where Raynes had been sitting the previous afternoon.

"Does that bring back memories?"

"Most certainly. Thank you for your note."

"I'm sorry you missed your cheese omelette."

"I was extremely hungry. All that fresh air gives you an appetite."

"It seemed quite a fierce confrontation?"

"They didn't want me digging up the past."

"None of us do. We want Derek's death to be forgotten as soon as possible."

Bill switched back to the castle station. He spoke into the

microphone. "There's six more passengers coming in from the car-park."

He turned back to the Inspector.

"Murder's not good for trade. Especially when your own staff are making the accusations."

"Is Mrs Barclay here today?"

Bill Naylor switched the security camera to the tea room and kitchen and looked at the eight people working there.

"No. I think she went home after telling you her story. Joyce Packer told her to leave the decision to you."

Raynes said quietly: "I have made my decision. I think it was murder. Virginia believes it was done by a member of the Railway. I'm not so sure. For all we know, there may be problems in Wolverhampton. Mr Barclay may have had enemies there."

Bill Naylor looked up.

"I hadn't thought of that."

"Might be a lot easier killing him over here?"

"Indeed."

"There's also Sir David Cadwaller? No friend of the railway . . ."

" . . . and no friend of Derek! He also hates Simon Jacoby. I often wonder whether he might take a pot shot at our Chairman whilst he's driving the train up the line. I'm told Sir David is a crack shot. I always tell Simon to keep his head down when he's approaching the castle."

Bill looked at the screen.

"They're getting ready to go."

He pressed another button and the signal at Caercraig promptly rose.

"No down train to contend with. They should arrive at Abernirvana in good time. That'll push up sales."

Smoke filled the screen.

"Keep your head down!" Bill shouted. (Not that Simon could hear him.) He said to Raynes: "Actually, I doubt whether Sir David would recognize either driver or fireman. Their faces are completely covered with sweat and soot."

He switched the screen back to the booking hall.

"The peasants are arriving."

"I'd better go back."

"Thank you for your visit. Good luck in your investigations – even though I think you're wrong."

Raynes walked back along the platform.

Lady Sylvia had now raised a good head of steam and would soon be ready to collect her carriages. Then only the three reserves would be left in the sidings.

He returned to Dr Campbell.

"I thought I'd lost you."

"No. I went to see Bill Naylor. He showed me his security cameras. He can switch from tea rooms to car parks and can see everything that is going on." More provocatively, he said: "It's a pity they weren't in operation the night Derek died. That might have answered all our questions."

Dr Campbell issued four tickets to a family.

Then he said: "They aren't switched on at nights – so they wouldn't have been much use. And they cost an absolute fortune. We're spreading the cost over four years."

"Who's paying for them?"

Raynes was surprised by the answer.

"I am."

15: Sunday Lunch

Sunday lunchtime found Arlene Jacoby dining with James Thompson in a country house hotel about ten miles south of Pwddldwc. She had spent three hours in the tea room serving breakfasts and morning coffee – so she felt that she had done her bit. Simon would be on the footplate of *Sir Walter* for the next five hours.

Arlene was unwilling to sacrifice her creature comforts – and high among them was a good Sunday lunch in civilized surroundings. Excellent food; beautifully served. It was said that the chef had been trained in Gleneagles; and the menu certainly pointed in that direction.

She had already enjoyed a bowl of Highland mussels in Muscadet and cream; followed by a traditional roast of Scotch beef with homemade Yorkshire pudding, garnished with Dijon mustard and horse radish sauce.

She enjoyed the company of James Thompson, who was a quiet, reserved sort of man who liked to keep the world at arm's length but was totally dedicated in his care for animals. Arlene knew this from having watched him perform a delicate operation on her golden retriever. And his dedication to Dolly had been legendary. The old horse had spent its final years in a paddock at the bottom of his garden.

Arlene had found that once she had penetrated his reserve and won his friendship, James was a man of passionate beliefs and a very dry sense of humour. But she realized that he must be a very lonely man.

His wife, Catherine, had died of cancer two years ago. She was one of the victims of "too little; too late." He had nursed her himself – right to the end. Their two sons were now living in England. After her death, he had dedicated himself completely to his profession. He had publicly declared that no woman would ever take Catherine's place.

Arlene knew she was safe with Thompson the Vet. There would be no gossip or scandal. There would be no heavy drinking because he was terrified of losing his licence; and she was aware that, later that day, she would be driving Simon back to London. So their Sunday indulgence was limited to a couple of glasses of claret and perhaps a Cointreau with ice.

As they lingered over the cheeseboard and the coffee, Arlene said: "Do you think Tom was wise to bring that policeman down to the Puddleduck?"

"Probably not. But people still have strong feelings. Their views have to be respected."

"I saw him talking to her yesterday in the tea room. Then they went out into the railway yard where she gave him all the gory details. "

"It takes time to get over grief."

"That policeman said that Derek's death might have nothing to do with the Railway. He suggested that there might have been some problems back in Wolverhampton."

"I heard that too."

"I wish she'd stay in Wolverhampton and look after her wretched children."

There was a thoughtful silence. Should she have more Stilton? James poured himself another cup of coffee.

"I hear Marion's back on the farm."

"I hadn't heard that. I was up there on Tuesday looking at two of their sheep. There was no sign of her then."

Arlene asked: "Is Ifor really coping? When he was carried out of the pub last night, he looked completely legless."

"When he's not drunk, he's fine. He's looking after all his animals – and feeding them properly. It's only when he goes down to the pub that trouble starts."

"I feel so sorry for Marion."

"So do I. But what can one do?"

"Kill him! Then Marion could run the farm."

"I think she'd need some help. But, of course, she might be arrested and that would do nobody any good. Least of all the animals. Ifor's brother is a complete waster."

"Even worse than Ifor?"

"Far worse. I'd rather buy it and run it myself."

"Wouldn't they be better selling it to Mr Cadwaller?"

James Thompson shook his head.

"I think he's already got enough. There's only a few family farms left in the valley. When I was a lad, there were eighteen – now they're down to four. Sir David has taken all the best land. He doesn't really need any more."

There was another thoughtful silence. Mrs Jacoby wasn't really interested in Ifor or his farm. What she wanted to talk about was Joanne. Eventually, she said:

"Do you think Simon's interested in Joanne?"

"Possibly. But I don't think she's interested in him. She doesn't display any outward signs of affection."

"People say she's had lots of men."

"Well, perhaps she has. But they don't seem to last long enough for anyone to notice."

"Has she ever made a pass at you?"

"Not that I noticed. If she was a horse, I might have paid more attention!"

Both of them laughed.

"I think Simon goes into that restaurant every time the train pulls into Abernirvana. He's up there three times a day. Anything could be happening . . ."

James tried to dispel her fears.

"I don't think he has time. He's too busy moving the locomotive from one end of the train to the other. And people are constantly taking photographs. I'm sure they'd notice if he slipped away into a broom cupboard! All the staff would notice. You can't keep any secrets round here."

Arlene wasn't convinced. But her mind turned to other things:

"Is that girl still pestering you?"

"Are you referring to Miss Williams?"

"Who else?"

"She'll shortly be going away to university. At the moment, she's doing her final revision for her A-levels. So she hasn't any time to work in the surgery. But she's very good with the animals."

"How much have you given her?"

"A couple of hundred. You've got to remember she lost her father when she was six. It can't have been easy for Mrs Williams bringing up four daughters. It can cost a lot to put a person through university. And she's a very bright girl."

"I always think she's spying on people."

"It's a long-standing Welsh custom. Everybody watches everyone else. They love to know everything about their neighbours. You English are far less nosey. And Emily does want to be a reporter."

"I don't think it's right her fleecing you."

"I can afford it."

Arlene paid their bill and they went out for a walk along the cliffs. Arlene loved the view and James was glad of a little gentle exercise after an extremely good meal. They spent half an hour on the headland and then walked back to the hotel. Simon Jacoby's BMW dominated the car park.

"What time are you leaving?"

"About half past six. It takes us about four hours to get back to London. Simon sleeps most of the way. But I enjoy the driving. Once we get on to the motorway, she just floats."

They strapped themselves into their black leather seats.

"Have you got anything new in your menagerie?"

Arlene normally ended her Sunday afternoons feeding the birds and animals that were currently being cared for by the vet.

"I have a couple of baby badgers. Their mother was shot. I'm feeding them on milk."

"Would they be any use as household pets?"

Thompson the Vet sighed at such monumental stupidity. But he said politely: "No. In a few weeks time, they'll have to be returned to their natural habitat."

"Rather like that policeman! I'm sure he'd be happier splashing around in his own pool." Arlene looked at her friend. "Simon didn't want him brought over. It was Tom Hayward's idea. Simon's very annoyed. He's told P.C. Roberts to scare him off his patch."

Mr Thompson laughed.

"I don't think Mr Roberts would scare anyone! Certainly not a police inspector. But Mr Raynes has no jurisdiction in Wales. The case has been closed and the coroner has given his verdict. I don't think Simon has anything to worry about."

16: Dicing With Death

Once he had completed his duties at the ticket office, Raynes took the 1.45pm train to Caercraig. He didn't tell anyone where he was going; but he bought a return ticket – just as if he was an ordinary passenger. (That was all Archie Campbell was getting out of him!)

He sat in the second carriage and enjoyed the fifteen-minute run up to the castle. He planned to catch the 3.59pm train back to Pwddldwc. So he had a couple of hours to visit the Cadwallers.

He had looked at the Ordnance Survey map in the booking hall; so he had a clear idea where the Cadwallers lived. All he had to do was cross the car park, walk down a country lane for half a mile and then turn right. He hoped that he might still be in one piece when he returned.

He strolled up the short drive and came to the elegant house and its farm buildings. It seemed a bit presumptuous to walk up the front steps, so he went round to the back door.

He knocked and an old lady appeared.

"Good afternoon. Is Sir David in?"

"No. He's gone shooting."

"Would Lady Margaret be in?"

"Who are you and what is your business?"

"I am Richard Raynes. A police officer and a friend of Virginia Barclay."

"I'll see if she's willing to see you."

So Raynes was left to cool his heels in the farmyard for five minutes. Being Sunday afternoon, no one was working. There were two tractors and a Land Rover parked in the yard – also a silver Mercedes 300 and an Audi A4. Both were in immaculate condition.

Instead of the old lady, a much younger woman, in her forties, appeared on the back steps.

"Are you Lady Margaret?"

"Yes, I am. Come in."

She looked pleased to see him.

Raynes was conscious of passing through a very beautiful house. It was splendidly furnished and there were family portraits on almost every wall. The front sitting room had an excellent view, looking across the fields and down to the sea. He was seated in a very comfortable armchair and given a cup of delicious coffee. He found himself being treated as an honoured guest.

Lady Margaret looked at him.

"So you are a policeman?"

"Yes. But not in Wales. I work in Grasshallows."

"That's quite a long way away."

"It is. But I am hoping to get back there tonight."

"You're working on the railway?"

"Well, that was the plan. But I found there were other reasons why I had been invited. I was asked to speak to Virginia Barclay – Derek's wife."

Margaret Cadwaller nodded.

"You've met her?"

"No. But I've heard a lot about her."

"She doesn't believe that her husband's death was an accident. She is convinced it was murder."

"She could be right . . ."

Raynes raised his eyebrows.

" . . . The circumstances were very peculiar. Quite out of character."

"You knew him that well?"

"I did. I can't imagine Derek wandering round the station yard at any time of day or night. He always did the job he was doing till 4.30pm. Then he liked to go for a hot bath. He had his evening meal and then went down to the pub for a game of darts and a couple of pints. His movements were as regular as clockwork."

Raynes noted that Lady Margaret would make an excellent witness.

"Well, Virginia has asked me to re-open the case – but in a

personal capacity. Just to see if – after all these months – the truth can still be found. Maybe it was an accident . . ."

"It wasn't."

"How can you be so sure?"

"Because . . . I have reason to believe my husband planned his death."

Faced with such a stunning declaration, Raynes was silent.

Lady Margaret explained.

"My husband is a very rich, powerful, selfish man. He is charming when all is going well; but if he is crossed or opposed in any way, he is consumed by an uncontrollable and fierce anger. He was an only son – and totally spoilt.

"He spends most of his time as a hard-working farmer. He loves the lands handed down by his forebears and is constantly seeking to increase them. He cares for his animals at all hours of day and night. He is particularly obsessed by the pedigree of his cows, his horses and his pigs. Only the best will do.

"However, he has frequently been in court for losing his temper, lashing out and attacking his opponents. The local magistrates know what he is like and he usually gets off with a large fine.

"He was very enthusiastic about the railway when it was re-opened . . ."

"Was it he who provided the two horses – Glyn and Dolly?"

"It was. But if the Railway ventures on to his land in any way, it is a very different story. He allowed Derek to build his waterfall and he has encouraged Father Morris to block off the old quarries with an embankment. But he was totally opposed to the restoration of the castle. He believed it was his property.

"He took his case to the highest courts in the land – and lost. Apparently, the castle had belonged to another family who bequeathed it to the Railway.

"He could not accept this judgement. He objected most strongly to Derek doing the restoration – although he did it beautifully. He objected to the cafe being installed in the keep and the toilets downstairs. When those things happened, he became totally irrational.

"All his anger was focused on Derek. 'That horrible little man!' he called him. 'That Brummie bastard!' And he treated him shamefully. He attacked his van; slashed his tyres; covered it with liquid manure. Derek never reported it. My husband was never charged for any of those things. And for the last two years, he has frequently talked about killing Derek – especially when he had been drinking."

Raynes intervened.

"Was this not because of some more personal matter?"

Lady Margaret looked shocked.

"Who told you that?"

"Tom Hayward – the person who brought me here."

Lady Margaret looked less anxious.

"Tom's all right. He was a friend of Derek's."

"He told me the background last night. He said that this was almost certainly the real reason why Sir David hated him so much."

Tears came into Margaret's eyes.

"It was my fault. I should never have told him. When the baby was born, he was so proud at having a son and heir – we already had three daughters who were all his.

"But, one day, when he was being particularly beastly, sneering at my family – who, he said, had no class – no pedigree – I told him who his son's real father was. That stopped him.

"He went terribly silent for a week. I knew a storm was coming. One Sunday night, he beat me up. He started with a riding crop; he ended up using his fists. I thought he was going to kill me. I spent four weeks in a private nursing home. During that time, he arranged for Timothy's adoption. He made sure I would never find him. He said that I had totally humiliated him.

"I received my punishment – but Derek's took a little longer to arrange. I warned him . . . but he laughed it off."

"Did the police question your husband? Did they know

about his threats?"

Margaret smiled sadly.

"I said nothing to anyone. I didn't even tell my mother. But he had uttered these threats in public. And Derek's van was found just up the road.

"P.C. Roberts came to see him. He took him round the farm to see all his animals. Gave him a ride round the estate in his brand new Land Rover. Plied him with whisky. Sent him home sozzled."

"So he could have been guilty?"

"He says that he has an alibi. He says that on that Sunday night, he was with Thompson the Vet looking after a sick cow."

"Was that true?"

"I don't know. I keep out of his way. He doesn't sleep with me. I keep my bedroom door locked."

Raynes looked thoughtful.

Why should Sir David be claiming a cast-iron alibi on the Sunday night – when Derek could have been killed on the Friday, Saturday or Sunday nights? What was so special about Sunday?

There was a distant sound of an engine revving up as it entered the drive.

Lady Margaret jumped to her feet.

"That's him! He's come back early! He mustn't see us together. You'll have to leave immediately!"

She rushed Raynes out into the front hall; pulled back the bolts on the main door and pushed him out on to the steps, slamming and bolting the door behind him. It all happened in less than thirty seconds.

Raynes tried to decide quickly what he should do. He could run. He could hide. But perhaps it might be better to see Sir David before he left – even at the expense of violence or personal injury.

Having taken that decision, he walked round the side of the house and entered the farmyard where Sir David was unloading no fewer than three guns.

"Good afternoon."

Sir David quite literally jumped. He had not heard the Inspector approaching.

"I wonder if . . ."

The landowner's face – already red – turned purple with rage.

"I don't know who you are – but you are trespassing. This is a private estate. Did you see the notice on the drive? 'Trespassers will be prosecuted.' If you're not off my land in three minutes, I shall shoot you!"

"I was hoping . . ."

Sir David Cadwaller picked up a gun and slipped a couple of cartridges into the breech.

"It's three – and counting!"

He slipped off the safety catch.

"Off you go."

Raynes decided that it was no use provoking a psychopath. He remembered the old saying: 'He who fights and runs away, lives to fight another day.' He turned on his heel and walked slowly out of the farmyard.

As he passed through the gate, two bullets thwacked the wall on his right-hand side. Forsaking dignity, he ran. As he reached the bottom of the drive, two more shots came his way. He heard the buzz as they passed.

It had been a pointless confrontation – and quite dangerous. But he was glad he had seen Sir David and experienced his brutality at first hand. Everything that had been said about him was true.

He made his way back to the castle station – and sat in the April sunshine, glad to be alive.

17: A Marked Man

Raynes had plenty of time to think about his weekend in Pwddldwc whilst he was waiting for his train.

Two nights with Mrs Williams; two visits to the *Railway Inn*. Some lovely food. The joy of the little trains. Helping to carry a drunk man home. The pleasure of spending a couple of hours in a Forestry Commission car park with Marion Davies. Naughty but nice!

It had been a colourful weekend; but had he really got anywhere with the murder? He had spoken to Virginia Barclay. He had hoped to speak to her again – but she had gone. He must go and see her in Wolverhampton.

Tom Hayward seemed to be convinced by her story. So did Joyce Packer. She had even told him how the murder was done. Was this the result of an over-active imagination or an accurate portrayal of what had actually happened?

Father Morris had been helpful in describing the murder scene. He had given a vivid picture of the Amos sisters finding the body. He had told him who had the keys to the station and access to the diesel locomotive. He had not ventured any opinion as to whether it was a murder.

The local policeman had insisted that it was an accident and told him to keep his nose out of it. Other people had threatened him – Lydia Naylor and Joanne Kennedy. They were both reputed to have had affairs with Derek. So also had Margaret Cadwaller. She had carried his child.

She had said that her husband had wanted to kill Derek. He had talked about it for the past two years. Dr Campbell was equally hostile. And Ifor Davies would never forgive him for fornicating with his wife. There might be other males bent on revenge.

He had met a lot of people over the weekend; but he still had no clear lines of inquiry. He couldn't be certain about anything.

He looked at his watch. 3.10pm. There was still another fifty minutes before his train departed. He could probably walk to Pwddldwc in that time.

But he suddenly remembered that there was a small cafe in the castle. He would perhaps be able to get that cheese omelette which had been denied him the previous day. Failing that, he could always have some ice cream. A Knickerbocker Glory. He headed rapidly up the path to the castle. Where he had a surprise.

Anna, from the *Railway Inn*, was standing behind the counter.

"What are you doing here?"

"Local licensing laws. We're not allowed to open the Inn till 7.00pm. So I often do a shift on Sunday afternoons."

"It's not very busy."

"Not at this time of year. But there'll be quite a few coming off the 3.15pm – and then people catching the down train."

"What have you got to offer?"

"Pastries, pies, bottles of coke, ham rolls, crisps . . ."

"Ice cream?"

"Yes. I can offer you chocolate, strawberry or vanilla – or a scoop of all three."

"That would be nice. Nothing alcoholic?"

"No. The licensing laws." Anna grinned. "But you can have a swig at my hip flask – any time!"

"Better not," said Raynes. "Bill Naylor could be watching us on his security camera."

Anna pointed to the hidden camera.

"He probably is. But he can't hear what we are saying."

"Are you sure?"

Anna nodded.

"He has to get his pleasures from somewhere."

"You don't think he gets it from Lydia?"

"No."

Anna put together a large bowl of ice cream and handed him a long-handled spoon. Raynes sat on one of the high stools and tucked in.

Anna looked at him with a friendly smile.

"How are you getting on with the murder?" she asked.

"I've just been thinking about it. I don't think I've got very far."

"I think you've got a lot further than you think. At least people are talking about it again. For the past seven months, it's been a no-go area. A conspiracy of silence."

Raynes felt encouraged.

Perhaps his visit had not been in vain.

"Virginia has certainly kept the subject alive."

"She certainly has. But only in the last four weeks. Remember – the railway was closed from October till March."

"You mean the locals didn't talk about it?"

"No. Even Ifor kept his trap shut – which is unusual for him."

"He seemed very bitter about Derek."

"He had reason to be."

"You think so?"

"If Marion was really interested in Derek, she should have left him. I know she says she was worried about the farm – but she used Derek . . ."

" . . . against her husband?"

"Yes. Derek was often here – out of season – during the winter months. She invited him up to Penbass farm. She made out that she needed protection from Ifor. But she only needed protection because of what she was doing with Derek. If she had just gone home with Ifor, there might have been a fight or a row; but she was more than capable of dealing with him. Especially when he was drunk."

"Last night, she was threatening to pour a kettle of boiling water over him."

"She wouldn't have done it. She was just saying that to stimulate your protective instincts." Anna smiled. "Did she succeed?"

"I have no regrets in saying she did."

"Well, you've fallen into the same trap as Derek. But he believed it. And, of course, it really upset Ifor."

"Do you think he did the murder?"

"He could have done it. He had the means – and the motive." She wiped the top of the counter with a wet cloth. "But . . . it was such a horrible way of killing someone . . . At heart, Ifor is a gentle soul. I've known him for the last twelve years. He's never raised a fist against anyone – except when he's drunk." She squeezed out the cloth. "But he was severely provoked – over a long period of time. And that can do things to a man."

As she spoke, he could hear the distant sound of *Sir Walter* setting off from Pwddldwc. He looked at his watch. The little train was about ten minutes late.

"Are you going up to Abernirvana?"

"No. I'm waiting for the 3.59pm back to the village."

"Did you come up to the castle to see me?"

"No. I'm sorry to disappoint you. I came up here to see Sir David Cadwaller."

Anna opened her big eyes.

"Was that wise?"

"Probably not. People have told me what he did to Derek's van. He certainly hated him. I've also been told that he announced his intention of killing Derek quite publicly."

"So you went to see him?"

"I did. But he was out. I spoke to his wife."

"Margaret? She's a lovely woman."

"Very gracious. She told me what he was like – and what he had done to her." Raynes smiled sadly. "But our conversation was interrupted."

"He came home unexpectedly?"

"How did you know?"

"I guessed. These things happen. What did he say?"

"He didn't say anything. The moment Margaret heard the sound of his car coming up the drive, I was shoved out through the front door . . ."

Anna laughed.

" . . . But I went round to the farmyard to speak to him. He just ignored me. He picked up one of his shotguns, loaded it and ordered me off his land. As I left the farmyard, he fired two shots – and two more as I ran down the drive."

"You're lucky to be here."

"Very lucky. I think I'll have another ice cream to celebrate my survival. How much are they?"

"For you – nothing."

"That's very kind."

Anna smiled.

"You never know. Like Marion, I might need you one dark night!"

Raynes expressed his astonishment. "You expect to win my heart with a Neapolitan ice cream?"

Anna looked at him knowingly.

"You're easy," she said. "You'd fall for any woman!"

Anna scooped out more ice cream and put it in a clean glass bowl. She put it on the counter.

"Margaret hates him."

"She's terrified of him."

"Did she tell you what he'd done to her?'

Raynes nodded.

"He whipped her and then he beat her up. She told me that she'd been in a private nursing home for four weeks. She thought he was going to kill her."

"I'm surprised he didn't. She'd broken every rule in the book. She'd committed adultery – and produced a bastard child. She never told her husband till the child was four or five. When he found out who the father was . . ."

Anna looked cautiously at the Inspector. Did he know who it was?

" . . . It was Derek Barclay. Tom Hayward told me."

Anna sighed.

"Not exactly pedigree stock! You know how obsessed he is with blood lines – only the best will do. Well, she'd been trying to pass off this child as his son and heir. Deceit on the grand scale. There was no doubt that he would get rid of him. Which he did." Anna stared angrily in the direction of Castle Farm. "We were all told that the child was adopted. But I've often wondered if he had him put down – and buried his body."

Raynes was interested.

"No one knows where he's gone?"

"No one would dare ask! It's a complete mystery. He did it whilst she was in the nursing home. Moved the child, his bed, his toys, his clothes. All sign of him – gone. When Margaret came home, he forced himself on her night after night till she conceived a son. It's a good job it wasn't another daughter! But it was a brutal business. And she hasn't been allowed to see the child – or hold it. I doubt whether she'd want to. He's being brought up by a wet nurse in Caernarfon – or so we're told. No expense spared. But at least he's got a male heir. Though if it's anything like him, he'd be better dead as well."

Anna sounded exceedingly bitter – as indeed she was.

In the silence that followed, they could hear *Sir Walter* approaching the platform.

Anna looked anxiously at Raynes.

"Were you thinking of going to see him again?"

"Not on this visit."

"If I were you," she said, "I would keep clear of the railway – and Pwddldwc. I would never come back. Once he finds out who you are . . . A police inspector investigating his private affairs . . . he'll go through the roof. He'll ask Margaret who the visitor was. She'll tell him. She wouldn't dare hide it. And he'll never rest till he's brought you down. You may not realize it – but you're a marked man – for life."

18: Battered – But Not Beaten

Carlisle asked politely: "Did you have a good time in Wales?"

"The short answer is 'No'."

"They didn't let you drive one of those little trains?"

"No."

"What did you do?"

"I worked in the ticket office."

Carlisle realized that – for his colleague – the weekend must have been a great disappointment. Perhaps the less said, the better?

Raynes sat down behind his desk.

"Working in the ticket office was regarded as a privilege. When I wasn't working there, I was free to move around the place, talk to people and go for a run up the valley on Saturday afternoon."

"Did you enjoy that?"

"The train? Yes. It was wonderful. The countryside is beautiful. The Railway is splendidly organized. An excellent team of volunteers. The food was fine and the weather remarkably good."

"So?"

Raynes brow darkened.

"I was invited under false pretences. Tom Hayward waxed poetic about working on the railway. But I found myself re-opening a murder inquiry in the most hopeless and ridiculous circumstances. Tom promised that he would say nothing about my job – but everyone knew! And he kept blurting out 'Inspector', so my cover was completely blown. I was clearly seen as a wolf in sheep's clothing; but for most of the time, I felt like a sheep!"

Carlisle maintained a respectful silence for a few minutes. Then he asked: "Was it an interesting murder?" He knew that the Inspector normally enjoyed a good murder.

Raynes shrugged his shoulders.

"The man died in July last year. He was run over by a railway carriage and his two legs were chopped off. There were no witnesses. He died from loss of blood. The body was not found for another five days. The local police drew the obvious conclusions and the coroner decided it was an accident.

"But the widow disagreed. She felt his alleged behaviour before his death was out of character. His shirt and jacket were drenched in whisky and an empty bottle was left nearby. He didn't drink whisky. Also, his body was found in a locked station yard; but his van was found four miles away – very near the home of one of his avowed enemies.

"On Friday and Saturday nights, Derek slept wherever he could. On Sunday nights, he went home. We do not know where he slept on the weekend when he died. Everyone denies seeing him or entertaining him. He was one of the most industrious workers on the railway. He was universally admired. Many ladies succumbed to his charms; and very few of their husbands objected. Perhaps they didn't know what was going on.

"The widow is certain that he was murdered. And I agree. But the case is long since closed. Everyone has moved on. No one wants to revisit his death. In fact, they reacted to my questions with great hostility. I was threatened with a knife. Then I was shot at by some maniac with a double-barrelled shotgun. The local policeman, who is a brainless idiot, ordered me off his turf. And I have been undermined and deceived by a treacherous teenager, whose boyfriend is in jail for burning down English holiday cottages! She is a fanatical Welsh nationalist – and is planning to come to Grasshallows University this October. I am certain she knows who the murderer is; but, like everyone else, her lips are sealed.

"Tom Hayward asked me to decide whether it was an accident – or a murder. If it was an accident, he wanted me to say a few strong words to the widow. Since it is murder, I have given her my support. But the obstacles to re-opening this case are immense. In fact, I would say impossible."

Carlisle listened carefully to the Inspector's brief summary. He could understand his frustration. But Raynes had faced many equally difficult cases in time past. He would find a way through this one.

"Do we open a file on this case?"

"Privately."

"Have we anything to go in the file?"

Raynes laughed sourly – and reached into his inner pocket. He took out a small paper envelope containing the postcard photographs of Lydia Naylor in her lilac cat-suit pouring oil on to the piston rods of *Lady Sylvia*.

He walked over to Detective-Constable Carlisle and threw them down on his desk.

"My sole evidence!"

Carlisle laughed.

"Was she one of his mistresses?"

"I think so. But you will appreciate the difficulties I had – even in getting this postcard. I bought two. One for us and one for Dr Stewart to cheer him up when he's working in the mortuary!"

"Are you expecting anything else?"

"Well . . ." Raynes stared blankly out of the window. "I am expecting a list of railway members. And also a rota of those who were on duty the weekend the man died. I am expecting some newspaper cuttings and the coroner's report. I'm hoping to get them in the next couple of weeks."

He didn't like to say who would be sending them. It was so humiliating – being at the mercy of that wretched Welsh girl. He just hoped that – encouraged by Tom Hayward and driven by her own natural greed – she would stick to their deal and send him what he had asked for.

In the meantime . . .

"Are you thinking of doing any visits?"

Raynes cheered up.

"If you can think of any good reason why we might be visiting Wolverhamton, we could go and see Mrs Barclay."

Carlisle smiled.

"I'm sure we can think of something!"

19: Ladies' Day

Having delivered an upbeat – and entirely satisfactory – report to the Police Committee on the Wednesday afternoon, Inspector Raynes felt justified in playing truant on Thursday morning. Grasshallows Police Force was not facing any serious problems at that moment; the students were busy revising for their exams; and "drugs enforcement" was always a convenient euphemism for a little private enterprise. They travelled in the Inspector's Rover – not exactly an inconspicuous vehicle; but, on the other hand, no one was likely to look too closely at the mileage.

They had arranged to be in Wolverhampton by 11.00am and they reached Mrs Barclay's home at 11.15am. Raynes was glad to see that the children were either at school or with their grandmother.

He introduced Detective-Constable Carlisle. He had the feeling that Mrs Barclay had expected him to be on his own. She was smartly dressed; had had her hair done and was nicely made up. She was almost a different woman to the tired and bitter drone he had seen on Saturday afternoon.

Both men were made extremely welcome. They were offered coffee or wine. A bottle of Australian Chardonnay was sitting on the table – with two glasses. For once, Raynes decided to opt for wine; Carlisle chose coffee.

Despite the paucity of information available, Raynes hoped to create an impression of "things being done" – when, in fact, nothing was happening and there was little to report. He was hoping that Virginia herself would be able to fill that vacuum and provide some clues for him to follow.

"I'm sorry I was unable to see you again before you left; but I believe you spoke to Tom."

"Oh, yes. He told me that you had stirred up quite a hornets' nest. Various ladies worried about their reputation! Someone throwing a glass at the upper station and smashing a valuable mirror . . ."

"It wasn't as bad as that!"

"I was told that P.C. Roberts spoke to you – and told you to keep out of his parish. And you told him that if he had done his job properly, you wouldn't be there."

Raynes laughed.

"A bit of an exaggeration. But it does show how sensitive they are."

"I've known that for months. I shall probably get the blame for bringing you in on this."

"It was Tom."

"Of course it was."

"Now," said Raynes, "I would like to get some basic facts. Such as – how long had Derek been working on the railway?"

"About fifteen years."

"He wasn't there at the beginning?"

"Not quite. I think he turned up just after they got their first engine – and it had an accident."

"And how did he get involved?"

"I think he saw a notice asking for volunteers. It was in some railway magazine."

"Has he always been interested in railways?"

"As a boy, he had a huge lay-out. Him and his father. It's still there – up in the attic. When Peter's old enough, it'll be his."

"So when he saw the notice in the magazine, he thought it would be fun to be involved in the real thing?"

Virginia nodded.

"He loved the Railway. It was his first love. I always came second." She smiled. "A very close second!"

"He must have spent a lot of money on the railway – over the years . . .?"

"He charged for the materials; but not for the labour. That saved them a lot of money. But he always bought in bulk. The cement and the paint, he would take with him. But if big things like breeze blocks or timber were needed, he had them delivered to the site."

"So what did he actually build?"

"The ticket office and the booking hall – that came first. They used to have a tin shed. Very cold and uncomfortable. Then he moved on to the upper station. He did that beautifully. The engineering workshop, the cafe, the waterfall and the castle. He loved that. I'm just sorry he never finished it."

Tears came into her eyes.

Carlisle lifted his pencil.

Virginia looked at him.

"Are you writing all this down?"

Raynes said: "It helps me to remember what's been said. No one else will see it – except me."

"I won't have to sign anything?"

"No. Once this case is over, all my notes will be shredded."

Mrs Barclay showed signs of anxiety.

"Do you think you'll be able to find out who killed him?"

"We have quite a good track record," said Raynes, sounding more confident than he actually felt. "Don't we?"

Carlisle nodded.

Raynes returned to the subject in hand.

"The castle. It caused him quite a lot of trouble, didn't it?"

"Well, the restoration was no problem. It was the local farmer who caused all the trouble. He brought in the conservationists. They said it should be left as a ruin."

"I believe Sir David said the castle belonged to him?"

Virginia pouted.

"Well, it didn't. The Society took him to court and the judge said it was part of the Railway. But he treated Derek very badly. He attacked his van, clamped his wheels and covered it in . . . manure. But it was easily washed off."

"He also slashed his tyres."

"Derek didn't tell me that."

Raynes looked thoughtful.

"Do you think that Sir David would have wanted to kill Derek? After all, he'd cost him a lot of money. He'd lost a legal case. He must have felt extremely angry."

Virginia nodded.

"I'm sure he was. Derek's van was found up near his house. Of course, he always left it in the car park when he was working on the castle. I don't think Sir David would have known all that much about the station yard."

"But it is a possibility?"

"It is."

Raynes did not say anything about his visit to Castle Farm or about his encounter with the farmer. In his opinion, Sir

David was a very dangerous character – paranoid, vindictive, cruel. He had the means and the motive. But the local people were frightened to move against him.

"Were there any people in the Railway who actively disliked your husband?"

"Well, I don't think he wished Derek any harm; but Dr Campbell, the Treasurer, always said nasty things about him. That was because he objected to all these big projects which Derek undertook. When they started, no one knew how much they were going to cost. The Society gave him the go-ahead; but sometimes they turned out quite expensive.

"For instance, the cafe at Pwddldwc was twice the size they originally planned – and much more elaborate. The bigger it became, the more equipment it needed. A bigger boiler and more central heating. A bigger cooker. More tables. More flooring. Three chest freezers!

"Dr Campbell blamed Derek for his projects getting out of control. Even though it wasn't his fault. He just did what the members wanted. Dr Campbell said the bills always came in when the Railway had no spare cash. He said Derek did it deliberately – but of course he didn't."

"Derek must have saved them thousands of pounds?"

"Dr Campbell never mentioned that. But you're right. He gave all his labour for nothing. But it didn't cause us any problems. We've always lived comfortably. He always had plenty of jobs here in Wolverhampton. It was his father's business and he had good contacts amongst the business community." Virginia smiled happily.

"Of course, it also worked the other way. Through his dealings with the Railway, Sir Walter Greenaway . . ."

Raynes looked at Carlisle.

"The railway's chief benefactor."

"He gave him some important jobs in Birmingham. His nephew, Nigel, recently had a double garage built at his home in Henley-in-Arden – and he gave the job to Derek."

Raynes was now approaching the most delicate part of his interview.

"Well, if we eliminate Sir David and Dr Campbell, were there any other people who disliked Derek. What about outraged husbands?"

Virginia laughed.

"Tom told me Derek was a bit of a ladies' man. Did that cause any trouble?"

"Sometimes it did. But the husbands were usually more angry with their wives than with Derek. You see, women always liked Derek. They came to him with all their problems and he would listen to them. He was a good listener. Very gentle; and he had a good sense of humour. He used to tease them. Thy loved him. Usually, they seduced him – and he didn't say 'No'. When they needed him, he was there."

"Didn't that upset you?"

"Well, he'd known some of his lady friends long before he met me. He introduced them to me when we got engaged."

"You weren't jealous?"

"I think they were more jealous of me. After all, he was my husband. I knew he loved me – and would never leave me. He adored the children. But when he was working on the railway, I always knew someone would look after him, give him a meal, provide a bed. There was no deceit. If I asked him where he'd been, he told me. I knew he would always come back to me . . ."

Virginia broke into tears.

Raynes held her hand.

" . . . but this time he didn't."

Raynes waited till she had poured out her grief – and squeezed her hand. It seemed to help.

When he felt she could cope with a few more questions, he asked: "What about Anna Patterson?"

"Oh, she's a lovely person. Derek got her the job at the *Railway Inn*. She married the owner – and then he conveniently died. So she took over. She's a very good businesswoman."

"And Black Bob?"

"Ah, well, he can be very protective. He watches her like a

hawk. But she can run rings round him."

"Is he her husband?"

"No. He was the local darts champion. He'd worked behind the bar for years. When Anna took charge of the Inn, she got Bob as well. Derek often used to challenge him to a game of darts. That kept him sweet. He liked to win."

"Lydia Naylor?"

"He's known her for ages. She came down to Pwdlddwc with one boyfriend – and then ditched him. She flung herself at Derek. That was long before my time. Then she went back to University and came back with Bill. He's a lovely man. She two-timed him for several years. I don't think she'd like to be reminded of how close to Derek she had been."

"I did ask."

"But she denied it?"

"She did."

"She makes out she's very prim and proper – but she isn't."

"Emily Williams said that Derek told her that Lydia and Joanne were like two animals!"

Virginia laughed.

"Well, she's no shining angel herself! I can tell you that. Even at the age of twelve, she was casting longing eyes in Derek's direction. She's very different to her three sisters. Being the youngest, she's been spoilt. She's had affairs with all sorts of people. I think she targets them. Then she uses them. And once you get into her clutches, it's very difficult to escape. I warned Derek about her."

Raynes said nothing. He reckoned the warning had come too late.

"Her boyfriend's in jail."

"Best place for him. He was a nasty piece of work. Yes, I'd forgotten about him. Derek gave him a labouring job on the railway; but he was hopeless. He had to sack him. After that, he went round burning down English holiday homes. Before he torched them, he used to pinch all the valuables and sell them at car boot sales in Aberystwyth. I would imagine he shared the proceeds with Miss Williams. She's always been very money-minded. She should have been jailed as well. But I would imagine some people in the community pulled strings on her behalf."

Raynes said: "The boyfriend would have been around last July. I'm told he wasn't jailed till November."

Virginia paused to think.

"It's possible." But then she dismissed the idea. "He was a coward. He wouldn't have killed Derek. I'm sure it was one of the Railway members who did it."

Raynes moved on.

"Joanne Kennedy?"

"Drink's her problem. When she's had a few, she's anybody's. I don't know how Graham puts up with it. If anyone deserved to be murdered, it was her."

"Margaret Cadwaller?"

"The farmer's wife? I didn't know about her. There were so many, over the years, it's difficult to remember all of them. Katie Thompson, Angie Thornton, Ingrid Fox, Ariel Stevenson . . . Derek used to call her the 'Trapeze Artist' because she used so many different positions."

"You never met Margaret Cadwaller?"

Virginia shook her head.

"A complete blank. But I would imagine that would have been a very dangerous liaison. Her husband hated Derek. If he knew Derek had been bedding his wife, that would have been the last straw."

Raynes didn't mention about the illegitimate child. Some things were better left unsaid.

He saved his chief suspect to the end.

"Marion Davies?"

"Yes. I thought you'd come to her. That's a difficult one."

Raynes nodded.

"Derek's known her for fifteen years. She's had a tragic life."

"It's still tragic."

"She married the wrong man. The person she should have married – Keith – committed suicide. Then she married Ifor –

on the rebound. Their only child was run over by a tractor on the farm. Fortunately, it wasn't her husband who did it. But it pushed him over the brink.

"He had to have psychiatric treatment. And she had to run the farm. She did her best; but it wasn't good enough for him. He blamed her for spending his money. He beat her – several times. He was sent to jail – for assault."

Virginia sighed sadly.

"Ifor can be a lovely man – when he's sober. But when he's had three or four pints, he becomes a devil. You can't imagine it's the same man. He becomes a raging lion. Anna refuses to serve him more than two pints of special – but he persuades the other people in the Inn to buy him a few more – with drastic consequences. Many's the night Derek and Bob have had to drive him home. Sometimes, Bob's had to knock him out before they could get him into the car. I can't tell you how many times Marion's left him . . ."

"She's left him again."

" . . . but she keeps coming back!"

"I think she's worried about the farm. She's frightened something happens to the animals."

Virginia shrugged her shoulders.

"She should think of her own needs. At least, when Derek was alive, she could always turn to him. She called him her 'guardian angel'; but I don't think angels are supposed to have sex with the people they protect! But she did. Derek described it as a pastoral necessity; but I'm sure he enjoyed it as much as she did. He said she used to make him the most marvellous breakfasts." Virginia laughed. "They say that the way to a man's heart is through his stomach . . ."

Raynes agreed that it was certainly true in his case.

Mrs Barclay looked ready to offer him any number of cooked breakfasts. Her eyes glowed with anticipation. It was embarrassing.

As to whether Ifor was capable of killing Derek, she thought it unlikely. Her husband had always been very watchful whenever he was in Ifor's company. He avoided him as much as possible; but both men met at the *Railway Inn*. There was no doubt that Ifor could be extremely violent under the influence of drink; but Virginia found it difficult to think of Ifor – in that condition – would be capable of moving carriages in the station yard. True, he had a tractor; but would he be able to drive it when he was half cut?

Raynes asked whether Ifor had ever done any work on the railway or driven either of the little trains.

"Not recently," she said. "Only in an emergency."

She remembered Derek telling her that Ifor had been called out to rescue *Sir Walter* once or twice. In the absence of Brian Williamson, being a trained engineer – he could usually identify a mechanical problem and do a temporary repair. He could mend broken couplings and release jammed points. He had his uses. This was the other side of the man.

Raynes had been keeping an eye on the time. He wanted to make sure they were back in Grasshallows by four o' clock so that they could deal with any problem which might have arisen in their absence.

Carlisle closed his notebook. Both men stood up. Raynes thanked Virginia for all the information she had given them – especially about Derek's lady-friends. As he edged towards the door, she held him back. Carlisle went out to the car.

She gave the Inspector a warm hug and a couple of kisses. She said: "Next time you come – come alone!" She smiled. "And don't leave it too long. When you come next time, I'll show you Derek's railway in the attic."

* * * *

Raynes returned to his car. They waved to Mrs Barclay, who was still standing on the doorstep. He then drove a hundred yards down the road and pulled into the kerb.

He said to Carlisle: " You'll never believe this. She has just invited me to come back – alone – to see her. And when I come, she's going to take me up to the attic to see her husband's railway set!"

"Lucky you!" said Carlisle.

"So much for the grieving widow!"

"It is a year since her husband died. She must need a little love to keep her going. She is an attractive woman. She has a good sense of humour. And you do have something in common with her husband!"

"Do I?"

"You both like a good cooked breakfast!"

Raynes laughed.

"I daresay we may have a few other things in common. But I never expected to meet such a merry widow. She was so drawn and distressed last Saturday. I can't think what's come over her."

"You must have given her fresh hope."

Raynes stared through the windscreen.

Carlisle asked: "Shouldn't we be going?"

Raynes returned to earth.

"I just wanted to check on one or two things she said."

"Whereabouts?"

"Derek's lovers."

"I've got about fifteen pages on that."

"Read me out what she said about Margaret Cadwaller."

"She said she didn't know her. She'd never met her."

"I think she was lying."

"Do you know the lady?"

"I've spoken to her. She's another woman trampled into the dust by a psychotic husband. She had a child by Derek. Some people say the child has been adopted. Others think it has been murdered. If Derek was so open about all his lady friends, I think he would have mentioned her. He might not have said anything about the child; but I feel sure they must have met."

As they were talking, a very large Jaguar saloon passed them, heading down the street. Raynes watched its progress through his wing mirror. The car seemed to have pulled into the empty space outside Virginia's house.

"Where's he going? The blue Jaguar?"

Carlisle looked in his wing mirror."

"He's taken our place. Another visitor for Mrs Barclay. Ah! There she is, coming out to the gate. Giving him a big hug. They're going inside."

Raynes thought quickly.

"She must have phoned him after we left. He can't have been far away. He's come to find out what we were doing – and she's going to tell him." He looked at Carlisle. "I wonder where he fits in the picture. We'll find out."

Raynes drove away from the kerb.

"I'll turn round the car. As we pass the house, you get his number – and we'll check his identity with the car registration people."

The operation was speedily performed – and an answer swiftly received.

Both men looked at each other with surprise.

"Nigel Greenaway! Derek built a double garage for him last year before he died. Nigel is a sworn enemy of the Puddleduck Railway. He tried to stop his uncle, Sir Walter Greenaway, leaving a large legacy to the Society. He took the matter the court – and lost. Why should he be visiting Mrs Barclay?"

Carlisle smiled.

"Another suspect?"

"Very much so. I'm glad we stopped. If we'd rushed away, we would have missed him."

"And what do you think he's doing now?"

Both men laughed.

"Playing with Derek's train set!"

"The dirty beast!"

20: The Enemy Within

On the Saturday morning, Raynes drove up to the front door of a substantial country residence in Henley-in-Arden. As one would expect of a property in that affluent area, it was beautifully maintained – and it had a brand-new double garage. Derek had managed to finish it before he died.

Raynes was not entirely sure why he was here. It was a gut instinct. The sight of a top-of-the-range Jaguar coasting down a street in Wolverhampton, visiting a house he had just left – together with the identity of its owner – set many alarm bells ringing.

He hoped that his early morning arrival would catch Nigel Greenaway when he was least prepared. At least he succeeded in that hope. The early morning start from Grasshallows paid a handsome dividend.

Raynes rang the doorbell.

A minute later, he rang it again.

A man in a camel-coloured dressing gown opened the door.

Raynes gave him a brief glimpse of his police identity card. "Detective-Inspector Raynes."

Nigel was so surprised that he automatically said: "Come in."

A smell of toast filled the hallway. Raynes followed the smell into the kitchen and sat down. Nigel followed – feeling quite perplexed.

Why was the Inspector here? What had he done? Or not done? Was he being arrested? How did Inspector Raynes know where he lived? How did he even know of his existence?

To buy time, he said: "Coffee?"

"Thank you. Black with two sugars."

Nigel made a second cup for the Inspector. His own was sitting on the table beside a copy of the *Financial Times*.

"What brings you here, Inspector?"

"I believe you were a friend of the late Derek Barclay?"

"Yes, indeed. He's a local builder."

"He built your garage . . .?"

" . . . Yes . . ."

" . . . before he died?"

Nigel picked up his coffee; but the tone of the Inspector's voice made him put it down again.

"I was very satisfied with his workmanship."

(As indeed he was.)

"Did he build anything else for you?"

"No. But he did quite a few jobs for my uncle."

"Sir Walter?"

"Yes."

Where was all this leading? Had he broken some building regulation?

Raynes hoped to keep him confused.

"I think you know his wife, Virginia, quite well?"

How on earth did the Inspector know that? Had she spoken to him? Surely not?

"I do."

"You visited her house on Thursday, shortly after I left. I saw you at the house."

Was he being watched by the police?

"Have you known Mrs Barclay for some time?"

"Yes."

No use denying it.

"Before her husband died?"

That was a difficult one. Nigel put on a brave face.

"No."

Raynes instantly detected a lie.

"I think you meant to say 'Yes'."

Nigel felt very uncomfortable. He was beginning to see where the questions might be going.

He quickly corrected himself.

"For a short while before."

"Thank you."

Raynes smiled – a dangerous smile.

"You are having an affair with her?"

There was a silence. The answer was obviously yes – but it

was difficult to admit it.

"Did this affair begin before Mr Barclay's death?"

Another silence. Another silent admission.

Inspector Raynes was glad that he had followed his instincts. This was an unexpected catch. He would not have thought that the woman he had met in Pwddldwc was having an affair with anyone. She was so weepy and distressed.

But the woman he had met in Wolverhampton seemed to be much more cheerful. Flirtatious, even. "When you come next time, come alone!" A fairly blatant invitation.

There were clearly two sides to Mrs Barclay.

"Since Derek died, have you taken Virginia down to Pwddldwc?"

"No."

"You know where the village is – in Wales?"

"I know very well where Pwddldwc is. Our family has been closely connected with the Railway for many years."

"You are a great admirer of the Railway?"

Raynes put his head slightly to one side, giving Nigel Greenaway the chance to utter another lie. But he was learning . . .

"No," he said honestly, "I am not an admirer of the Railway."

"You have in fact sued the Railway to prevent part of your uncle's estate going to the Society?"

"Yes."

"And lost?"

"Yes, I lost."

It was still hard to admit it. He had been sure he would win. But Simon Jacoby knew the best QC to represent the Society and he had not only defeated him – but also humiliated him.

Raynes adopted a more thoughtful tone.

"Would it be true to say that you are encouraging Mrs Barclay to make a claim against the Railway for negligence over her husband's death?"

It was an entirely spurious question. If Virginia genuinely believed that her husband was murdered, she couldn't be claiming that his death was an accident.

Most surprisingly, Nigel said: "We have considered it."

"Really?"

"But Virg . . . Mrs Barclay still believes that her husband was murdered."

Raynes stared hard at Nigel.

"Were you in Pwddldwc the weekend of July 10 last year, when Derek died?"

"No."

Raynes paused – and then asked more quietly: "Do you have friends in – or around – Pwddldwc who might have been glad to see Mr Barclay dead?"

Raynes had been expecting the answer "No" but the way he phrased his questions had unnerved Nigel – and his silent reaction was most revealing.

"You do have friends?"

Nigel stared back.

"And who would those friends be?"

"I don't have to tell you."

"You've told me everything else!"

Nigel was silent.

A picture suddenly flashed into Raynes' mind.

"A wealthy landowner perhaps?"

Nigel's face crumpled. It was impossible to put up any defence against all these leading questions. The Inspector seemed to have sixth sense of what he was thinking. Raynes was feeling glad that he had scored another bulls-eye.

"Sir David . . .?"

"I was at boarding school with him. And I was his best man when he married Lady Margaret."

Raynes felt like twisting Nigel's tail a little further.

"Were you perhaps godfather to his son, Timothy?"

"Yes, I was." There was a grim look on Nigel's face.

"He turned out not to be the heir."

"So I believe."

"You know he's been adopted?"

"That's what I've been told."

"Have you ever seen him?"

"Not since the baptism."

Raynes was amazed at the way the conversation had developed. He had never expected such riches. All paths, it seemed, led to Sir David Cadwaller.

"And, presumably, you encouraged him to sue the Railway and prevent them restoring the castle?"

Nigel nodded.

"I believed it belonged to Sir David."

"But it didn't?"

"No."

"So, like you, Sir David must have lost a lot of money?"

"He did."

"He must have felt very bitter towards Derek when he was rebuilding the castle?"

Nigel nodded again.

"And making love to Lady Margaret?"

"I wasn't aware of that."

"The child was his."

"I don't think he ever ascertained whose child it was. He was so angry."

"He beat up Lady Margaret quite badly. Smashed up her face."

"That was quite unforgivable."

"Wouldn't this have provided two perfectly good reasons for Sir David and yourself to get rid of Derek Barclay? First of all, for Sir David to punish him for seducing his wife; and secondly, for you to grab Virginia?"

Nigel looked horrified at the suggestion.

Raynes continued: "Derek's car was found in the castle car park – just a few hundred yards away from Castle Farm. The body was found elsewhere. Would I not be right in accusing you of being involved in the death of Derek Barclay?"

There was no answer to that question because a third person had entered the kitchen. Mrs Greenaway was anxious to get her breakfast. Normally, on a Saturday morning, her husband brought her a cup of coffee, a slice of toast and a copy of the *Daily Mail* – but, this morning, there had been no toast and no *Daily Mail*. As she opened the kitchen door, she heard Inspector Raynes' final words:

" . . . Would I not be right in accusing you of being involved in the death of Derek Barclay?"

She looked at Raynes with a hostile glare.

"And who are you?"

"I am a Detective-Inspector investigating the death of Derek Barclay – the man who built your double garage."

"And what has that got to do with my husband?"

"Because he has been having an affair with the dead man's wife and may therefore have been involved in Derek's death."

Anger, fury and fear all combined in one terrible scream. Followed by several more – as Mrs Greenaway rushed at Nigel, lashing out with both fists. Even the coffee cup was smashed on his head. Coffee poured down his face.

Raynes left the kitchen as quickly as possible. All his gut feelings had been confirmed – and more. The last words he heard as he left the house were: "Don't just sit there! Get a solicitor!"

Raynes reflected that the costs of the divorce might eat heavily into Nigel's estate.

21: The Welsh Letter

Carlisle deposited a large envelope – recorded delivery – on Raynes' desk.

"Fan mail – from Wales."

The Inspector looked at the postmark.

"About time too."

He tore open the envelope.

Emily had certainly done her stuff. There was the expected list of names; a photograph taken at a dinner dance when many of the ladies were present. There was a copy of the Society's membership list for 1989, details of the Railway's elected officials and a duty rota for the weekend on which

Derek had died. There was a photocopy of his obituary from the local newspaper together with more cuttings reporting the finding of his body and the coroner's inquest.

Emily seemed to have done her job most effectively; but Raynes did wonder whether she had had some professional help. He detected the hand of Tom Hayward in some of the material. Was there more in this than met the eye?

Raynes picked up the photograph of the dinner dance.

Carlisle looked over his shoulder.

"Derek's harem!"

"Are they all Welsh?"

"No. Members of the Society come from all over the country. But there is a certain amount of local talent."

Raynes pointed out the people who had been mentioned during their visit to Mrs Barclay.

"That's Anna Patterson – the woman who runs the hotel. And her partner, Black Bob."

"He looks lethal."

"Positively satanic! And that's Ifor and Marion Davies . . ."

"She looks sad."

"Do you blame her?"

Carlisle identified Virginia and Derek.

"They both look happy."

Raynes said cynically: "So we are told."

Carlisle also identified Lydia.

"That's the lady in the cat suit . . ."

" . . . And her drunken friend, Joanne."

"She looks quite pretty."

"She is."

Emily had also supplied a separate photocopy with each of the women numbered in red.

"That will be helpful."

Raynes looked more closely at the photograph.

"I do believe that is Tom Hayward hiding in the back row!"

"The proprietor of the *Echo*?"

"Yes. Who's that woman with him?"

They checked the photocopy.

"No. 16. Lisa Gray. Ever heard of her?"

"No."

"Well, it's certainly not Mrs Hayward."

"He's a dark horse!"

They went through the rest of the names and the photographs.

"Have we got the trapeze artist?"

"Sadly, no," said Raynes. "I was looking for her. She sounded quite exciting."

He checked the names again. "No. No Ariel Stevenson. What a pity! I must find out what happened to her."

Carlisle put his finger on one of the dinner guests.

"Who's that Smart Alec in the front row? He looks very pleased with himself."

"He's the President of the Society. Simon Jacoby. And that's his wife, Arlene. I'm told she's not as dim as she looks."

"Aristocratic disdain!"

"That just about sums it up."

"Did Mrs Barclay tell us that Arlene had an affair with her husband?"

"No, she didn't. But it's quite on the cards. Not the sort of thing you would want to admit to. Especially if you're married to a high-flying QC – destined one day for the Bench!"

"Is there anyone else of interest?"

"Well, Mrs Packer's not there. I don't suppose anyone would want to be her partner. She's stout and rather mannish. Drinks gallons of Tequila Sunrise. But, despite it all, she has a good mind. She gave me a very vivid account of how the murder might have been committed."

The tone of the Inspector's voice suggested that he was not entirely sure about Mrs Packer.

"Could she have been involved?"

"Not without help."

"Mr Packer?"

"No. He's dead. Tom said he died in mysterious circumstances some years ago."

"Would you like me to run a check on her?"

Raynes smiled.

"Why not?"

Raynes checked to see if there was anything else in the envelope. He found a letter from Emily written on scented notepaper with neat black handwriting – and a bill for £225 – including expenses.

He raised his eyebrows.

"We agreed on £200."

"You paid for all this?"

"I offered a hundred."

"Enterprising young woman!"

Raynes said: "I'm used to women charging me for their services. No ties. No comeback. You get what you pay for."

Carlisle uttered a warning:

"You get what she chooses to give you."

"Yes. You have a point there. All these details point me in the direction she wants me to go. I must be careful to take everything with a pinch of salt. Though I don't suppose she could have doctored the membership list, the obituary or the coroner's report."

"But it's only the press coverage of the inquest."

"That's true."

"Perhaps Dr Stewart will help us get the real thing?"

Raynes said: "We need to get the exact details of Derek's death. I've never dealt with anyone who's had their legs chopped off. This is new territory for me."

He picked up the coloured postcard which had been lying on his desk.

"This may be the price of unlocking the oracle!"

"Did he like it?"

"Ecstatic. He says he likes his women beautifully packed. Like expensive chocolates! He's planning to go down to the Puddleduck at the first opportunity."

Carlisle picked up the list of the Society members which helpfully contained all their home addresses. Mrs Packer lived on the outskirts of Bath.

He wasn't expecting to find anything exciting. But

Grasshallows was going through one of its quiet spells and it would give him something to do. He went through to the police computer and entered the word: "Packer" together with the address in Bath. Almost immediately, the screen began to fill with information and photographs. There were several pictures of Philip James Packer – a wealthy businessman, who had been the subject of a major police investigation.

Mr Packer had owned two hotels and specialized in restoring Georgian mansions and then re-selling them at a high price. He had been married four times and had three children. His firm still existed in Bath. It was now run by his brother. Mr Packer had died in September 1975. His wife had been abroad at the time.

It was reported that Philip had been having an affair with his secretary whilst his wife was away. The secretary's husband was suspected of being responsible for his death; but the man had an impeccable alibi and there was no forensic evidence linking him with the corpse.

Carlisle read through the police reports and looked at the photograph of Philip's body and where it had been found. He had a strong sense of déjà vu. When he felt he had acquired sufficient information, he returned to the Inspector's office.

"Mr Packer," he said, "was murdered."

"When?"

"September 1975."

"By whom?"

"Persons unknown."

"No arrests?"

"I think there were several arrests. But nothing could be proved – so no trial."

"And where was Mrs Packer?"

"In the south of France."

"With a cast-iron alibi?"

"I would imagine so."

Raynes was interested. Here was a second murder to brighten up his day.

"And how did Mr Packer die?"

Carlisle smiled.

"You'll love this! Mr Packer died on the Bristol to London railway line – just inside the Box tunnel, ten miles east of Bath. He was decapitated and lost one arm. Before he died, he had taken a substantial dose of valium. Despite an extensive investigation, the coroner decided that it was suicide whilst the balance of his mind was disturbed."

Raynes shook his head in disbelief.

"No wonder she described the murder so well. She'd done it all before!"

Carlisle was cautious.

"Someone had done it before. But not necessarily her. She was interviewed twice by the police – but never arrested. This could have been the perfect murder."

Raynes was thoughtful.

He could remember Tom telling him that Mrs Packer had once asked Simon Jacoby to be her defence counsel if she was ever prosecuted! Why would she say that? Did she still suffer from a guilty conscience?

To Carlisle, he said: "Well, if she didn't kill her husband, she could have passed on the idea to someone else. But who? Tom told me that he didn't know how her husband died. You'd think – being a newshound – he would have made a point of finding out. But perhaps he did know . . .? He just wasn't telling me. Was he trying to protect Joyce?"

"Diplomatic amnesia?"

"Quite probably."

Carlisle put his notes down on the Inspector's desk.

"Something to mull over on your holiday!"

22: *The Broken Reed*

When the Inspector returned from his holiday in Nice with Mrs May, he phoned Tom Hayward, the publisher of the *Grasshallows Echo*.

"Have there been any developments whilst I have been

away?"

There was a silence at the end of the phone. Raynes wondered whether he had been cut off. But eventually, Tom said: "One or two. You may be interested to know that Virginia has not returned since you spoke to her. This has provided some people with a little comfort."

"And why was that?"

"Well, I would imagine that her non-appearance is connected with the visit you paid to her home in Wolverhampton, which caused her great embarrassment. You didn't tell me you had gone to see her."

Raynes was surprised.

"I wanted to find out what she knew about Derek's relationships with other ladies in the Society. To try and see if any of them – or their husbands – might have a motive for killing him."

"Well, she objected to your questions."

"She seemed perfectly happy at the time. She gave me a lot of information. I have a complete record of our conversation. She raised no objection. In fact, she invited me to come back for a second interview."

Tom's attitude was beginning to annoy him.

He said: "Perhaps you could tell me a little bit more about Ariel Stevenson?"

There was another silence at the end of the phone.

"Do you remember Ariel?"

"Of course I remember Ariel! She was a disgraceful woman. She was expelled from the Society for making love to a driver on the footplate."

"It wasn't you?"

"Certainly not!"

"Do you still have her phone number?"

"No."

Raynes changed the subject.

"I'm free to go down to Pwddldwc this weekend. Will you be going over to the Railway?"

Tom Hayward said very firmly: "I shall not be going down

to the Railway this week."

Raynes looked at his diary.

"What about Friday the 15th?"

Mr Hayward finally made his feelings clear.

"I shall not be able to take you – either that week – or any future week."

This sounded like bad news. But Raynes decided that he would twist the publisher's tail a little bit further. He said: "Have you been expelled from the Society?"

"No, I have not!" Mr Hayward sounded very angry. "And, if you must know, the Society does not wish you to pry any further into their affairs. They were very angry that I brought you down at the end of April. They have made their feelings quite clear to me. They do not want your investigation to go any further. They are satisfied with the coroner's report. They believe it was an accident – and that's an end to it!"

"But you know it was murder!"

"I've changed my mind."

"Has Sir David issued an ultimatum? Has he threatened to shoot you?"

Raynes could almost hear the publisher grinding his teeth.

"No. Sir David has said nothing. But Nigel Greenaway has issued a writ against the Railway for failing in its safety procedures – and causing Derek's death."

"Really?"

"Yes. Really! This will cost the Society thousands of pounds. Dr Campbell is furious with you. Apparently, you went round to this man's house at Henley-in-Arden and accused him of killing Derek. This is his riposte!"

Raynes was irritated by the unfounded accusation.

"I didn't accuse him of killing anyone. I simply asked whether he had been in Pwddldwc on the weekend Derek went missing. I also asked him whether he had taken Mrs Barclay over to the Railway on any weekend since Derek died. These questions are important because I discovered that he had been having an affair with Virginia since before Derek's death."

"I believe he is also suing you for slander."

Raynes looked at his empty desk.

"Nothing has been received here. Not yet anyway."

Turning back to Mr Hayward's problems, he said: "Nigel told me that he – and Mrs Barclay – were planning to sue the Railway. That was before either of my visits." He laughed coldly. "And I hardly think he will sue me. There were no witnesses present during our conversation. If he says there were, he'll be committing perjury."

"Don't try to get out of it!"

"I'm not trying to get out of anything. I'm just giving you the facts. But there is one thing . . . If Mrs Barclay is joining him in suing the Railway on safety grounds, that means she can no longer accuse them of killing him!"

A note of triumph came into Tom's voice.

"Precisely. That is why you are no longer needed down in Pwddldwc. We have moved on. You are *persona non grata*. I should have realized that right from the start."

Raynes realized that Mr Hayward must have received a very hostile reaction after his visit in April. And yet he had encouraged Emily to send all that information – most of which she could not have obtained without his help.

Raynes sounded a little more understanding in his reply.

"I'm sorry I've caused you so much trouble. But surely Simon Jacoby will be able to deal with Nigel Greenaway?"

"Of course he will. But all these things take time. This is the beginning of the holiday season. An allegation such as this can cause the Railway a lot of trouble. When people hear about a breach in safety regulations, they will think the Railway is unsafe. The number of visitors will fall. Income will fall. The Railway will be unable to pay its bills. It's an absolute disaster. And it's all . . ."

Mr Hayward was going to say: "It's all your fault . . ." But, remembering his enthusiasm in getting the Inspector over to Pwddldwc, and encouraging his investigation, he had the humility to say: " . . . And it's all my fault!"

Raynes decided that there was no more point in pursuing

this conversation. Mr Hayward was a broken reed. There was a need for speed in winding up the investigation. He would have to act quickly.

He said briefly: "Thank you very much for letting me know."

He put down the phone.

Carlisle looked up.

"That didn't sound a very friendly call."

"No," said Raynes, "Did you hear it?"

Carlisle smiled.

"I recorded most of it. Once he started getting hot under collar, I pressed the record button."

"That's very useful," said Raynes. "It'll be a great help to have a full report of our conversation."

Carlisle asked: "So do we close the Pwddldwc file?"

Raynes was shocked.

"Of course not! The search for the truth goes on – with or without Mr Hayward. I shall have to wrap up this case quickly." He thought for a few moments. "Mr Hayward is not going down this weekend. So I shall go on my own. He won't be expecting me to go. And the people in Pwddldwc won't be expecting me either. There will be shock on all sides."

"And where will you be staying?" As always, Carlisle was concerned with the practical details. "With Mrs Williams and her beautiful daughter?"

"No," said Raynes, thinking quickly. "I shall stay at the *Railway Inn*. I shall be the spider at the very heart of the web." He smiled. "The lady who runs the Inn has a soft spot for me."

Carlisle said: "I wouldn't trust any of them."

Raynes laughed.

"I'm told she makes an excellent seafood paella."

He flipped open his diary.

"Could you provide me with an alibi for Thursday and Friday? I can't be seen to be having any more holidays."

Carlisle looked at the calendar of national police events.

"An Immigration Conference in Nottingham?"

"That sounds perfect!"

"But I need to know where you are so that I can get you back in a hurry. What's the phone number of the *Railway Inn*? You may need reinforcements."

Raynes grinned happily.

"You may be right. The Welsh police won't like it either."

Carlisle smiled.

"You'd better find their phone number as well. Just in case you get arrested!"

23: A Silent Witness?

Raynes set off early on Thursday morning. He gave himself four days to crack this case. He must have a solution by Sunday night. During his lengthy journey across middle England and central Wales, he analyzed all the facts he knew and all the personalities he had met.

Of the seventy or eighty people working on the railway, he had met only fourteen. Of the actual villagers he had spoken to, he could count nine. Even among this select circle, there was enough combustible material to generate several murders. But he was conscious that there must be at least sixty railway people and a couple of hundred villagers who might have played some part in the murder about whom he knew absolutely nothing.

For his own peace of mind, he decided that he would concentrate on just those people whom he had met – and if he did not unearth a murderer amongst them, he would let the case go.

As his Rover ate up the miles, he had no distractions. He could bring up each character; analyze their possible motives; assess their reaction to Derek Barclay's death; imagine how they might have dealt with his body; consider how they might have covered their tracks. He could talk aloud to himself – both asking and answering questions as if his suspects were actually sitting beside him in the car. Was he being told any lies?

Perhaps he could follow up Virginia Barclay's outrageous suggestion and ask Derek himself what had happened; and then see what answers came into his mind? In his routine police work, he would never have dreamed of involving the supernatural; but this case was rather different. It was a piece of private enterprise, where any help would be welcome.

Quite clearly, Derek had died in the station yard. There was the evidence of the blood which had seeped into the ground from his wounds. That suggested that he was still alive at the moment when the carriage wheels rolled over his legs. He would have died soon after – from shock or the loss of blood. Probably both. But how did he get there?

Three suggestions presented themselves. Firstly, he was using the carriage as a cheap bed for the night. He had been dragged out of the carriage; rendered unconscious and then prepared for his gruesome death.

Secondly, he had come to the station for some secret assignation – a kiss and a cuddle in one of the old carriages. His female partner might have been followed by an angry husband or a dangerous rival. Both of them could have attacked him. It might be revenge – or a deliberate trap.

Thirdly, Derek could have been captured much earlier. He had not been seen all weekend. He might have been attacked on the Friday or Saturdays nights. Tied up, drugged, locked away; and then brought to the station yard when all the railway workers had gone home

All three scenarios suggested that Derek's death had been carefully planned.

It was certainly not an impulse killing. Careful thought had been given to the timing. His death had been arranged to look like an accident. The empty whisky bottle and the whisky spilt over his clothes suggested drunkenness. It created doubt and uncertainty. In the absence of any witnesses – or any other injuries to his body – Derek could appear as the architect of his own doom.

Raynes felt the third scenario was the most likely. For if there had been two people involved, there would have been a fight. Derek would not have passively submitted to his fate. He was a fit and healthy man. There would have been scratches, blood, traces of other people's skin under his finger nails. Derek would have received a few bruises in the process. These could not be disguised. Presumably, the police would have considered all these possibilities and eliminated them.

This pointed to an earlier entrapment. A spiked drink. Not being a whisky drinker, he might not have noticed a difference in the taste. He would have been effectively knocked out. How long had Derek been kept sedated – and where?

Would it have happened at Sir David's elegant country home – close to where Derek's van had been found? Or was he kept in some locked outhouse or barn till he was brought down to Pwddldwc and killed in the station yard?

Had Derek's own van been used for the transportation of the body? Would it have been powerful enough to pull the single carriage forward about twenty yards?

Would it have had the strength to push the coach backwards quickly enough to slice off his legs? Even if the van was not powerful enough, both Sir David and Ifor had tractors or Land Rovers sufficiently powerful to do the job. And the keys to the station yard would be in Derek's pocket.

But, on the other hand, the attack on Derek could have come from within the station itself. Raynes had noticed – from the very first moment – the proximity of the engineering shed to the scene of the murder. The doors of the shed, where all Derek's materials had been stored, were only yards from the sidings where his body had been found.

Very few people worked in the engineering shed. In the building, there would be store rooms and locked doors. After a "friendly" cup of tea or coffee, Derek's body could have been stored close by. It could have been transported on a porter's trolley from the engineering shed to the siding for the old carriages in less than five minutes. No chance of being seen on the open road. No need to open the gates to the station yard. If it was an inside job, the maintenance diesel was also parked in one of the sidings, ready to be used. An extra key could have been cut many weeks before. With the departure of the other Society members on the Sunday night, would anyone notice the diesel being moved?

Had there been any witnesses?

Raynes was assuming that the murder had taken place at night, but it could have been done early on Monday morning. The murderer would have known that the station yard would be deserted for the next four days. An early morning visit would ensure that no mistakes were made – no tell-tale evidence left behind.

But whether it was done late at night – or early in the morning, someone might have seen a person entering or leaving the station yard. Had they been a leading member of the Railway – such as Simon Jacoby, Brian Williamson or Dr Campbell – it would be assumed that they were delivering some essential items or doing a security check. Their entry or departure would not have been questioned. But once Derek's body was found, that nocturnal visit would have been remembered.

If there had been a silent witness, why had they not spoken to the police? Who was protecting whom? Raynes felt that this might be the murderer's weak point.

This brought him back to his most abiding and tantalizing question. Who would have been so ruthless and cruel to render a man helpless and then cut off his legs, leaving him to bleed to death. That suggested real hatred. Raynes could imagine Sir David firing a couple of shots or Ifor Davies battering him over the head with a hefty spanner; but Derek's death was cold and calculated. It required a very special type of murderer. Raynes had narrowed down his list of suspects to four; but Derek Barclay's spirit seemed to be suggesting someone else. Someone he would have regarded as a 33-1 outsider. Fortunately, at this stage, he still retained an open mind.

24: The Unwanted Guest

Raynes passed the station at Abernirvana at 3.35pm. Eight minutes later, he arrived at the *Railway Inn*. He parked his car behind the hotel and walked in through the back door. The place seemed deserted. He went through to the public bar.

Anna Patterson was polishing the wooden shelving behind the bar. She looked up with surprise.

"Inspector Raynes! What are you doing here?"

"I've come to book a room."

"At the *Railway Inn*?"

"Why not? Are you fully booked?"

"I thought I told you to keep away."

Raynes smiled.

"Excellent advice – which I have thought about carefully – but have decided to ignore."

"Hasn't your friend, Tom, spoken to you?"

"He has. But I've decided to ignore him as well."

"Why?"

"There are too many people trying to discourage my investigations. There has to be a reason . . . There must be a cover-up." He grinned. "Derek's ghost is urging me on!"

Anna laughed.

"He was persuasive enough in real life. Don't tell me he's pursuing you from the grave!"

"No. I've been thinking about this case. I've been thinking what people have told me. I've read the coroner's report and the newspaper cuttings. I've been to see Mrs Barclay at her home in Wolverhampton and I'm beginning to see the picture. There are so many people involved, I can quite understand their reluctance to re-open the case."

"Well, it's on your own head."

Anna put down her polishing cloth.

"Would you like a whisky?"

"I think I would prefer a gin and tonic at this time of day. I've had a long run in the car and I think that would be more refreshing."

Anna poured him a generous measure of gin, threw in two or three cubes of ice and handed him two bottles of Schweppes.

"Help yourself."

Raynes emptied in one bottle of tonic water.

"Am I really that unpopular?"

"Well, as I said to you – the last time you were here – when you started asking questions, you opened up a real can of worms. A lot of people had secrets. They thought they were all nicely hidden away when Derek died. But you rattled the bones and their fears all came flooding back."

"Fears?"

"Husbands finding out what had been going on. It was better to keep Derek dead and their secrets buried with him. Now they've shut the coffin lid a second time, they won't want to open it again."

Raynes sipped at his iced drink.

"Do you think my life is at risk?"

"How long are you staying?"

"Till Sunday night."

Anna looked happier.

"I think you might survive three nights. You will have me to protect you! Or perhaps you would prefer Marion Davies?"

She laughed.

"Is she back home?"

"She is. And the two of them are very lovey-dovey. You'd never have known there had ever been a split. Mark you, your return might change things." Anna looked at the Inspector. "She quite fancied you."

"I liked her."

"You were both playing with fire. You were lucky you didn't get burnt."

"I think I would prefer the *Railway Inn*. But do you have a room?"

"I have an excellent room. The best room in Pwddldwc. It is vacant this weekend. And if you can afford it, you can have it."

Raynes was suspicious.

"Who normally has it?"

"Mr and Mrs Jacoby. Arlene likes the best of everything. But, apparently, I'm not good enough for her. She's gone to some flashy establishment down the coast."

"Did you fall out?"

"Not at all."

"There must be some reason."

"There is. And now she is no longer a valued customer, I will tell you. Joanne and Graham Kennedy also have a room in the hotel most weekends. Arlene has noticed – I'm surprised she took so long . . . She has noticed that Simon had his eye on Joanne. And she is worried about a midnight romance on the top landing. I've been wondering about it myself. But Simon is very discreet."

"So she has spirited him away?"

"Yes. She's taken him to the hotel where she entertains her boyfriend to lunch most Sundays. I won't tell you his name – but he's not one of the railway people."

She looked at the expression on the Inspector's face. "I am assured it's completely platonic – and I'm sure it is. She wouldn't risk her reputation. She has too much to lose. Simon Jacoby is a very rich man – and is set to become even richer. He's a senior partner in Brick Court."

Raynes smiled.

"So his loss is my gain?"

"If you can afford it."

Anna topped up his gin and poured in the second bottle of tonic water.

"£130 a night including dinner, bed and breakfast. And if you want Bob to guard your door at night, that would be another £20. If you were wanting me to protect you, the cost would of course be much, much higher."

Raynes smiled.

"I sure it would be worth it."

Anna changed the subject quickly.

"Will you be working on the railway?"

"No. I shall visit people on the railway. I will speak to them in the bar when they arrive tomorrow night. But I promise not to cause any fights."

"You better not tell Sir David Cadwaller you are here. When he heard from his wife who you were, he said that he was sorry he hadn't shot you on the spot." She paused. "He said you were an interfering little ****!"

Raynes sighed.

"It's been said many times before. But how did you hear about it?"

"His wife, Margaret, told me. She does her shopping in the village. I asked her if he had found out who his visitor was. She said he had. She had to tell him. You don't say no to a man like that. But he was surprised at your audacity in penetrating his castle."

"Others have done it before."

"He doesn't like it. Apparently, you also visited a friend of his . . ."

Raynes nodded.

"Nigel Greenaway. Sir Walter's nephew. Who is now suing the Railway – or so I hear."

"I hadn't heard about that."

"He is claiming that Derek Barclay's death represented a serious breach of safety regulations. Tom Hayward is quite worried about it."

Anna looked serious.

"I would be quite worried about it, too. It might lose me a lot of trade. That railway's a gold mine to people like me. Make sure you don't kill the goose that lays the golden eggs."

Raynes said: "I have no intention of killing anyone – or anything. Least of all the Puddleduck. I think it's a wonderful railway. It's been beautifully restored. And Derek was responsible for some of its best features . . . No. I intend to save the railway from any further disasters. I hope that, by the time I leave, I will know who killed Derek Barclay – and why. And that should be the end of the story."

The Inspector showed more confidence than he actually

felt. But he convinced Anna that it was worth providing him with a roof over his head – and full protection – for the next three nights.

She picked up her keys.

"Let me show you the room."

25: *All Creatures Great And Small*

James Thompson was coming to the end of his 5.00pm surgery. There had been four patients – none of whom had any serious problem. He had been out for most of the day visiting farms. Now he was looking forward to a lamb casserole with baked potatoes. After that, he would watch the news and read the evening paper. Then he would go up the road to the *Railway Inn* and have his usual two pints of Guinness and smoke a pipe of peace in his favourite corner seat.

As he was examining his fourth patient, who had torn the skin pad on his front paw, he heard the door of the waiting room open and shut. He sighed. Another fifteen minutes before he could shut up shop and have his supper. He completed the bandaging of the paw and let the animal test his foot. It gingerly lowered its leg; but, at the first touch, lifted it again.

Mr Thompson looked at the dog's owner.

"The injection will help. Bring Buster in tomorrow night and we'll see if there's any improvement."

The dog looked at the vet with a mixture of resentment and fear. The injection had hurt and the paw was still sore. Now it was all wrapped in a white bandage. He would tear it off the moment they got home.

Mr Thompson knew what the dog was thinking. He finished the job by wrapping some white sticking tape around the bandage.

"Give him something else to chew on. A nice bone or some tasty biscuits. Otherwise, he'll gnaw at it all night."

The patient departed.

Mr Thompson made a note of the visit – its time, its cost, the materials used – and the address to which the bill would be sent. He knew all his customers. Some were slow payers – but they all paid in the end.

He was suddenly aware that the fifth patient had not come through to the surgery. He went to the door and looked into the waiting room.

"Good evening, Mr Thompson."

It was that police inspector from . . . somewhere. What was he doing back in Pwddldwc?

"I didn't expect to see you again."

Raynes smiled.

"The rumours of my death have been greatly exaggerated!"

The vet laughed.

"I suppose you had better come in."

He walked back into his surgery.

"Are you seeking professional advice? Or is there some animal needing help?"

"I am seeking some professional advice. I would like an answer to a single question. I believe that on the night of Sunday July 10, last year, you were dealing with a sick animal at Castle Farm, the home of Sir David Cadwaller. Would you like to tell me what kind of animal you were treating?"

Mr Thompson looked at the Inspector.

"You're not the local police."

"No, I am not P.C. Roberts. This is a personal question which has been very much in my mind since my previous visit."

"Does it have something to do with Derek Barclay's death?"

"I simply wish to confirm some information I was given – in April. I did try to ask Sir David himself; but he picked up a shotgun and made sure I left his estate as quickly as possible."

The vet laughed.

"I heard about that. In fact, we all did. And you were right to run. Sir David doesn't like people on his land and he's often winged the odd trespasser. It's taken him to court several times, but he doesn't care – even if he gets fined. To him, it's a matter of principle. It's his land."

"I'm very aware of it."

The conversation was non-threatening. The Inspector seemed in an agreeable mood. He only wanted an answer to a simple question. No harm in that.

The vet remembered the night in question. He was fairly sure it was a Sunday night. He had been at Castle Farm till almost ten o'clock. The animal had been ill for several days and eventually had to be put out of its misery. Sir David called her "Princess". Mark you, he called a lot of his cattle "Princess". Normally when they were ailing. By giving them a special title, he impressed upon the vet the importance of curing the animal. This was an expensive and valuable beast.

Mr Thompson got up and went over to his filing cabinet. He was a tidy, methodical man; and his secretary kept his papers in excellent order. He opened the drawer containing the Cadwaller account. A green file for 1989. He took it out and returned to his desk.

He opened the file and flicked through the pages.

July 1989.

"Here we are!" He raised his eyebrows. "Three nights – not one! I was called out on Friday, Saturday and Sunday. I was asked to inspect the cow – a Friesian – on Friday afternoon. Suspected BSE. No sign of the disease. I took some samples. Gave her an injection. Said I would return on Saturday. Called Saturday – half past six. No improvement. Two more injections. The animal was de-hydrated. Wouldn't drink. We did everything we could for the "Princess". But no response. The animal was beginning to suffer. Sir David wanted to shoot her. Put her out of her misery. He phoned on Monday to say she had died. Do you want to know the fee?"

"Not really."

"It was £87."

"That's quite cheap."

"Sir David's one of my best customers. He calls me out for the slightest thing. He's very particular about all his animals."

He looked at Raynes.

"Why are you so interested in this cow?"

The Inspector looked thoughtful.

"I'm not really interested in the cow. But I was told that Sir David couldn't possibly have murdered Derek Barclay because he was with you, looking after a sick cow. You were his alibi. If you were there, that clears him. At least for Sunday night . . ."

"Is that when Derek died?"

"I think so. It couldn't have been Friday or Saturday night – or his body would have been seen. Most people think he died on the Sunday night when all the volunteers had gone home. Of course it could have been done early on Monday morning. The police seem to think he had been there for four or five days."

"So you think this puts Sir David in the clear?"

"Well, he seems to have been the person with the most reason to kill Derek. And Derek's van was found near Castle Farm. His body had to be brought down to Puddleduck by someone. You didn't give Sir David any extra medicine?"

"Certainly not. I have here a list of the injections which were used."

He handed over his notes to the Inspector.

Raynes quickly read through the two sheets of paper. It all looked above board. Thompson the Vet had recorded the time spent, the work done, the medication used, the advice given. He was a very methodical man. He would make a very useful witness.

Raynes handed back the papers.

"Does that answer your question?"

"It does."

"And will you now be able to return to Grasshallows . . .?" He was going to add: " . . . as quickly as possible?" – but the conversation had been pleasant thus far.

It was better to keep it that way.

Raynes looked grim.

"I'm afraid not. All this does is to eliminate Sir David from my enquiries. I hardly think that he could cope with a sick cow on the same night as he was chopping off Derek's legs."

Mr Thompson spoke quietly.

"I don't think anyone chopped off his legs. It was an accident."

Raynes gave him a long, hard look.

"I think we both know that is not true. Mr Barclay was murdered. He had several enemies. For some reason, they decided to kill him that night – in a particularly horrible way. There has been a cover-up. A very successful cover-up. It will be difficult to pin the murder on anyone – especially since a year has passed. But I intend to find out who it was." He looked at the vet. "And, as one professional to another, I would appreciate your help."

Mr Thompson said nothing.

There was very little he could say.

He looked sadly at the Inspector.

"I do not know anyone on the railway – nor in this village – who would have done a thing like that."

"Sir David?"

"You have cleared him."

"Only for Sunday night."

The vet looked anxious.

"If he knows that you are still pursuing him, he won't take it very kindly. You better watch your back. Sir David doesn't tolerate any opposition."

"I'm aware of that."

26: Friend Or Foe?

Raynes left the surgery. As he came down the steps, he saw Emily Williams coming towards him. The moment she saw him, she stopped. Her jaw dropped.

"Surprised to see me?"

"Tom said . . ."

" . . . that I had been paid off?"

"Something like that."

Raynes smiled.

"You shouldn't believe everything Tom says."

Emily recovered from her surprise at seeing him.

"What are you doing here?"

"Same thing as I was doing on my last visit. Asking people questions. Trying to find out who killed Derek."

"They don't think he was murdered."

"I know. But there's been a cover-up."

"You're not going to be very popular."

"I'm aware of that."

"Where are you staying?"

"Not with you, I'm afraid. I don't want to upset Tom or embarrass your mother."

"Why were you visiting Thompson the Vet?"

"I just wanted to ask him a few questions."

"About what?"

"About a cow he was looking after on Sunday July 10 last year."

"A cow?"

"Yes. I was told that Mr Thompson was with Sir David Cadwaller at the Castle Farm on the night Derek died. I just wanted to make sure that Sir David had an alibi."

"Did he?"

"Yes. Mr Thompson has a complete record of his visit. The facts prove that both men were at Castle Farm that night. Sir David could not have been in two places at once."

Emily looked relieved.

Raynes looked at her.

"And why are you going to the surgery? Is this a professional visit – or are you going for a kiss and a cuddle?"

Emily was shocked at the suggestion.

"I work here."

"Do you? Why?"

"For money, of course. I clean out the cages. Feed the animals. Then I mop the floors and empty all the bins. I vac the waiting room and the surgery carpets."

"And how much d'you get for that?"

Emily looked shifty.

"Five pounds."

"A week?"

"No. A night. I get £25 a week."

"And is all this going into your bank book? To pay for you going through university?"

Emily nodded.

Rather unwisely, she added: "It also pays for me to go and visit Marc once a fortnight."

The Inspector welcomed this opportunity to talk about her boyfriend.

"Which prison is he in?"

Emily immediately regretted that she had mentioned Marc. Reluctantly, she said: "Swansea. The first place they sent him was dreadful. Winston Green . . ."

"In Birmingham?"

She nodded.

"And how much longer will he be in Swansea?"

"Well, he got two years last November. But they say that if he keeps his nose clean, he should be out by Christmas."

Raynes tried to sound reassuring.

"You'll be glad to have him back. Do you think you'll be able to pick up where you left off?"

Emily smiled provocatively.

"You mean – burning more cottages?"

"No!"

"I don't think he's changed that way. But he'll have to be more careful. He knows everyone will be watching him when he comes back."

Raynes laughed.

"Does that include P.C. Roberts?"

"Oh, he won't worry about him. He's useless. Even if he saw you with a bunch of firelighters in your hand, he'd never guess what you were up to."

"So it wasn't P.C. Roberts who caught him last time?"

"No. Someone saw his car."

Raynes looked thoughtful.

He distinctly remembered what Marion Davies had said. She had shopped him once to the police. She would gladly do it again."

"Would that have been on Sunday July 10?"

"No, Mr Raynes, it would not!"

There was a glacial tone to her voice.

Raynes continued to sound friendly and light-hearted.

"Can you remember what you were doing on that Sunday night?"

"Yes, I can . . . I was with Marc all evening in his flat."

"Did you stay the night?"

A severe look of disapproval.

"No. He brought me home."

"And where was Marc living at that time?"

"He had a small flat in Abernirvana – opposite the station."

"Does he still have the flat?"

"No. He cannot afford to keep it. When he comes out of prison, I am hoping that he will be making his home with me in Grasshallows." She glared at the Inspector. "We shall do our best to make your life more exciting!"

Raynes laughed.

"It's quite exciting already. But at least we can keep an eye on both of you. I don't think your mother would like to see you put inside." He changed the subject quickly. "How have the exams been going?"

"Very well. I am hoping to see you in October."

Raynes cast a glance back at the vet's house.

"Providing your sugar daddy keeps paying!"

Emily smiled confidently.

"He will."

27: A Quantum Of Wickedness

When the Inspector returned to the *Railway Inn*, he enjoyed half an hour of sheer bliss in his luxury en suite bathroom. It was equipped with an up-market jacuzzi which maintained an invigorating torrent of hot water. Of course Mrs May had one of Signor Candido Jacuzzi's splendid creations, but this was on a far larger scale and much more powerful. He was surprised to find it in such a small Welsh village.

He tried to decide which wine would suit his mood. A Piesporter would do for the first course which would probably be seafood – mussels or crab. (One had to remember that one of Wales' national dishes – laverbread – was made from seaweed.) For the main course, roast lamb would probably require a rich, full-bodied claret.

With some reluctance, he got out of the bath and wrapped himself in a large, warm towel and walked back into the bedroom with its highly romantic four-poster bed. Mrs May would enjoy that; but he couldn't think of any way of enticing her over to Wales.

So, instead, he concocted a tantalizing picture of Arlene Jacoby gliding round the room in a peach satin negligée. Sadly, the picture caused him no joy. He did not find Arlene very exciting. Cold, reserved, calculating was his reading of her character. He would prefer Marion Davies – or even Anna. They were both more passionate individuals.

Very quickly, he reminded himself that he was not in Pwddldwc to pursue women – but to solve a particularly unpleasant murder. And he had set himself a target of four days. He must keep focused on that one over-riding objective.

* * * *

As he descended the staircase, he was met by Anna in her stunning red dress.

"I'm putting you beside Father Morris."

"Is he here?"

"He usually comes down on Thursday nights. He likes to get things ready for the weekend."

Raynes remembered that it was on a Friday morning – with the Amos sisters – that Derek's body had been found.

"That's fine."

He would enjoy a long chat with the padre.

The dining room was fairly empty; but Anna had put them in a quiet corner near the open fire. Father Morris rose to his feet.

"I wasn't expecting to see you."

"No. Tom has warned me off his patch; but I couldn't let the matter rest."

"A true professional!"

"I like to think so." Raynes looked down at the table. "What would you like to drink?"

"I normally have a pint of special."

"Rat's piss!" Raynes laughed. "Would you like to share a bottle of Piesporter? I was going to have that, followed by some claret."

"I should be delighted."

Raynes sat down.

"Not very busy, is it?"

"It fills up at the weekend. Not just with railway people. The locals come here in force on Saturday nights. You have to have a thick skin to venture here on a Sunday night. The chapel people violently disapprove of any pleasure on the Sabbath."

"And yet they break the ninth commandment without a flicker of conscience, slagging off their neighbours!"

"I think there's a quantum of wickedness in every community."

"Including the railway?"

Father Morris laughed.

"You should see some of the letters they send to the Editor of the Society's newsletter. They obviously don't expect them to be printed. They're just letting off steam. But it's amazing how much aggro there is under the surface."

"What is the current *bête noire*?"

Father Morris looked serious.

"It may surprise you to learn that it is *Lady Ermintrude*."

"Really?"

"There are a lot of people who think two engines are quite enough. There was no need to buy a third locomotive – especially when almost everything in her has had to be replaced."

"Not just the piston rods?"

"That was the last straw! But a lot of questions have been raised about the cost. Did Brian Williamson not know the condition of the engine he was buying? How much did he pay for her? How much money did the Society raise in their Appeal? How much has been spent on all the repairs? None of these questions have been answered. It's caused a lot of unrest amongst our members."

Anna came to take their order.

Father Morris looked up at her.

"How much did you give to the *Lady Ermintrude* Appeal?"

"Five hundred."

"Did you receive an official receipt?"

Anna looked thoughtful.

"No. But Dr Campbell thanked me for my gift. Is there a problem?"

"I don't know. I was just telling the Inspector that there had been many complaints about the Railway buying a third engine. People say they've never been told how much she cost – or how much was raised by the Appeal."

Anna shook her dark locks.

"I don't recollect anyone being told. Is it important?"

Raynes said: "Father Morris says that he's had quite a few letters about it."

"Perhaps you should ask Archie?"

"I have. But he says the money is still coming in – and still pouring out! He says that he thinks it would be better not to say anything till *Lady Ermintrude* is up and running."

"He may be right."

Anna looked down at her pad.

"So what's it to be?"

Raynes said: "A bottle of Piesporter – with a nice claret to follow."

Father Morris looked at the menu.

"French onion soup – and a steak with a Béarnaise sauce. Well done."

Anna turned to Raynes.

"What is in the seafood pancakes?"

"Haddock, scallops, wild mushrooms and prawns; a dash of cream and Gruyere cheese."

Raynes felt weak at the knees.

"That sounds perfect. Could I have two?"

"And the roast lamb?"

"It is Welsh lamb?"

"Of course."

"From Sir David Cadwaller?"

"I'm afraid so. We have to support local producers. And his lamb is of the highest quality."

Anna departed with their order.

Father Morris looked across the table.

"You don't like that man."

"Neither do you. It was you who told me what he had done to Derek. But even if I do dislike him, I won't let it prejudice me against his sheep!"

Black Bob arrived with a bottle of Otto Dunweg – a distinctly upmarket Piesporter with a predictably upmarket price. Raynes, looking at the label, wondered if it might be too sweet; but to Bob, it was just a bottle of wine. There were only two bottles left on the rack. If it was half-decent, the Inspector might take the final bottle the following night.

Raynes tasted the wine anxiously. It was not too sweet and it had retained its freshness and fragrance. He gave Bob a nod of approval.

Whilst they were sampling the wine, Raynes asked Father

Morris whether there had been many other complaints from his correspondents.

The padre grinned.

"There have been plenty about you! Quite a lot of people have written in criticizing Tom Hayward for bringing you over to the railway. I'm sure most of these people have never met you. To me, it has the appearance of an organized campaign."

"Organized by whom?"

Father Morris looked guarded.

"Simon Jacoby, I should think . . ."

"Really?"

"He's also ditched Tom Hayward as his fireman."

Raynes was even more surprised.

"Who's he taken on instead?"

"Charlie – the Communist. Everyone is surprised. But Charlie's been longing to get on to the footplate for some time."

Raynes instantly remembered some interesting information given him by Tom Hayward.

"Wasn't there someone else thrown off the footplate – and expelled from the Railway?"

Father Morris looked astonished.

"How on earth did you find out about that?"

Raynes smiled.

"A little bird told me!"

"Well, whoever the little bird was, it had access to highly classified information."

"I believe she was called Ariel Stevenson. She was also known as the 'Trapeze Artist'. Whose girlfriend was she?"

"Didn't the little bird tell you?"

"I think it wanted to."

Raynes looked thoughtfully at the burly clergyman who was reluctant to reply.

"Would it have been Simon Jacoby?"

Father Morris took a deep breath.

"It was many years ago. Long before he met Arlene. Ariel

grew up in a circus family. People turned against performing animals. The circus closed down. But Ariel had been taught all the tricks of the trade. She also moved in high circles. I think Simon met her at the Henley Regatta. He was instantly smitten. Besotted. He brought her down here during the summer vacation. It was hilarious – but quite disastrous. Ariel was a complete nymphomaniac."

"She was one of Derek's conquests, I believe."

"I think it was more likely the other way round. She had to go."

"It wouldn't have done Simon's reputation much good."

"It wouldn't do anyone's reputation much good!"

"Did you meet her?"

"Pass."

Raynes said: "We all have our secrets."

Father Morris agreed.

"I'm quite certain Simon would be horrified if that was brought up again; now he's such a high flyer." The clergyman looked at the Inspector. "Who was it that told you?"

Raynes had no hesitation in saying: "Tom Hayward".

Father Morris shook his head.

"Tom could do Simon a lot of damage. He knows too much."

Raynes agreed.

In the hope of further indiscretions, he topped up the other man's glass – and was instantly rewarded.

"I probably shouldn't tell you this, but the knives are out for Tom. I had an anonymous letter last week, accusing him of having an affair with a schoolgirl!"

"Emily Williams?"

"I don't believe it. Emily has many faults – but Tom has been very kind to her family. He stays in their house under Mrs Williams' eagle eye. He wouldn't be there if she thought anything untoward was going on. And for most of the time he's over here, he's hard at work shovelling coal into the fire box. I don't think he'd have the time or the energy for an affair."

Black Bob arrived with their first course. The French onion soup was still bubbling in its earthenware bowl with the croutons sinking under a rich thatch of cheddar.

Raynes looked at his own plate – and felt that he had chosen wisely. The pancakes were generously filled and the prawns and scallops were already trying to leap out of their velvet jackets.

Once they had enjoyed their first few mouthfuls, Raynes asked: "Do you get many anonymous letters?'

"Quite a few."

Father Morris wiped his lips on his napkin.

"None of them can be printed."

"Are they all true?"

"No."

"Are they written by the same person?"

"No."

Raynes waited for the clergyman to say more – as he knew he would. Father Morris took two more spoonfuls of soup – then he looked up.

"Most of the correspondents are identifiable. Some of them have been writing for quite some time. When they first send in a letter, they probably sign it. Two years later, they send in an anonymous screed. Well, you cannot help noticing the handwriting, the typewriter, the kind of paper they use, the lay-out of the envelope, the mistakes in spelling, the use of adjectives and punctuation – all these are dead giveaways. I file the letters under their own names."

He looked over his shoulder.

"I keep an eye on the hotel register and the Secretary of the Society occasionally compares any unknown envelopes with correspondence she has received. It doesn't take much detective work. So I get a very clear picture of what people are feeling – without letting on that I know who they are."

"Who is the Secretary?"

"Kathleen Williamson."

"I've not met her."

"She's a very capable woman. She handles all the

membership applications and draws up the weekly rotas. Simon Jacoby deals with the business correspondence. Or, at least, his Secretary does. But Kathleen does all the bread and butter work."

"So who is your most vicious correspondent?"

"You wouldn't expect me to tell you that!"

"I can probably guess. Would it be Virginia Barclay?"

Father Morris nodded sadly. The Inspector was too quick for him.

"You're quite right. She's always sent in letters expressing her views; but, since Derek died, she's been attacking everyone. She changed to a different typewriter and used a different colour of paper; but her style is unmistakable."

"Is she accusing people of murder?"

"Well, to start with, she was asking for help. She wanted people to demand a full inquiry. She called on everyone to say what they knew – not to remain silent. But, after the inquest, she started naming names, trying to provoke a reaction. But, of course, it didn't; because I was the only person who saw her letters. I didn't show them to anyone else. Her energy was entirely wasted."

Raynes was sorry to hear that. If Virginia's anxieties had been addressed earlier, there would have been no need for him to get involved.

"So who is she accusing?"

"At this moment, her chief suspect is Brian Williamson. She seems quite sure Derek was killed in the Engineering shed whilst he was unloading cement and sand. She says he was hidden in a locked room. Once the volunteers left on the Sunday night, Brian brought him out and laid him beside the track. Then he got the diesel going and within ten minutes Derek was dead. Then he went back home to Crewe."

"Was Brian's wife with him that weekend?"

"Apparently not."

"And how did he manage to keep Derek for two or three days in a locked room?"

"Drugs. First of all in his coffee. Then regular injections

every few hours. She blames Dr Campbell for supplying the drugs."

"I see. Plausible."

"Very plausible."

Father Morris added: "One or two other people have pointed the finger at Archie Campbell."

"Why?"

"He seems to have had a habit of supplying drugs to people. Recreational drugs. The suggestion is that he sells them to his better-off patients in Cheltenham – and does the same thing for people here on the Railway. Certainly quite a few people have been smoking cannabis and snorting cocaine. They don't seem to have any trouble getting it."

Raynes digested Father Morris' information.

He smiled.

"He didn't try to sell any to me."

"He wouldn't dare. He knew who you were. He wasn't very happy about you being placed in the ticket office."

"That was Tom's idea."

"It wasn't appreciated."

Raynes could imagine that his presence in the ticket office would have been most unwelcome. No wonder Dr Campbell had been willing to give him a lengthy lunch-break, with plenty of time to talk to Virginia, and to encourage him to leave his post early for a ride on the train. He must have been terrified lest any of his regulars turned up and asked for a fix!

To Father Morris he said: "Most of our conversation was about the security cameras. He told me that he had paid for them."

"I didn't know that. I assumed that he had used the money from the Appeal."

"No. I think he's innocent on that charge. Dr Campbell blames Derek for using up all his money on his building work. Sending in huge bills. He said he still owed Virginia a couple of thousand."

Father Morris disagreed. "It wasn't so much the building materials which cost the money. It was all the furnishings. The large cookers, chest freezers, a commercial dishwasher, non-slip flooring, good quality chairs and tables. Mrs Packer insisted on the best of everything. They were expensive – even though Derek bought them at trade prices."

"I am sure Mrs Packer could have paid for them herself. I believe she's quite a rich woman."

The roast lamb and the steak arrived together. Both were accompanied by generous helpings of roast potatoes and cauliflower *au gratin*. Bob put down the plates and hurried off to the bar to collect the claret.

Raynes waited till the claret had been poured before he started his main course. It was delicious. A perfect match for the roast lamb. Again there was silence whilst both men tucked in.

But Raynes' mind was still focused on the problems of the little railway.

"So Dr Campbell supplied drugs?"

"He wasn't the only one."

Raynes raised his eyebrows.

"There have been allegations . . ."

"From Mrs Barclay?"

" . . . from a number of people that Lydia Naylor has also been peddling drugs."

"Where does she get them?"

"From a contact in the University where her husband works."

"Nottingham? Or was it Keele?"

"I'm not sure. But they said she was selling them under the counter at the top station. There is a possibility that Joanne may also be involved."

Remembering his experience in the restaurant at Abernirvana, Raynes was not altogether surprised. He had thought that the two ladies were guarding their restaurant, but perhaps they were protecting their other business. The arrival of a detective-inspector must have given them a nasty shock. No wonder they had prevented him speaking to anyone and driven him back on to the train as quickly as possible.

Raynes wondered how much Bill Naylor knew about their drug-dealing. He must know what was happening because the security cameras covered both the shop and the restaurant. He would be able to keep an eye on all their customers and warn them if there was any sign of a police raid. Not that P.C. Roberts was likely to cause them much trouble.

The Inspector had assumed that the cameras had been installed to protect the Railway, the stations and the passengers. But perhaps they were designed for a more sinister purpose. Mr Naylor was sitting in his signal box, like a spider at the heart of its web, watching everything.

Raynes was also aware that he would be keeping an eye on Dr Campbell as well. After all, he had paid for the cameras with his own money. The Inspector had thought it was a generous act; but it was nothing of the sort. He was simply protecting his own vested interests.

Raynes said: "It's amazing that they can get away with it. You'd think someone would notice."

"Someone has noticed."

"And what are they doing?"

"They are making money out of it."

"In what way?"

"Blackmail. I believe that both Lydia and Joanne have been buying silence. The blackmailer apparently has documentary proof – or photographs – to show what they are up to. If they fail to pay, the evidence will be sent to the police. The sums being asked for are not great. The victims obviously feel it is price worth paying."

Raynes stared up at the ceiling.

"What a way to run a railway!" he said.

But then, another thought flashed through his mind. He looked at Father Morris – a piercing look.

"Is anyone blackmailing you?"

"What do you mean?"

Raynes thought it was pretty obvious what he meant. The Reverend was simply playing for time.

"Well," he said, "you've talked about this 'quantum of

wickedness' on the Railway. You've spoken about accusations being made against various people. You've talked about poison pen letters and drug-dealing. Possibly we shall get round to child murder. And now you've mentioned blackmail. There's a lot happening behind the scenes. I just wondered if you yourself were a victim?"

Father Morris was cutting up his steak. He dipped it in the Béarnaise sauce but did not put it to his lips. He remained – staring down at his plate. He was afraid to look the Inspector in the face.

Raynes said quietly: "I take it the answer is 'yes'?"

The padre put down his knife and fork and took out his handkerchief. He wiped his eyes. Raynes did not hurry him. He poured out two more glasses of claret.

"Anything you tell me will go no further."

Father Morris looked at the Inspector. Could he really trust this man? He drank more than half his glass of claret to give himself courage to speak.

"Yes," he said at last. "Yes, I am being blackmailed. I have been for quite a while."

"How much?"

"A hundred a month."

"That's quite a lot!"

"It is for me. I only get half a salary for my work in Manchester because I'm often away at weekends. The bishop would like to sack me . . ."

"And this could be the opportunity?"

"I'm afraid so."

Raynes was speculating on the possible reasons why Father Morris was being blackmailed; but the padre quickly came clean.

"I'm in a relationship with another man. We don't live together; but we share a caravan when we're down here. I've already had two warnings about my relationships with other men. I was told that if there was any recurrence, that would be it.

"We've tried to keep the lid on things for the past two

years; but Derek Barclay found out about us. He got his hands on a couple of photographs of us at a gay party. We were showing off our crown jewels. I don't know how he got the pictures – but he never did us any harm. In fact, he used to joke about it: 'If I have any trouble from you young fellows, I'll send the pictures to the bishop!'

"Unfortunately, when he died, those photographs passed into other, less scrupulous hands. Derek must have spoken about my warning from the bishop because I received a rather nasty letter, threatening me with exposure if I didn't pay up or if I missed my monthly deadline."

"Did you think of going to the police?"

"To P.C. Roberts? You must be joking!"

"To a higher authority, perhaps?"

"The letter said that if I went to the police, the photographs would be sent immediately to the bishop. I couldn't afford to take any chances."

"So you paid up?"

"I've been paying for almost a year."

"Do you know your blackmailer?"

"Yes."

"And do I know your partner?"

"Yes."

Raynes ran his mind over the people he knew on the railway and in the village. One person stood out in his mind.

"Charlie – the Communist?"

"He's not a Communist. I think he's probably a Liberal-Democrat."

Raynes smiled.

"That's just as bad!"

Raynes reflected: "Charlie does a lot for the Railway."

"We both do."

"Would you like me to crunch up your tormentor?"

"Very much. But I don't see what you can do."

Raynes said: "Well, I can't do anything without a name. Is it Dr Campbell?"

"I think he's being blackmailed as well."

"Anyone else?"

"I believe Arlene Jacoby has been desperate to get back some old love letters she sent to Derek Barclay. He refused to hand them back. She threatened him with murder – just two weeks before he died."

"So this could have been a motive for murder?"

"Very much so."

"And Derek's successor is making it difficult for all of you?"

"She is."

A woman! Raynes was not surprised.

He knew that there was only one person in the village who had been accused of blackmail. She had tried it on with Marion Davies and got her fingers badly burnt. Marion had reported Marc to the police; he had been arrested, charged, found guilty and sent to prison. She seemed to be having more success with her other victims.

He said: "Emily Williams!"

Father Morris was amazed at the Inspector's telepathic powers. On three occasions, he had come up with the right name.

"How did you manage to think of her?"

"I was told that she had already tried to blackmail someone in the village – but they wouldn't submit."

"Good for them!"

"She is a very dangerous young lady."

"I wouldn't have told you if you were still living in her mother's house. But since you are staying here, it might be easier to deal with her. But one false move – and she'll drop us in it!"

"I think you're probably right."

"But how can you stop her?"

"I don't know. But I have dealt with blackmailers before. You have to crunch them up good and hard. You soon discover they are complete cowards. If I succeed, I shall make sure you get back your photographs and all the money you have paid. If she hasn't spent it . . .! How do you pay her?"

"By cheque."

"That should be traceable. Cash would be more difficult. But you deserve to have this axe removed from your neck. You both do. Even if I cannot find Derek's murderer, I can certainly deal with this one."

Raynes had already begun to have a few ideas about what he might do to Emily. Mr Hayward wouldn't like it. But the poor man had no idea of the viper he was nursing so close to his bosom. He could easily become one of her victims.

Raynes said: "When I speak to her, I shall not mention either of your names. I'll pretend I'm acting on behalf of Arlene Jacoby – trying to get back her love letters. If anything goes wrong – if things blow up in my face – then Simon Jacoby will have to intervene. I'm sure he won't take blackmail lying down."

"No."

Father Morris could already see the wisdom of Inspector Raynes' approach. Mr Jacoby would not have been willing to act for him or Charlie; but he would certainly intervene to protect his wife.

For the first time in several months, Father Morris felt a genuine sense of relief – a glimmer of hope. He felt very thankful that the Inspector had had the courage to come back to Pwddldwc and continue his investigations. He would cut Miss Williams down to size.

"Do you think she will go to jail?"

Raynes finished his roast lamb. Despite all his eager anticipation, he had hardly noticed what he had been eating. He was so excited by the way the plot was developing. His mind was racing ahead.

"She should be in jail already. I have no doubt that both she and her boyfriend were involved in burning down the holiday homes. She has an intense hatred of the English. I saw the full depths of her feelings on my first night. She is a political fanatic. And now we know she has blackmailed several people. I imagine that, last year, Mr Hayward must have employed a very astute lawyer to defend her. I shall be interested to see what he does this time."

Raynes reckoned that providing Father Morris with a good meal and plenty of wine had proved an excellent investment.

Thanks to him, he had now discovered a great deal more about the "quantum of wickedness" which seemed to afflict both the Railway and the village.

He wondered if he could still garner a little more information before the padre collapsed or fell asleep.

Once the plates had been cleared away, Raynes said: "Would you like a glass of port with your coffee?"

"I should prefer an Irish whisky."

"Let's make it two!"

Father Morris smiled.

"I feel there must be an ulterior motive for all this generosity."

"Of course there is," Raynes admitted. "I'm still trying to decide what happened to Derek's son. Anna told me that the official line was that Timothy had been adopted. But she felt sure the child had been killed."

"Anna's very close to Lady Margaret."

"Birds of a feather?"

Father Morris looked uncertain as to whether he should say any more; but then decided to throw caution to the winds.

"It's a very serious allegation. No one wants to talk about it. They know that if they say anything – and Sir David gets to hear of it, he'll be down on them like a ton of bricks. He would throw any tenant out of his property. Drive them out of the village. He could close down the *Railway Inn* . . ."

"Really?"

"He owns it. Anna rents it from him, so she has to mind her Ps and Qs. That's why she was worried about you staying in the hotel. She knows that it will annoy Sir David. She doesn't want any trouble from him."

That was food for thought. But Raynes' mind kept returning to the fate of the child.

"What do you think happened to him?"

"Well," said Father Morris, "my personal view is that the

child was killed and his body was buried in Lake Nirvana. I have no proof. But we had a very dry summer at the time the child disappeared. The lake began to dry up. We all wondered how long it would take to refill.

"Whilst the water level was low, Sir David built a slipway running out into the lake. He used stones from the old slate quarries, so it didn't cost him very much. And he built it quite quickly.

"A lot of people use the lake during the summer months. It's a handy way of getting your yacht or dinghy into the water. The windsurfers use it as well. I've often wondered whether Timothy is buried under that slipway."

"It won't be easy to find out,"

"They'll have to wait till the next drought."

Raynes said: "It is a nice, peaceful place to be buried . . ."

Father Morris laughed.

"Perhaps Sir David will bury you beside Timothy?"

Both men drank their whisky coffee in a thoughtful manner.

To cheer up the Inspector, the padre raised his glass.

"A successful end to your investigations! May you find the truth before Sir David finds you! And may he never discover that I have been discussing his private affairs with you!"

28: *The Green Goddess*

Raynes was up early on the Friday morning – but not as early as Father Morris. He had gone across the road at 8.00am to open up the station for the Amos sisters who always arrived punctually at 8.30am to clean the carriages.

Raynes enjoyed a good breakfast and then followed him across the road and into the station yard, where the cleaners were already halfway through their work.

Father Morris introduced him to the two elderly ladies who were immediately overcome with admiration:

"The famous Inspector . . ."

"Come all the way over to Pwddldwc to solve our murder!"

Raynes congratulated them on their discovery of the body. They had done all the right things. They chirped happily about all they had seen and done:

"It was terribly exciting!"

Father Morris rescued the Inspector.

"Have you come over to see *Lady Ermintrude*?"

"Is she ready to receive visitors?"

Father Morris gave a wry smile.

"As ready as she'll ever be!"

He looked towards the engineering shed.

"Brian's already in there."

Raynes was surprised.

"When did he come?"

"Late last night. He stays in a very impressive mobile home with all mod cons. But Saturday will be a very special day for him. He's come down early to make sure nothing goes wrong."

Raynes looked at the engineering shed with its open doors, disgorging endless supplies of timber, sand and cement.

"Go through the door; walk straight down the passage and you'll find her ladyship gleaming like a French tart!"

Raynes wondered how much Father Morris knew about such things. He said: "You should treat '*une respectueuse*' with more respect!"

The clergyman looked at his yellow diesel.

"I prefer something practical which doesn't break down. If anything goes wrong on Saturday, it'll be this fellow who'll bring them home."

Raynes walked down the main passage of the engineering shed. At the far end, under powerful halogen lights, stood a small engine in rich green livery, lined out in gold. There was a strong smell of polish and brass wadding with an equally pervasive smell of oil and grease from her pistons and connecting rods.

He walked round to the front of the locomotive. *Lady Ermintrude* had a cheerful face. She had a bright red buffer beam and her name was emblazoned on a brass plate on her smoke box. Her small coal bunkers were already filled to the brim – and the large porthole windows in the spectacle plate made her look almost human. Raynes felt that *Lady Ermintrude* was a mischievous lady who had a mind of her own.

There was a sound of footsteps – and Brian Williamson appeared, clutching a mug of tea. He was clearly not expecting visitors. When he got over his surprise, he said: "Lovely, isn't she?" Then he realized who his visitor was. "Good Lord! What are you doing here?"

"I've come back to the Railway to see *Lady Ermintrude* make her maiden voyage."

"Have you been given a special ticket?"

"No. I shall watch her leave Pwddldwc and then I shall drive up to Abernirvana to see her arrive there. It'll be a wonderful occasion."

Brian looked unconvinced.

"You're still following up Derek's death, aren't you? Even though you've been warned off."

Raynes said quietly: "I've been warned off many times in my career. Each time, there was something to hide. Once you find what's hidden away, you discover something pretty gruesome underneath." He paused. "And a prosecution swiftly follows."

Brian was silent.

Raynes changed the subject.

"Is *Lady Ermintrude* ready to go?"

"Completely. We've done several test runs up the valley. She hasn't broken down. Nothing serious has happened. I think she'll be a splendid addition to the Railway."

"Was a third locomotive really necessary?"

Brian Williamson looked at him sharply.

"You've been talking to Father Morris!"

"I have. He says that, amongst his readers in the Society's newsletter, one of their chief concerns is the cost of *Lady E*. No one has ever said how much she cost to buy; and no one has said how much has been spent on the repairs. People are surprised that you bought a machine that needed so much doing to it. The suggestion is that you bought a dud and there has been a cover-up. No one will say how much the Appeal has raised. Donors have not received official receipts. Father Morris says that Dr Campbell will not publish any figures till the locomotive is up and running."

Mr Williamson was again silent.

He looked a worried man.

Then he said: "Would you like a cup of tea?"

Having only just had his breakfast, Raynes really didn't want another cup of tea. But if it helped Brian to talk, then the opportunity was not to be missed.

They went into a small office where the Chief Engineer switched on an electric kettle and put a tea bag into a mug. When the hot water, sugar and milk had been added, Brian sat down – and sighed.

"It's very difficult, Inspector. There has been an element of deceit – but not in the direction you might think. The first thing to note is that *Sir Walter* is in need of major repairs. It is a miracle that the engine has kept going for so long. You will probably have noticed how difficult it is for *Sir Walter* to climb the incline up to the Gushers of Idris with a full load. Since April, we've been using *Lady Sylvia* when traffic is likely to be at its heaviest. But it is quite a lot even for her.

"It is true that we have had to do a lot of work on *Lady E*. But we knew this when we bought her. We paid a fair price. The Appeal took a long time to get going; money was very slow in coming in. Dr Campbell had no money to spare. Derek Barclay had put in huge bills for the castle and the tea room. Bill Naylor was pressing for CCTV cameras all the way up the line.

"So I had to take out a personal loan to pay for her. I had just bought a large house with a hefty mortgage; so it wasn't the ideal moment to be raising another £30,000."

"Dr Campbell told me that he paid for the security cameras himself."

"He did. But he wasn't prepared to put up a penny for *Lady E*. It caused a lot of rows. Once the money did begin to come in from the Appeal, it was all used for repairs. But, inevitably, we could only move at a snail's pace on the repairs."

Brian looked apologetic. "I must confess that it was me who spread the story about *Lady E* being in a worse state than we had expected."

Raynes raised his eyebrows.

"Broken pistons? New forgings?"

"Untrue! I did it for two reasons. One to boost the Appeal; the other to explain why the job was taking so long. Simon – Simon Jacoby – knew what I was doing – but no one else. Believe me, in lying, I prepared a rod for my own back."

"So you do need a third locomotive?"

"Desperately. But it'll be a long time before the Society is in a position to pay me back for my loan. And I can tell you this! It'll be even longer before we can face the cost of rebuilding *Sir Walter*."

"How does your wife feel about all this?"

Brian looked down at his empty mug.

"Disgusted. Fed up. She would like to leave the Railway; but too much of our savings are tied up in all this. We might never get it back. I shall have to peg on."

"Father Morris tells me that Kathleen is the secretary of the Preservation Society."

"She is. But she's decided to resign at the next annual general meeting. They can find someone else to do their donkey work."

Raynes looked thoughtful.

"Has she received any poison pen letters?"

"She hasn't. But I have. How did you know about that?"

"I didn't. But several people have received them. When did you get it?"

"In April. That's why she stopped coming down each weekend."

"It wasn't because he mother was ill?"

Mr Williamson looked puzzled.

"That was your excuse when I came here in April. You said that she had gone off to see her mother."

"It was a lie . . ."

Raynes thought that Brian Williamson seemed to be in the habit of telling lies.

" . . . but Simon persuaded her to come back . . . which she did."

"What did the letter say?"

Brian looked grim.

"It accused me of killing Derek Barclay. It said that I had hidden his body in this shed. The letter pointed out that I had the keys to the station, to the diesel loco and to this building. It said that I had killed Derek because he had discovered that I was using the money raised for the Appeal to line my own pockets. And I had been frightened the truth might come out."

As he spoke, Brian sounded increasingly bitter.

Raynes asked: "Was the letter hand-written or typed?"

"Typed."

"What did you do with the letter?"

"I tore it up."

"Did you notice the postmark – before you tore it up?"

"It was posted here. It was sent to Crewe – where I work. Not to my home address."

Raynes was silent.

He was sure he had been told another lie.

"Are you quite sure you tore it up?"

Brian breathed heavily.

The last thing he wanted was for the Inspector to see the letter. But the Inspector had already detected the lie. It was no use lying any more. The letter was locked in the filing cabinet right behind him.

He took his keys out of his pocket and unlocked the cabinet. He pulled open the third drawer. He handed over a plastic file containing both letter and envelope.

"Thank you," said Raynes. He looked for a while at the print on the envelope. The local postmark. The stamp – second class. It was all very ordinary.

He took the letter out of the plastic file and read it. The first thing he noticed was the misspelling of Derek's surname – "Barkly" instead of "Barclay". Was this a deliberate mistake?

As he read the letter, he realized that Brian was not being accused of embezzling funds. He was being told of the infidelities of his wife, Kathleen, both before and after their marriage. It was suggested that Brian had found out about these indiscretions and had decided to kill Derek before they became public knowledge. The writer suggested that there were one or two juicy stories which could cause both of them acute embarrassment.

The Inspector looked at Brian.

"Would you let me show this envelope to Father Morris?"

"He's already seen it. And my wife immediately recognized the typing."

"Virginia?"

"It was quite stupid her pretending she couldn't spell her husband's name."

Raynes agreed.

"Who else but Derek would have known about what he and your wife got up to? He must have told Virginia. Laughing at you behind your back?"

He looked at the engineer.

He had tears in his eyes.

Raynes continued: "If your wife knew Virginia had written this letter, she must have found it very difficult to face her in the tea room – or around the station?"

Brian nodded.

"That's why she stopped coming. The letter was posted from Pwddldwc on the opening weekend. I got the letter on the Thursday. I showed it to Kathleen right away. She was deeply upset. Fortunately, she'd already told me about her affair with Derek – so that didn't cause any trouble. It was the sheer nastiness of the letter . . . Pure poison.

"Kathleen insisted on coming down the very next weekend, determined to have it out with her. There was a terrible scene. Virginia was absolutely hysterical – she denied everything!

After that, my wife refused to come over to the Railway. But, after your visit, Virginia stopped coming. And now we know why! Her new boyfriend – that toffee-nosed twit – is suing the Railway on her behalf! Causing us even more misery!"

Brian looked angrily at the Inspector.

"Simon blames you for stirring up a hornet's nest!"

Raynes said quietly: "I know he does. But he's wrong. I went to see Mr Greenaway and he told me what they were planning. The decision to sue the Railway was already in the pipeline – before my visit. I did not provoke him."

The Inspector hoped that Brian Williamson did not posses the same gift for detecting falsehood.

But Brian was only thinking about Nigel Greenaway.

"It was obviously his idea. She would never have thought of it. She might enjoy all the bad publicity. The damage to the Railway. But she'll certainly not get any money. Simon will see to that!"

29: Pandora's Box

Later that morning, Raynes saw Mrs Williams going into the hairdresser's. He knew her daughter was working in the station bookshop. He decided that this might be a good moment to make a quick search of No 14 Chapel Road. He knew where Mrs Williams hid her key, so there would be no difficulty getting into the house. But, in case he was caught – or a neighbour reported him to the police, he needed an excuse.

It would have been helpful to produce a letter or an article of clothing left behind during his previous visit. He could easily have brought something from Grasshallows; but he had never thought such a thing would be necessary. Fortunately, he remembered that his AA card was tucked into the back of his sun visor. What was more natural than for it to have slipped down behind a bookcase or a chest of drawers?

He walked slowly up Chapel Road to see if anyone was

working outdoors; but the street seemed empty. There were no parked cars outside No 14. He walked up the garden path and round to the back door. He moved a plant pot – and there was the key. He opened the back door and put the key back in its hiding place.

He shut the back door and went through the hallway to the front door to make sure he had a second line of escape. When he was sure that his visit had attracted no attention, he went upstairs to the room he had occupied in April and dropped his card behind the dressing table. It was something anyone could have done.

He then moved directly to Emily's room. It was surprisingly tidy. A single bed with a collection of bears and dolls; a desk; a bookcase with quite a number of textbooks and dictionaries. On the wall, there was a reproduction of Monet's "Water Lilies" and a picture of some raunchy jazz players sweating profusely. There was a Victorian wardrobe, a large comfortable armchair and a chest of drawers. There was a picture of some dark-haired young man and a photograph of Mrs Williams and her four daughters. Emily looked about eight.

Raynes peered under the bed. Then he looked on top of the wardrobe. He checked through the bookcase to make sure nothing was hidden there. He ran through the drawers of her desk. He looked under the chest of drawers and deep into the depths of her wardrobe. He could not see what he was looking for. But it would not be placed anywhere her mother might find it.

Also missing were all her school notebooks, files and letters. He could not imagine that she had thrown them away – even though she was now going to University. There were no personal letters from Mark. No cheque book – or bank book. But, of course, they might be in her handbag.

Clearly, there was another place – perhaps a less accessible place – where her most personal belongings would be stored. Somewhere her mother would not be visiting on a regular basis. Raynes walked out on to the top landing and tried all the other doors. Mrs Williams' room. Tom Hayward's. The fifth door led to a very steep staircase up to the attic.

Raynes smiled quietly to himself. This was more hopeful. But before he went up the stairs, he went into one of the front rooms and looked down on the street and the garden path. Was anyone watching the house? Convinced that he was still unobserved, he shut the door of Emily's room – but left his own open.

He climbed up the stairs to the attic and there, on the right hand side, was a large pile of box files and lever lock files. There was a bookcase full of children's books, two boxes of jewellery and more photo albums.

Raynes opened the box files one by one. No 3 contained what he was looking for. Her passport, private letters, bank statements and a bank book. No cheque book. She obviously had that with her.

There were a couple of recent diaries and an envelope full of keys. From their labels, it appeared that Emily had access to most corners of the two stations at Pwddldwc and Abernirvana. There was even a key to the castle tower.

Box No 4 also had a lot of letters and packages. Raynes decided that there was too much to examine in the house, so he decided to take both boxes back to the hotel and examine them at leisure.

He descended the staircase, put off the light and shut the door. He was conscious that his fingerprints would be everywhere and that he had deliberately left his AA card to provide a suitable excuse for a second visit when he returned the files. He locked the front door, let himself out of the back door, locked that door and once more hid the key. Then he strolled calmly down to the gate.

He stood there thoughtfully for a minute or two as if waiting for someone to appear. Then he shook his head sadly, looked at his watch and then walked down the road. It was still deserted. He made his way back to the *Railway Inn* and locked himself in his room. He did not want to be disturbed. He settled down in a comfortable arm chair with the two box files sitting beside him on the bed.

He went straight for the bank statements and the savings book. £8104 – with money still coming in. He looked back to see how long she had been using it. Three years. In 1987, there had been a succession of small entries – £20, £30 and the odd fifty. Raynes guessed that the larger sums might have come from Tom Hayward. Christmas seemed to be a good time – and so did her birthday, which appeared to be in November. Miss Williams was a Scorpio. He should have guessed that. Secretive, two-faced, with a sting in the tail!

He looked at her passport. A dreadful photograph. There were better photos of her taken by Marc. And there was also a collection of his letters from prison, written on lined paper. The Inspector read a few of them.

Her boyfriend seemed to be a rather selfish, soulless creature. There were few endearments; no sentimental slush; no rampant expression of desire. *Cariad* (Darling) was about as far as he went. It didn't appear that Mark spoke any Welsh. What did she see in him?

The answer, of course, was money. She was the treasurer of their fire-raising operations. In a small blue book, there was a careful record of money found in the houses which were later burnt. To this was added the proceeds from the sale of jewellery and antiques which they had stolen. This was neatly divided between E and M.

Raynes then returned to the bank statements to see where the money went. It went first into Emily's current account. If her share of the robbery was – say £362.63, three hundred and sixty was banked. Soon after, it was moved into the savings book – keeping her current account quite small.

The bank she used was in a nearby town. Pwddldwc and Abernirvana were too small to have a bank; but in the place where she went to school, the local branch of the TSB seemed to supply all her needs. Raynes was amazed that no one had questioned how a schoolgirl could be doing all these financial transactions.

From the evidence, it appeared that, in the year up to July

1989, seven houses had been raided, but not all had been burnt. Theft seemed to be the dominant motive.

The Inspector looked in particular at the weekend of July 8 -10, the weekend when Derek Barclay had died. Emily had said that she and Marc had spent the Sunday night at his flat in Abernirvana. But what were they doing on the Friday and Saturday nights?

Raynes compared the division of spoils with the dates when the money finally appeared in her bank account. There seemed to be an interval of about ten days. The goods were stolen one weekend; they were sold the following Saturday; and on the Monday, there was an addition to the account. The next entry after Derek's death was on Monday July 18. So there had been a raid on the weekend Derek died.

Having identified the money received from theft, the Inspector moved on to other sources of income. From July 1987, there was a regular £25 a week which went into the main bank account. This was presumably the money she received from Thompson the vet. It stopped suddenly in August 1989. That would have been when Marc was arrested. As Emily had said, the money was then used for her fortnightly visits to Swansea prison to visit her boyfriend.

But each week, there was another £50 which was paid into her savings account. This was not spent on visiting Marc. This payment had begun at the end of July 1989 and was still being paid into that account every week. It now amounted to £2000. This was serious money.

There were also a number of other payments which went in every month. There were two regular contributions of £100, others of £20 and £40. These smaller sums were more irregular. They had not been paid between October 1989 and March 1990, when the railway was closed. But they resumed in April. Was this blackmail money?

Digging deeper into Emily's blue notebook, Raynes came across a list of names. Many of them he did not know; but top of the list was the Methodist minister! Apart from drinking whisky at a wedding, what other sins had he committed? And poor Father Morris was being stung. A couple of photographs in an envelope revealed him naked, embracing Charlie at a party. Raynes noticed that Marion's name had been crossed out. That had been a serious misjudgement. Emily had got nothing from her.

Arlene Jacoby was one of those paying a hundred pounds a month. Archie Campbell and Lydia Naylor also paid Danegeld. And Raynes was beginning to see how Emily operated. Around the village, Mrs Williams picked up the latest gossip – and her daughter exploited that information. But, on the Railway, much of the material came from Derek Barclay. He had had many lovers over the years and they had told him their secrets. He had also passed some of them on to Emily and she had realized their value.

In fact, from the circumstantial evidence of the blue notebook, it looked as if she had begun to tap the Railway people in April 1989, two months before Derek died. The villagers had been paying for their sins since January 1988. Raynes wondered if her career as a blackmailer might have led to one of her victims killing Derek? There might be a connection there?

Further evidence in both box files revealed photographs, personal letters and cards, letters from drug dealers, hotel bills and other embarrassing documents which could easily send people to jail or ruin their careers. This was how the victims were squeezed. And as Raynes discovered very quickly, all this material had belonged to Derek.

Raynes' mind moved quickly to the set of keys – notably the key to the castle tower. Could Derek have hidden all this stuff in a safe place at Caercraig? Had he told Emily where it was hidden? So that, when Derek died, she had gone straight to the tower and moved it? But how had she laid her hands on the keys?

The Inspector's mind moved further. Derek had not kept all this material at his home in Wolverhampton. He had told Virginia about his past romances. They had happily discussed all the goings-on at the Railway. So she was able to write her poison pen letters with a fair degree of accuracy. But Emily, with the evidence in her hands, was able to use it more profitably. Had Emily worked hand-in-hand with the murderer? Was Marc not just an arsonist and thief, but also a killer?

Raynes was interested to note that Tom Hayward was not included as one of her victims. Presumably, Mrs Williams was doing very well out of him already. And Emily had high hopes of the publisher providing her with accommodation in Grasshallows – and perhaps even a part-time job.

One thing was certain. She would be one of the richest students in the University. She had feathered her nest most effectively.

Raynes felt that Derek Barclay's ghost must be working overtime to lead him to this Pandora's box of treasures. Obviously, he should not have broken into Mrs Williams' house; but the results had been amazing. He now had facts, figures, names, motives, even photographs. He had always believed that one small fact – one small clue – would burst open this case. He had never expected such a wealth of information. It was too precious to be returned to No 14 Chapel Road. He would have to store it in some safe place.

But he now had a complete picture of the whole background to Derek's death. He knew the name of the person who killed him – although he still did not know why. With Emily's unsuspecting help, the case was now an open book.

30: Dead Men Tell No Tales

When Raynes entered the restaurant of the *Railway Inn* on Friday night, he found the place absolutely packed. Many people had come down to Pwddldwc that weekend to see *Lady Ermintrude* make her maiden journey. Even though they were living in tents or caravans, they had decided to start their celebrations with an excellent meal.

Raynes hovered at the door, wondering if he should just go

to the public bar and have a couple of pints of Special and a bag of peanuts. But since he was paying for an evening meal, he felt he should have one. The dilemma was – how long would it take to get a table?

Black Bob, who was busy delivering drinks, took pity on him. He came over and said: "There's one spare seat next to Mrs Packer."

Raynes smiled with relief.

Any port in a storm!

He worked his way through the crowded tables.

Mrs Packer looked up with surprise.

"Inspector!"

He noted that she had almost finished her coffee. She would not be there for long.

"Is this seat taken?"

"No. No one wants to sit beside an old battle-axe. I would have preferred to eat upstairs; but they were too busy to look after me."

She looked at Raynes.

"Did I hear that you were staying in the hotel as well?"

"They had a spare room. Apparently, Simon and his wife have moved elsewhere. Anna feels quite affronted."

"They'll be back. The food may be good at the other place, but the facilities are decidedly primitive. I wouldn't like to take a bath in something the size of a bidet!"

Raynes laughed.

"I have a splendid jacuzzi. It's most refreshing."

"I know. I've slept in that room. But Anna charges quite a high price for her honeymoon suite." She looked at the Inspector quizzically. "Are you putting it on expenses?"

"No. I'm paying for it myself."

Mrs Packer's eyes twinkled.

"And what have you been doing since I last saw you?"

"I've been on holiday in France. In Nice . . ."

"Trying to get away from all your criminal associates?"

"Indeed. But then I discovered the French have quite a few of their own."

"Don't tell me you had another murder?"

Raynes smiled.

"I had a frozen body dumped in the swimming pool of the villa where I was staying."

"And did you find who did it?"

"I did."

"And what about the French police?"

"I gave them a helping hand."

Joyce Packer shook her head with amazement.

"Some people have all the luck."

A waitress came to take his order.

"Tournedos of beef. Well done. And the Raspberry Fiesta."

"Anything to drink?"

"A bottle of rosé."

He turned to Mrs Packer. "Would you like to join me?"

"No, thank you. I'll just have another coffee."

"A half bottle of rosé."

Raynes sat back comfortably in his chair.

"I believe you also enjoy the south of France?"

"I do very much. I have friends who live in Vallauris."

"That's the place where Picasso had his studio?"

"Yes. You can see some of his work in the local museum."

"Was that where you were staying when your husband died?"

The question was put so simply – and so naturally – that Mrs Packer said: "Yes. It was." And then began to wonder why the Inspector should be interested in her husband's death.

"How did you know about that?"

Raynes smiled inoffensively.

"I read about it in the newspapers."

For one ghastly moment Mrs Packer wondered if her husband's death might have been revisited by one of the tabloids. It was now over ten years since Philip died. She had hoped that, by now, the story might be dead and buried.

"A recent newspaper?" she asked nervously.

"No. It was a police report way back in 1979. There were some cuttings from the local newspapers. I had a feeling that there had been some other case of a man being run over by a train. So I looked back on the police computer – and there it was. What surprised me most was to see your husband's name come up with it."

Mrs Packer's face seemed to have lost some of its colour; her eyes had become watchful and guarded. Raynes knew exactly what she was thinking.

"It wasn't quite the same as the murder here."

"No, it wasn't. Philip had the upper part of his body cut off by the train, didn't he? The train must have been going quite quickly?"

"About 60 mph."

"I think the coroner's report said it was suicide?"

"Yes, it was."

"But your husband had been taking some medication before his death. Valium, I think?"

"That's what they said."

"And Derek was drugged up before he died?"

Mrs Packer relaxed a fraction. So long as the Inspector kept talking about the Pwddldwc murder . . .

"Well," she said, "he wouldn't have gone willingly to his death, would he?"

"No." The Inspector looked thoughtful. "But this raises the question of who supplied the drug and where Derek was staying on the night before he died. Do you have any ideas?"

Mrs Packer had one or two very good ideas; but she had no intention of sharing them with this nosey detective. She could see that he was well on the way to accusing her of performing a copycat murder.

The half bottle of rosé was delivered to the table – and his glass was filled. Raynes took a small sip.

"In the course of my holiday in Nice, I found time to visit Vallauris. I can see why Picasso liked it. One of the great centres of indigenous pottery. Lots of little workshops and studios. Highly coloured ceramic bowls and plates spilling out on to the streets.

"I asked one or two people if they'd heard of you; but they

hadn't. I had more success at the local hotel – The *Hotel des Mimosas*. They knew all about you. 'A valued customer', they said. 'A regular visitor'. They had details of all your previous visits. Including the one in September 1979 with an Australian lady called Alison Gifford."

Raynes had often found it useful to assemble a collection of circumstantial facts to bombard and unnerve an interviewee. In themselves, the facts did not amount to very much; but taken together, they tended to demoralize the opposition.

People always assumed that the Inspector knew a great deal more. In this case, he did.

"Only thirty minutes from Nice airport? Two hours from London? You could have got home remarkably quickly. You could have been back in Vallauris before your husband's body was even identified. Nobody would have taken much note of a much-valued guest who had been confined to her room for twenty-four hours!"

Although the Inspector had given her a very nasty shock, she could not help admiring him for the subtle yet graceful way in which he had presented her husband's tragic death. How, in just a few moments, he had come so close to the truth.

She looked at him with steely determination.

"Mr Raynes! Which murder are you actually pursuing? My husband's or that of poor Derek? I can assure you that the bones of my own domestic tragedy have been picked over many times by a team of very skilled police officers.

"And I can assure you that, although I may have been the chief beneficiary of his estate, his three children also benefitted substantially from his death. And as the investigation revealed, his murder required some considerable athletic prowess. It would have been completely beyond my physical powers to transport a man's body to the Box tunnel and then down a steep embankment to the railway track." Her eyes sparkled with gleeful malice. "Even if I had performed such a hideous murder, my dear friend, Anne, would have been willing to perjure herself for a few bucks!"

Raynes said: "Is that why you said that you would like

Simon Jacoby to defend you in the event of any future prosecution?"

Joyce Packer looked surprised.

"Who told you that?"

"Tom Hayward."

"That man knows too much!"

Raynes said: "When I asked him how your husband died, he said he didn't know . . ."

"Of course he knew!"

The Inspector poured himself more rosé.

"That is the point I have been trying to decide. Whether you killed your husband or not, your description of Philip's death may have given someone else the idea of how they could kill Derek Barclay. Also on a dark night; also on a deserted stretch of railway track. With no spectators. Another body drugged up and unable to escape. A diesel locomotive ready to move a carriage – or, as you said, a tractor – leaving him to bleed to death."

"My husband died quickly. Very quickly."

"Yes. Derek's death was much nastier. And in his death, there was a strong element of revenge."

Now that Raynes had turned to the more recent murder, Joyce Packer felt that she had emerged from a tunnel.

"I think you are quite right, Inspector. There was an enormous bitterness of soul – a deep anger – that fired this murder. I had nothing whatsoever against Derek. He was a good, kind, hard-working man. He did an excellent job building our tea room. He put in all the things we asked for – even when we changed our minds. It was 'no expense spared'. I know that didn't make him very popular with Archie; but we were delighted. The only thing I couldn't stand about Derek Barclay was his wife. She's just a self-pitying wimp!"

Mrs Packer drained her coffee and stood up.

"I hope you enjoy the rest of your evening, Inspector. I shall look forward to attending your funeral!"

Without a single backward glance, she headed back to her room.

31: Red For Danger

Raynes had just finished his *tournedos* and was looking forward to his Raspberry Fiesta, when Tom Hayward slipped into the vacant seat across the table. He did not seem to be in a good mood.

"I told you to keep away from the Railway."

The Inspector looked at the distinguished Rotarian.

"You said I was no longer needed. I had offended many important people. They didn't want any further investigation."

"It was for your own good."

"You believed my life was in danger?"

"It still is. There are a number of people who want to silence you."

Raynes looked surprised.

"Wouldn't they be better shooting you? After all, it was you who invited me over. It was you who sent me all that documentation. You set the wheels in motion . . . You were the one who wanted to find out the truth . . ."

He paused.

"Mrs Barclay had already given up any hope of finding out who killed her husband. That was why she was willing to go along with Nigel Greenaway and sue the Railway. Even if Simon does fight the case – and win – which I am sure he will; the damage had been done long before I appeared on the scene."

The waitress picked up his empty plate.

"Would you like another bottle of rosé?"

"No, thank you." He returned to Tom. "And why was Simon Jacoby so rattled by my questions? Has he something to hide? Was Arlene seeking revenge? Was she involved in Derek's death?"

"Don't be ridiculous!"

"Has she received poison pen letters?"

Tom Hayward looked flustered.

"She may have done."

"Is she being blackmailed?"

"Of course not!"

From his extensive rake through Emily's box files, Raynes knew that she was. Arlene had been paying up for almost a year. That afternoon, he had read two letters from Arlene to Derek Barclay begging him not to tell people about their association. It could endanger Simon's career. At the end of the second letter, there had been a direct threat. If he didn't return the letters to her, then other – unspecified – action would follow. That letter had been written on 20 June, 1989 – less than three weeks before Derek's death.

But the letters had not been handed back. They were still in one of the box files in a big white envelope, entitled "Mrs Jacoby" in Emily's neat handwriting.

Raynes had no desire to read the letters. But he had every intention of returning the letters to their rightful owner.

So the Inspector said quietly: "I think she has been paying quite a lot of money to prevent a scandal."

Tom Hayward looked shocked.

"Don't tell me that you didn't know."

"I didn't."

"I'm afraid that's a lie. I've seen the letters she sent to Derek. Simon must have told you."

"Has Virginia kept them?"

Raynes had no intention of revealing his source of information – to anyone.

He said: "And you also told me another lie. You said that Joyce Packer had married a rich man – but no one knew how he had died . . ."

Tom looked mystified.

"You told me that on my first night – whilst we were walking home from the *Railway Inn*. You said that she had asked Simon Jacoby to defend her if she ever ended up in court."

"Oh, yes."

"Well, I think you must have known how Mr Packer died.

Just as the person who killed Derek Barclay knew. I think Joyce gave them the idea."

The publisher said nothing.

"Philip Packer died in July 1979. He died on the main Bristol to London railway line just as it enters the Box tunnel. He had his head and one arm sliced off . . ."

Mr Hayward winced.

". . . Mrs Packer was in the south of France at the time. She had a very good alibi. And so did everyone else. I believe that, more than once, she talked about his death in the public bar – here in Pwddldwc; and her story gave our murderer the idea of doing a similar murder in the station yard."

Raynes looked hard at his former friend.

"Did you know about Mr Packer – or not?"

"I did know."

"Well, why didn't you tell me? It was a very important fact."

Tom Hayward hesitated.

"I thought you had enough on your plate at that moment."

Raynes said briefly: "You were wrong!"

Mr Hayward quickly changed the subject.

"Are you any nearer to solving the murder?"

Raynes raised his eyebrows.

"Much nearer. I hope to have the full details by Sunday night."

The publisher tried to sound helpful.

"Mrs Williams thinks it was Ifor Davies. She was convinced he had the motive and the means. His wife has been covering up for him. That's what they're saying in the village."

"Is that what Emily is saying?"

"Well, yes, I suppose it is. But why should that matter?"

Raynes received his Raspberry Fiesta. It did not look as exciting as he had hoped. But there seemed to be plenty of raspberries.

He looked up.

"'Why does that matter?' Well, it matters because your

little friend has already tried to blackmail Marion Davies!"

"No!"

"Yes. It was nothing to do with the murder – but there is plenty of bad blood between them. It was while Marion was away from her husband – during one of their separations. Emily received confidential information about where she was staying. Emily threatened to tell Ifor unless she paid £100."

"Did she pay it?"

"No. So your little friend told Ifor where she was staying and he went round, dragged Marion out of the house, beat her up and punched her in the face."

"I didn't know that."

"There's a lot of things you don't know about Emily. Your little friend can be very spiteful and malicious."

Raynes took a spoonful of the raspberries. They needed a lot more sugar – and more cream.

He looked at the publisher.

"You remember that first night, when you brought me down here – to the *Railway Inn*. You wanted to keep my identity a secret . . .?"

"Yes."

" . . . But when we got here, everyone knew who I was?"

"Yes. I remember that."

"Well, dear Emily phoned from the house – and told them. That's how it leaked out."

"Why should she do that?"

"To warn the murderer!"

"Does Emily know who the murderer is?"

"Yes. And that person is also paying her money every month to keep her mouth shut. She's doing very well out of it."

Tom Hayward looked horrified.

"You would have done much better asking her who killed Derek Barclay. She could have told you – and saved me from wasting a lot of time and money!"

Raynes stood up and threw down his napkin.

"The answer was on your own doorstep. She's been pulling

the wool over all our eyes. If the police knew what she had been doing – and what she is still doing, she'd be in prison along with her boyfriend, Marc. She was actively involved in robbing and burning down those holiday homes."

"Does her mother know all this?"

"No. Are you going to tell her?"

"I couldn't."

"So she's going to get away with it?"

Mr Hayward was almost in tears. He obviously had a deep affection for Emily. He said: "I can't believe she is as bad as that."

Raynes said: "By this time next week, you'll know the full story. Then it's up to you. To report her to the police – or do a cover-up."

Mr Hayward felt a deep anger towards Inspector Raynes. He hated him attacking a girl he had cherished since childhood. A strong note of defiance came naturally to him.

"I shall protect her!"

Raynes shook his head.

"You always have. You always will. But you will regret it."

He turned on his heel and walked out of the dining room. He would seek better company in the public bar.

32: A Bullet Train?

But it was to be some time before Inspector Raynes reached the public bar. As he crossed the hallway, he suddenly saw Sir David Cadwaller, sitting in a wing chair, holding a double-barrelled shotgun. The gun was pointing in his direction.

"Don't move an inch, Inspector."

Raynes stopped instantly.

He looked at the farmer.

"This is not the place to be using a firearm. There are a lot of people in this building. Someone could get hurt."

Sir David sneered.

"There's only one person who is going to get hurt, Mr Raynes – and that is you! I have the reputation for being a good shot. Compared with a flight of wild geese, you'll be a piece of cake!"

Black Bob suddenly appeared with a trayful of drinks for the dining room. He looked shocked.

"You can't do this!"

"I can do what I like in this hotel. You rent it. I own it."

Bob could do very little to help the Inspector; but he shouted: "Anna! Anna!" There was a note of panic in his voice.

Several people came out of the public bar to see what was happening. It seemed that a public execution was in the offing. There was the Inspector at the foot of the stairs. Alone. Unarmed. About to be shot.

Anna came into the hallway.

"What on earth do you think you are doing?"

Sir David stood up.

"This man has been interfering in my private life. He has accused me of killing Derek Barclay."

Raynes could not let this accusation pass unchallenged. He said: "Thompson the vet will vouch for the fact that I merely confirmed your alibi. That you were – both of you – looking after a sick cow on the night Derek died."

He looked into the crowd beside the door to the public bar. He could see the vet smoking his pipe.

"Is that not true, Mr Thompson?"

With some reluctance, the vet took his pipe out of his mouth and said: "You asked me to check my records. Which I did."

Attention moved back to the man with the gun.

"You spoke to my wife!"

"She told me that you had been threatening to kill Derek Barclay for almost two years."

"That is true. But I didn't kill him."

By now, the hallway was quite full. People had also come out of the dining room to see what was happening. They were very much in the line of fire.

Raynes decided that if he was to go down, he would go down fighting. And he would give as good as he got.

"I have never accused you of killing Derek Barclay. But I have reason to believe you may have killed his child!"

There was a sudden buzz of excitement.

His child!

Sir David was visibly taken aback.

Raynes continued: "Your wife, Margaret, told me that you had taken away the little boy and had him adopted. But no one knows where that child is – and many people suspect that you killed him. They've been too frightened to call in the police – but there are questions which need to be answered. And even if you kill me, those questions will not go away."

The atmosphere in the hallway was electric.

Sir David said nothing. But in the silence, everyone could hear the click as he released the safety catch on his gun.

He seemed to be shaking. It may have been Raynes' accusation. Or it may have been his uncontrollable anger. Perhaps both.

Anna stepped forward.

"Stop this nonsense – immediately! If you shoot the Inspector, you'll go to jail. You'll be imprisoned for life. You'll never see your farm or your animals again. Is it really worth losing all you've spent your life building up?"

Sir David coolly ignored Anna's warning.

He lifted up his shotgun to his shoulder – and then lowered it a fraction.

Raynes said quietly: "Can you tell everyone if that child is alive? Can you tell us where he is living? Or did you shoot him?

Sir David said: "Mr Raynes, you have said too much! I came here tonight with the intention of wounding you. But after all you have said, I believe that any court – any Welsh court – would agree that I have been severely provoked. You have accused me of killing my wife's child . . ."

"Derek's son!"

"You have tried to humiliate me. You have accused me of murder. This will be an honour killing. And it will be a pleasure!"

Someone called out: "P.C. Roberts, arrest that man!"

Sir David laughed.

"Don't bother about him!"

He raised his shotgun again and took aim. Straight between the eyes.

At which moment, there was a sudden movement behind Sir David. A flash of copper. A shadow that swung dramatically across the wall – too fast to be taken in. An object smashed down on the gunman's head. And Sir David crashed to the floor.

As he fell, his gun fell with him. When it hit the floor, the two cartridges were discharged. There was an extraordinary crackling sound as the Victorian grandfather clock in the far corner was riddled with pellets at almost ground level.

Its casing was shattered; the clock suddenly jerked forward and crashed down face-forward on to the tiled floor.

Several women screamed and ran.

Miraculously no one was injured.

Raynes was rooted to the ground. His feet felt like lead. He just couldn't have moved. Had Sir David fired – at almost point-blank range, it would have been instant death. Something – someone – had saved him. He stared into the crowd.

Marion Davies stepped forward. She had been standing behind Sir David's wing chair. No one had noticed her removing the copper bed-warming pan which had been hanging on the wall. Everyone had been looking at Sir David – not her.

She had held the long handle firmly and – at the vital moment – smashed it down on the farmer's head.

All the men in the hallway cheered.

She came up to the Inspector.

"You were too young to die!"

She hugged him and kissed him with great passion.

As the tension lifted, Raynes broke into tears.

A voice in the crowd said: "Fetch a doctor!"

Dr Campbell said irritably: "I am a doctor!"

He went over to Sir David and took his pulse.

"Alive!" he said.

"Pity!" said Marion. "He deserved to die!"

"We need an ambulance," said Lydia Naylor.

"We need the police," said Father Morris.

Raynes looked around the assembled company. Was P.C. Roberts in the building? He suddenly saw the wretched policeman standing at the back of the crowd – saying nothing, doing nothing.

P.C. Roberts moved into the limelight as if he was in a dream.

"I can't deal with this," he said.

Raynes said quietly: "You'll need to clear the hallway – immediately. This is an area where a crime has been committed. The police will want to see where all the pellets have gone. You'll need a pair of handcuffs to secure the attacker. And the shotgun will have to be wrapped in some form of plastic bag so that the forensic team can obtain fingerprints. You will need statements from witnesses. If you go and get the handcuffs, I'll make a list of witnesses."

P.C. Roberts continued to look down at Sir David's body. Blood was oozing out of the wound at the back of his head and the body was beginning to twitch.

The policeman said again: "I can't deal with this."

"Why not?" asked Raynes.

"Because he's my friend. I can't arrest my friend. If I arrest him, he'll turn on me and my family. He'll drive me out of the village. He'll report me to the Welsh Constabulary. I'll lose my job."

Raynes listened patiently.

Then he said: "This man has attempted murder. You have a public duty to arrest him. The quicker you phone the local police headquarters, the sooner they'll be here and take charge of the operation."

Brian Williamson said to James Thompson: "Can't you give him something to sedate him?"

The vet looked horrified,

"My treatment is restricted to animal welfare. I should get into terrible trouble if I started prescribing for the general public."

Black Bob appeared with a roll of old window cord and a sharp knife.

"This'll probably do the trick."

Anna Patterson looked across the hallway.

"I think he might have spared my clock."

Tom Hayward put a comforting arm round her shoulders,

"We have an excellent firm in Grasshallows who can deal with it. Munn's. I'll take it back with me and get it restored as quickly as possible."

The Inspector gave Mr Hayward a cold hard look.

"You knew this was going to happen, didn't you? You knew Sir David was sitting out in the hallway with a shotgun."

"I did warn you."

Anna nodded.

"And so did I. But I never thought it would come to this."

"The man is completely unhinged."

Raynes turned to Anna with a gentle smile.

"You promised to protect me."

Marion returned from the kitchen with a pair of yellow plastic gloves and a large roll of black bin bags.

Raynes pulled on the gloves and put the shotgun into one black bag and then wrapped it up in two others. He put the package on to the winged chair.

Black Bob had tied Sir David's wrists together behind his back and started on his feet.

P.C. Roberts had begun to move the onlookers out of the hallway and people slowly drifted back into the dining room and the public bar. The excitement was over.

Anna said: "You fairly provoked him by mentioning that child."

"It's my fault," said Tom Hayward. "I should never have

told you."

Thompson the vet said: "You were lucky to escape. He's a first-class shot. When he puts his mind to killing something, he does it properly."

"It's about time he was put behind bars," said Marion. "He's taken the law into his own hands far too often – and got away with it."

"His wife will be very distressed."

"No, she won't," said Anna. "She'll be glad of a break. She lives in fear every day. A couple of years in Swansea jail will teach him."

P.C. Roberts looked appalled.

"Jailed?"

"You can't let people go round shooting each other."

Raynes turned to the policeman: "Or killing young children. Why didn't you investigate – or even report – the disappearance of Derek Barclay's son? Why didn't you arrest him for beating his wife, Margaret? She was in a nursing home for four weeks – covered in bruises and cuts."

P.C. Roberts looked utterly helpless.

"He was my friend."

Raynes said firmly: "He was nobody's friend. He loved no one but himself. And his own precious pedigree. He hated the Railway . . . he hated Derek . . . and he hated me . . ."

Father Morris re-appeared in the hallway.

"I've phoned the police and told them the whole story. They're on their way."

"Thank you," said Raynes. "I shall be glad to see them." He poked Sir David with his shoe. "And I shall be glad to see this brute taken away."

Marion said: "I shall take you back to the farm. I don't think you're safe in this hotel."

Anna looked angry at this slur on her management capabilities.

"I think he'd be a good deal safer here than he would be at Penbass. If Ifor got the slightest idea you were playing around, he'd be quite capable of killing the Inspector."

Father Morris said: "Well, the police will be here for most of the night, so I think he'll probably survive."

Raynes smiled a wry smile.

"Thank you for your kind thought. But what I'd really like to know is how Sir David knew I was here. I arrived in Pwddldwc twenty-four hours ago and only five people knew I was here. Someone must have told him."

Marion said: "It was probably that blackmailing little bitch from Chapel Road! She'd sell her grandmother's soul for five pieces of silver!"

Raynes looked at Thompson the vet to see how he would re-act to this attack on his employee. He looked very upset – but said nothing.

Tom Hayward defended Emily.

"She'd never do anything like that. Not when you've been a guest in her house."

Raynes asked Tom: "Who told you I was down here for the weekend? I didn't tell you. And you said you wouldn't be here. Was it Emily who told you?"

Tom Hayward ran a hand through his hair.

"I wanted to see *Lady Ermintrude* make her first official run."

His reply did not ring true.

Raynes turned to Anna.

"And is that why Simon Jacoby moved to another hotel this weekend? Was he told that he might be caught up in a murder? Not very advisable for one with such high legal ambitions?"

Anna shrugged her shoulders.

"How should I know?"

Sir David was beginning to show some signs of life. Trying to move his hands and turn himself over to see what was happening. There was blood on his nose and his lips. His eyes seemed to have difficulty in focusing.

He growled at Raynes: "Are you still here?"

"Yes."

"Why are my hands tied?"

"P.C. Roberts didn't have his handcuffs with him."

The policeman butted in: "I told him I couldn't arrest you."
"Quite right. Untie me immediately!"
No one moved.

Raynes said: "The local police are on their way. They've been told the whole story. They will be arresting you for attempted murder. There were over thirty witnesses. I don't think you'll get off so easily this time."

"Damn you!" Sir David struggled to loosen the cords. "I should have killed you when I had the chance."

"Indeed you should. But as Mrs Patterson told you, you would have been put away for twenty years and you would never have seen your home or your animals again. She gave you good advice. At worst, you should get about two years."

Sir David's eyes bulged.

"Two years! No one will jail me! I shall make sure I have first-class legal representation. If necessary, I shall take the case to the House of Lords."

Raynes said quietly: "There may be other charges brought against you. Wife-beating . . . child abduction . . . not to mention Derek Barclay's death . . ."

Sir David caught sight of the vet, who was standing in the hallway, re-filling his pipe which had gone out during all the excitement.

"James, come over and give me a hand."

Thompson the vet looked up sadly.

"I'm sorry, old boy, I can't help you on this one. You're for the high jump this time. The boys in blue can't turn a blind eye to attempted murder. They'll have to charge you."

Sir David uttered a stream of obscenities and then lay exhausted on the floor. His head was sore. He nose felt smashed in. His wrists were tied too tightly and no one was going to lift a finger to help him. He drifted in and out of consciousness. He had no idea how he had come to be in this position; but he blamed Inspector Raynes.

The few people left in the hallway said nothing. They were all waiting for the police to arrive. Raynes stayed very close to Sir David and the gun. He would not move an inch until the local police took over. He didn't trust anyone in the hotel – except perhaps Father Morris . . .

The silence affected all of them. P.C. Roberts went off to put on his official uniform. Mr Thompson was soon enveloped in a cloud of smoke with a delicious Turkish aroma. Joyce Packer would hate it.

Anna went off to the public bar to tell all her customers that their next drink would be on the house. Whatever they wanted.

She turned to Black Bob.

"Make sure Mrs Packer gets a Tequila Sunrise. A double!"

She went through to the dining room and offered each guest a brandy, a whisky or a liqueur. An extra drink would keep the punters happy – and stop them asking questions.

Fortunately, when they left, most of the restaurant customers went out through the back door into the car park – whilst those in the public bar would use the side door. Most of them were likely to be there until closing time.

So for about half-an-hour, everyone just stood and waited. Idle conversation seemed inappropriate. Mr Hayward stood biting his nails. This could be very bad publicity for the Railway. If it got into the Press, they could portray Pwddldwc as a wild outpost in the American Mid-West where law and order had broken down.

He cursed himself and Raynes for setting loose the dogs of war.

Eventually, they heard the distant sound of a police siren. And then another. Doors crashed open and four officers found themselves in the hallway, with the local bigwig trussed up like a Christmas turkey.

They showed him little sympathy.

"You've gone too far this time."

"You won't get away with this one."

The senior officer looked round.

"Who was he trying to kill?"

Raynes said: "Me."

"And who are you?"

"I am Detective-Inspector Raynes of Grasshallows police."

"And what are you doing down here?"

"My friend Mr Hayward invited me to come over and work on the railway. This is my second visit. I wished to see their new locomotive make its first run."

"Why should he want to kill you?"

"Well, I believe he spent two years threatening to kill Derek Barclay. He seriously assaulted his wife, Margaret. When I went to see him at his house, he refused to speak to me – and fired two shots at me as I left. I have been warned by Mrs Patterson there was still a danger of him attacking me. When I walked out of the dining room, he was sitting in this chair with his shotgun."

Father Morris said: "There are at least twenty witnesses in the public bar who will corroborate the Inspector's story."

Raynes indicated the shot gun in its plastic bag. "No one has touched it."

Anna said: "There are pellets everywhere. He has destroyed my grandfather clock. It is an heirloom."

The police recognized Thompson the vet.

"Is that how it was, Jim?"

"I'm afraid so. Mr Raynes was pinned down at point-blank range. This time, Sir David had no alibi."

Raynes thought this was a significant remark.

"And who stopped him?"

"I did." Marion stepped forward. "It was the only thing I could do. I grabbed that copper pan off the wall and bashed him."

The senior officer looked reproving.

"You could be arrested for assault."

Marion pouted contemptuously.

"I deserve the Queen's Medal for Gallantry."

Most of the men said: "Hear! Hear!"

The senior officer untied the cord round Sir David's ankles.

"Get this man into the car – and stay with him."

P.C. Roberts came forward with his pair of handcuffs.

"Thank you, mate, but we've got our own."

Sir David struggled to his feet, swayed and fell heavily. Two policemen helped him to his feet and led him out of the hotel.

The tension lifted. A thorough search was made of the hallway and the area cleared. It was now a crime scene. A police photographer would arrive later to take photographs. A statement would be required from Inspector Raynes and all the other witnesses. Names were taken and those who were willing to provide an immediate statement were encouraged to do so.

Raynes, no longer feeling quite so limp and drained, was escorted back into the public bar. Brian Williamson led the Inspector over to a corner seat, where a lady was twirling an empty cocktail glass.

"This is my wife, Kathleen."

Raynes smiled.

"I am very glad to meet you."

Brian said: "What can I get you to drink?"

Raynes breathed a deep sigh of contentment.

"A double Cointreau on ice."

"Make it a treble! All the drinks are on the house!"

33: Ladies Of The Night

When Inspector Raynes awoke the following morning, in his sumptuous four-poster bed, he could scarcely believe that the events of the previous night had really taken place.

They had the makings of some particularly repellent dream where he had been cornered by his enemies, threatened with instant death and rescued by a middle-aged woman bearing a copper warming pan – with which his assailant had been effectively pole-axed.

In this incredible mixture of farce and fear, shots had been fired, a clock had been smashed and people had cheered. But, throughout the entire ordeal, he had been utterly helpless; his legs immovable; his mind seemingly frozen in time.

He could remember drinking an orange liqueur with Brian and Kathleen Williamson who had been remarkably kind and caring. They had offered to help him up the stairs to his room; but he had managed it himself. By that point, he was beginning to feel a lot better. He was wondering whether fifteen minutes in the jacuzzi would wash away all the hateful memories.

But when he entered his room, he suddenly noticed that there was someone with blonde hair lying in his bed. She was asleep – but she soon woke up.

"At last!"

"Have you been waiting long?"

Marion looked at the clock on the bedside table.

"About an hour."

Raynes smiled.

"I take it that you are here to protect me?"

Marion laughed.

"I think once is enough – at least for one evening! Besides, the danger has now passed."

"You deserve a reward!"

"That's what I'm here for. I just hope you are up to it. I must say this bed is incredibly comfortable. Much more comfortable than the back seat of my car!"

Raynes took off his socks and shoes.

"What about Ifor? Where is he at this moment?"

"I think he will still be in Penbass, in his usual condition – blind drunk! But if he should be sober – which is very unlikely – he won't have the slightest idea where I am. Only Anna knows – and she's not going to tell anyone."

Marion sat up in bed.

"And it would help if you could shut that door and lock it. We don't want Joanne dropping in!"

"Joanne?"

"I believe she has a tendency to sleepwalk during the midnight hours and enter other people's bedrooms. I'm sure it's just an excuse." She rolled the sheets back a little further. "Anyway, I'm not sharing you with anyone."

Raynes locked the door and tore off his clothes.

"This is the perfect end to a dreadful day."

"Just make me as happy as you did in that car park and I'll make sure all your fears just fly away."

* * * *

Marion had kept her promise. But now, she had flown away. To milk the cows, feed the pigs or some other equally unromantic activity. He had not noticed her go. He had been in a deep, deep sleep.

As he slowly surfaced – and realized where he was – safe, warm, comfortable, physically satisfied – he felt an enormous sense of gratitude towards Marion – for saving him and healing his wounds. He hardly knew her as a person; but as a woman, she had given him everything.

Beyond the dark red, heavy velvet curtains, it was – he was sure – a most beautiful day. He would enjoy a glorious breakfast. He would feel the warmth of the sun on his skin. He would smell the smoke pouring out of *Lady Ermintrude*'s chimney. He would hear the clatter of small wheels as the little train set out on her maiden journey.

He would also tie together the loose ends of this perplexing case. He would put an end to Emily Williams' despicable trade. He would confront the person who had so brutally killed Derek Barclay. Everything was going his way.

* * * *

As Raynes was drinking his second cup of black coffee, Anna came up to his table. "Another lady to see you! You're having quite a morning!"

Raynes immediately recognized Margaret Cadwaller.

He stood up.

"It's very nice to see you again. Would you like some coffee?"

"I would."

Margaret sat down beside him at the table.

"I've come to apologize to you for the terrible ordeal you went through last night. My husband was out of his mind. He could easily have killed you."

Raynes admitted that he too had thought his last hour had come.

"If I had known what he was planning to do, I would have warned you."

"You didn't know?"

"He never tells me anything. He just went out of the house. I didn't know where he was going. All I heard was the sound of his Land Rover going down the drive. It must have been terrifying for you."

"I just walked out of the dining room – and there he was. The gun was pointing at me – and my feet turned to lead. I couldn't run."

Anna put Margaret's cup of milky coffee on the table. She looked at Raynes.

"Marion saved his life. Bashed your husband on the head good and hard. He went down like a ninepin." She smiled. "The Inspector's lucky in his choice of lady friends."

With that, she went back to the kitchen, leaving them to talk on their own.

Margaret Cadwaller said: "Marion has her own reasons for hating him. She knows my husband wants to get hold of their farm. He offered them money – twice; but they refused. He's just waiting for her to ditch Ifor – then he'll step in with an offer she can't refuse."

That was another interesting angle on village life; but Raynes was more interested in talking about the missing child.

He said: "Did you hear what the argument was about?"

"Timothy? Yes. I'm glad you had the courage to bring that up – in a public place – with a lot of witnesses. He wouldn't have liked that."

"Father Morris told me that he thinks that Timothy was buried in part of the lake. Apparently there was a drought . . .?"

"There was." She looked thoughtful. "He could be right."

"His body could still be found."

"That would prove it."

"Well, at least they could find out how he died."

Margaret Cadwaller seemed relieved. Perhaps there would be some light at the end of the tunnel.

"But he wasn't arrested because of Timothy?"

"No. He was arrested for attempted murder. He'll be kept in custody for a few days; but I'm afraid that with the help of his legal friends, he could soon be out on bail. And that might be rather dangerous . . . for everyone."

"That's why I came to see you. I wanted to warn you. Ever since you visited the house, he's been planning to get his revenge. When he heard that you had come back to the village – and that you were staying in the *Railway Inn* – he was determined to get you. To teach you a lesson . . ."

Raynes raised his eyebrows.

"Who told him I was here?"

"He had a phone call."

"From Emily Williams?'

"How did you know?"

"I met her on Thursday evening. I thought she would spread it around."

"She's a very nasty piece of work."

"A blackmailer."

"So I've heard."

Raynes looked at Margaret Cadwaller with fresh interest. "Has she been blackmailing you?"

"Certainly not! I haven't got any secrets!"

She laughed – nervously.

Raynes said: "I think you may still have one or two; but you are lucky not to be in her clutches. She has been blackmailing Arlene Jacoby for almost a year."

The Inspector waited for her response.

"I didn't know that."

A lie. A definite lie.

That made it a little easier to bring up the question he was wanting to ask.

"You told me that Timothy was Derek Barclay's child?"

"Yes."

"Was he?"

"Of course he was. I should know."

Margaret Cadwaller sounded angry. Some of the sweetness had gone out of her face. She was now on the defensive. It was not what she had expected.

Raynes said: "Are you really sure about that? You see – I am beginning to think that there may have been a cover-up. You told your husband that Derek was Timothy's father. You said that to hurt him . . . to humiliate him. But perhaps you were also intending to hide the identity of the real father? I think you hoped to provoke your husband into attacking Derek – perhaps even killing him – so that your husband would be arrested and put away for a long time. Your life would have been much happier. You didn't mind what happened to Derek; but you wanted to protect someone else."

Margaret Cadwaller turned immediately hostile.

"That's a terrible thing to say!"

"Nonetheless, I think it's true. And I think you were deeply shocked by what happened to Derek."

"Of course I was. We all were. But it had nothing to do with me!"

Raynes looked speculative.

"Could you have been protecting Thompson the vet? People have said that he was quite fond of you."

It was a complete lie – but it produced an immediate reaction.

Margaret Cadwaller was horrified.

"I've never had any dealings with him – other than professional. He was devoted to his wife. He wouldn't have gone with anyone else!"

"But he was willing to provide an alibi for your husband. He said that they were together on the Sunday night when Derek was killed. Looking after one of his precious cows . . ."

Margaret Cadwaller was scathing.

"James Thompson would do anything to protect my

husband. We are the geese which lay the golden eggs. He gets most of his income from looking after our animals. He would do anything my husband told him to do!"

"Even committing perjury?"

"He needs the money."

Margaret Cadwaller could be brutal. Raynes began to see another side to her character.

He shrugged his shoulders.

"Well, what about Simon Jacoby?"

Margaret's face flushed with anger – and embarrassment.

"He has been mentioned."

"He was not Timothy's father!"

Raynes, listening carefully, detected no lie.

He continued: "But Simon has caused your husband a lot of grief. It is thanks to him that your husband has lost several expensive legal battles. If he had also been the father of your child, that might have been the last straw?"

"He would have killed me."

"I think you are probably right. Bill Naylor has told me that he feared Sir David might have taken pot shots at Simon whilst he was driving the train up the valley. There might have been more than legal expenses to upset him?"

Margaret Cadwaller was cold and contemptuous in her reply.

"He certainly hated losing money. But there nothing more to it than that."

"Was Simon Jacoby ever your lover?"

"I'm not going to answer that question!"

She already had – but Raynes passed on.

"What about Nigel Greenaway? A good friend of your husband. I believe they were at school together. A tall, handsome fellow with a lovely home in Henley-in-Arden. The chief beneficiary of Sir Walter Greenaway's estate. Not averse to an affair with a younger woman. Might that be the reason for the cover-up?"

Raynes saw that he had achieved a palpable hit. Margaret Cadwaller's face had gone white. She was close to weeping.

She certainly wasn't going to answer that question.

Raynes said quietly: "You wouldn't expose him. That would have revealed real treachery. So you accused Derek Barclay of being the father. And because of that accusation, Derek died. And because of that cover-up, I almost died."

He looked at her.

"More coffee?"

Margaret Cadwaller flung down the napkin she had been using to wipe away the tears. She stood up.

"I'm not going to answer any more of your questions. If I'd known what you were really like, I'd never have come." She paused. "I understand now why my husband hated you. Why he wanted to kill you!"

"Well," said Raynes charitably. "I'm sure he'll soon be home. But I think that once he gets accused of child murder – which he will – a lot of unpleasant facts are going to come out. And you are going to be in the witness box, testifying against him. The Court will want to know who Timothy's father was. If you won't tell me, you'll have to tell them!"

Margaret Cadwaller ran out of the dining room.

Raynes finished his coffee.

Anna came back to his table.

"You upset her!"

"Yes. But I wanted to find out the truth. She told her husband that Derek Barclay was the father of her child. But I don't believe he was. Derek had affairs with a large number of women. None of them fell pregnant. Why should she?"

Raynes stared thoughtfully at his coffee cup.

"I suggested that one or two of her other lovers might have been responsible for the child – Simon Jacoby and Nigel Greenaway; but she denied both of them."

"Did she?"

"She lied. I could see from the look on her face that either man could have been the father of the boy. I think Mr Greenaway, Sir Walter's nephew, is the most likely candidate. She was covering up for him. But she blamed Derek Barclay. And Derek died . . . I warned her that when she stands up in court and testifies against her husband, she'll have to tell the truth. But she's not ready for that . . . Not yet."

Anna Patterson had acquired a healthy respect for the Inspector's skills and his determination to discover the truth. She knew the answers to most of the questions which were troubling him. She decided to give him a helping hand.

"There's one connection you haven't made."

"Only one?"

"You should have asked Margaret to tell you her maiden name."

"Should I?"

"Yes, you should. I think it could have been useful." Anna smiled. "Would it have helped you to know that her maiden name was Stevenson?"

Raynes whistled with surprise.

"Ariel Stevenson! The Trapeze Artist! The woman Simon Jacoby was making love to on the footplate of the little train. Well, of course, she had had an affair with him . . .!"

" . . . And probably many more! But in those days, she used her circus name . . . Now she's Lady Margaret. A stalwart member of the lesser aristocracy." Anna chuckled happily. "I thought you would like to know."

34: Daybreak Express

Whilst Raynes was talking to Anna, he was increasingly aware of the hubbub outside the *Railway Inn*. A large number of visitors were gathering in the street – all trying to make their way into the station.

Cars were still trying to get down to the parking area on the seafront; but other cars were stopping to drop off passengers and there was a complete traffic jam outside the gates to the station yard. Car horns blared. People were cheering. A brass band was trying to play "Men of Harlech" and "Cwm Rhondda"; but they were regularly drowned out by the noise.

Raynes decided that he should go out and mix with the

crowd. He plunged into the melée and let it carry him across the road, through the booking hall and out on to the platform. But people had gone even further and there were at least two hundred enthusiasts milling around in the station yard.

High in the air, there was a hot air balloon hovering above the village; whilst, at ground level, a camera crew from BBC Cymru were struggling to maintain their strategic position covering both the engine shed and the sidings where the six carriages were already filling up with VIPs.

One of the Railway volunteers said to him: "Have you got a special ticket?"

"No," said Raynes.

He was told – politely – to leave a clear path for those who had.

"How much are the tickets?"

"£150. But they were sold out weeks ago."

Raynes did a few quick calculations. Six carriages, each carrying twenty-four passengers at £150 a head, suggested an income of £21,600. That should be a healthy shot in the arm for the Puddleduck's finances. The sale of souvenirs would also bring in plenty of money. Perhaps Brian Williamson would be getting back some of his money sooner than he had expected?

Raynes could see the Railway's chief engineer standing beside *Lady Ermintrude*. He was wearing a large, black top hat, rather like the famous Victorian railway builder, Isambard Kingdom Brunel – but without the sideburns! Whilst the Inspector was watching, he had already been up on the footplate three times. He was now down beside the track, wiping his forehead with a red and white spotted handkerchief. The tension and the excitement were getting to him.

Raynes looked at the station clock. It was 10.30am. The train was due to go at 10.45.

It seemed that the new locomotive was ready to go. First of all, she would head up to the main platform before reversing into the siding to collect her six coaches. With a portentous shriek of her whistle and an immense wallop of smoke, *Lady Ermintrude* moved forward.

This was the moment for hundreds of photographs to be taken. Such was the size of the crowd standing on the edge of the platform that Raynes wondered if a few of them would tumble over into the path of the approaching train. Fortunately, it was moving quite slowly. The Inspector could see Simon Jacoby controlling the speed and, behind him, Charlie keeping his eye on the boiler pressure. Tom Hayward would be very disappointed not to be there.

Having taken her photo-call, *Lady Ermintrude* reversed steadily over to the siding to be coupled up to her coaches. Raynes could see that in the guard's van, at the rear of the train, there were people with saxophones, trumpets and trombones. It was clearly going to be music all the way. He wondered if they would be playing the "Chattanooga Choo-Choo" as they set off for Caercraig and what might happen to the musicians when they passed under the low bridge on the north side of the village.

There was another delay whilst the VIP passengers taking photographs were finally ushered into their carriages and the journey could begin. *Lady Ermintrude* emerged slowly from the siding, pulling a load of over sixty tons. She was quite a powerful little engine but she took time to gather speed. She passed through the station to be greeted with prolonged cheers. People were leaning out of the carriage windows, waving to the crowd; some had glasses of champagne in their hands. For them, the party had already begun. The jazzmen in the guard's van were playing: "Yes, sir, that's my baby!"

Raynes was glad to see the train going safely on her way. As he stood looking out over the empty yard, he noticed Father Morris standing beside his yellow diesel, waiting for the disaster call which he hoped would never come. Raynes gave him a friendly wave.

Many people in the crowd were waiting for *Lady Sylvia* to arrive. She was due in about fifteen minutes. Many of them were hoping to follow *Lady Ermintrude* up the valley and have another chance of seeing her on the way back.

In the meantime, they headed for the tea room, only to be told it was closed. The staff were preparing a buffet of fresh salmon, trout and smoked salmon for the special ticket holders. They would be having canapés up at Abernrirvana with bucketloads of champagne. By the time they returned to Pwddldwc, they would be ready for a superb lunch.

However, part of the engineering shed on the other side of the track had been converted into a makeshift cafe – serving tea, coffee and alcoholic drinks. Most of the crowd crossed over to Platform Two for their own celebration party.

Raynes went back to his car and opened one of the box files which he had hidden in a locked suitcase in the boot of his Rover. He took out one of the envelopes he had seized from 14 Chapel Road. It was a slim one containing eight photographs. He walked back to the station. Father Morris was now sitting on the steps of the signal box, drinking a bottle of beer.

"No call on your services so far?"

"No. Bill says she's reached the castle. And *Lady Sylvia* has just left."

There was no sign of Bill Naylor. He was presumably keeping an eye on the whole railway, making sure that everything went without a hitch.

"Raynes said: "Could you join me for a brief walk?"

"Of course."

They walked back towards the yellow diesel.

"You remember what we were talking about on Thursday night?"

"Yes. Most vividly!" He smiled. "But quite a lot has happened since then!"

Raynes said: "Well, I survived. And you were a great help. That policeman was useless." He looked at the burly cleric. "I followed up the information you gave me and I am pleased to hand over this envelope. I hope it will set your mind at rest."

Father Morris looked at the handwriting on the envelope.

"From Emily?"

"Yes. But please don't ask how." He looked towards the station bookshop where Emily was at work. "And don't say anything to her!"

Father Morris looked inside the envelope to make sure all the photographs were there.

Raynes said: "Don't give her another penny. And I shall do my best to recover all the money you have paid."

Tears poured down the clergyman's cheeks.

"You've saved my life – and Charlie's."

He put his arms round Inspector Raynes and gave him an enormous hug.

Raynes was taken by surprise.

"Make sure you don't lose them!" he said.

"I shall destroy them right away!"

Raynes walked slowly back to his car. One gone; many more to go.

* * * *

Raynes was intending to visit Swansea prison that afternoon. A visit had been arranged with the help of Detective-Constable Carlisle. And it would take a couple of hours to get there.

But before he left the Puddleduck, he wanted to bestow a similar gift on Lydia and Joanne – though they hardly deserved such kindness.

He was also uncertain about the documents and pictures contained in the envelopes. Lydia's were all to do with drugs; the names of dealers and the amounts due. They meant nothing to him; but the police in Nottingham would probably find it quite interesting. Joanne's seemed to involve the theft of two paintings from a local art gallery, which she had hidden away in her attic to help a friend called Malcolm. Doubtless, the authorities would be glad to get them back.

He put both envelopes into a green Marks and Spencer bag.

Raynes then got into his car and drove up the road to Abernirvana. On the way, he turned up a side road to Lake

Nirvana to see the exact location of the slipway that Sir David had built during the drought.

There were several small boats out on the lake and one or two families settling down for a picnic lunch. Raynes looked at the cobbled pathway running out into the water. He returned thoughtfully to his car.

* * * *

Abernirvana was quite busy. Many people were preparing to welcome *Lady E* when she reached the upper station; but the crowd was much smaller than the one at Pwddldwc.

Raynes walked through the main entrance and once again admired the Art Deco features of the station.

Two waitresses guarded the entrance to the restaurant, so he went into the souvenir shop, hoping to find Lydia. In the event, she found him.

Raynes was looking for a woman in a lilac cat suit; but on this special day, Lydia was wearing a pale cream chiffon dress, which seemed to flutter as she moved.

"Mr Raynes! Fancy seeing you here! I hope you haven't come for lunch. I don't think you are one of our special guests."

"No. I haven't come for lunch. I've come to see *Lady E* arrive at her destination. She had a splendid send-off from Puddleduck and I would like to see her rolling into Abernirvana."

"She'll be here in about ten minutes. She's late. There are too many people getting out to take photographs. She's also had to take on quite a lot of water at the Pistylloed o Idris. We're all ready for her."

She looked at the Inspector.

"You're not here to cause trouble, are you?"

"No. I come in peace."

Lydia could not resist saying: "Sir David missed a golden opportunity!"

"I'm afraid he did."

Raynes looked at Lydia sadly. She had the most wonderful grey eyes and a splendid figure. It was terrible to think that she was involved in something as sordid as drugs.

"So why are you here?"

Raynes said: "I am here to bring you a gift which will add to your happiness on this special day."

He indicated his green M & S bag.

Lydia said: "At my school, we were warned about the danger of Greeks bearing gifts . . ."

"I think Virgil was probably right. But the things in this bag belong to you and Mrs Kennedy. They have caused you a lot of grief and cost you both a lot of money."

A look of anxiety passed over Lydia's face.

What was this wretched man talking about?

Raynes pulled out the thicker envelope.

"This is yours. And I have another one for Joanne. I believe that you have both been the victims of blackmail. In fact, I know you have. I have found all the material which was being used against you. And I would like to return it at the earliest opportunity."

Lydia did not reach out her hand for the envelope.

"Is this a trick, Mr Raynes?"

"Not at all."

"Are you hoping to catch me with incriminating documents and then arrest me?"

"No. I am returning them in good faith to their rightful owners."

As he spoke, the carrier bag was torn out of his hand. Joanne had come up behind him and heard most of the conversation. Lydia had given no indication that she was there.

Joanne snarled: "Why can't you leave us alone? Can't you let us enjoy this special day without poking your nose into everything?"

Both women glared at him.

Raynes said quietly: "You have been blackmailed by a very unscrupulous young woman. I know she would not hesitate to shop you to the police. I am returning your personal property so that you can destroy it as quickly as possible."

Lydia remained staring at the Inspector. Joanne pulled her envelope out of the bag. She opened it – and then shut it quickly.

"Oh, my God!" she screamed.

Lydia looked at her with alarm.

"What is it?"

"All that stuff about the pictures."

"No?"

Raynes handed over the other envelope to Lydia.

She took it with great reluctance.

"If you are trying to deceive me, Mr Raynes . . ."

She peered inside the envelope.

One look was enough.

She took a deep breath. She turned to Joanne: "I think we should lock both these envelopes in my safe. Immediately. We can deal with them later." She turned to Inspector Raynes: "If you are going to watch the arrival of *Lady E*, don't stand too close to the edge of the platform. You might find yourself following in Derek's footsteps!"

Within seconds, both women had gone.

Raynes shrugged his shoulders.

"Ungrateful bitches!"

As he walked out on to the platform, there was a huge cheer. Not for him, but for *Lady Ermintrude* who was rapidly approaching the southern end of the platform. She had chugged up the steep incline from Lake Nirvana and was soon sweeping down the final hundred yards which would bring her to the end of her maiden run.

Then the doors of the carriages burst open and the one hundred and forty four guests poured out on to the platform – some of them still clutching their glasses and their empty bottles of champagne. They all looked a little tipsy.

The West Coast Jazzmen thankfully put down their instruments. It had been a very exhausting gig. Battling against the wind, the smoke, the noise. Trying to maintain high spirits all the way up the line. They had done their best with "Honky-Tonk Blues", "Pennsylvania 6-5000" and "Shuffle off to Buffalo". They had returned once or twice to "Daybreak Express" but it had probably fallen on deaf ears. Now, all they wanted was a very large cool drink. They might be more selective on the way home.

Raynes had taken Lydia's advice and kept well back from the edge of the platform. But now there was safety in numbers – even if his presence was unwelcome.

Tom Hayward was the first to challenge him: "What the hell are you doing here?"

"Waiting for someone to push me under a train!"

Mr Hayward looked annoyed.

"That's a joke in very bad taste!"

"I've just been threatened by two ladies. I think you could guess who they are."

Mrs Packer was in her best summer dress and had just opened her bright red parasol.

"I'm sorry I missed all the fun and games last night. I would have quite enjoyed it."

"At least you got your double Tequila Sunrise!"

"I should have much preferred to attend your funeral!"

Brian and Kathleen Williamson gave him a warmer welcome.

"Are you feeling better this morning?'

"Much better."

"Sometimes the shock comes later."

Raynes changed the subject.

"Seeing *Lady Ermintrude* has given me a great deal of pleasure. She is already extremely popular. I'm sure she will transform the Puddleduck's finances. Even Dr Campbell should be satisfied with today's turn-out."

"I hope so."

By this point, they had reached the door of the restaurant.

Kathleen said: "Are you coming in?"

"I'm not one of your special guests. I haven't paid my £150."

Brian laughed.

"If you pay up quickly, I'll give you my ticket. No one will refuse me entry."

Raynes opened his wallet and gave him three £50 notes. Brian handed over his ticket.

"I hope you enjoy the canapés."

There was still a lot happening on the platform. *Lady E* was being filled up with water. The front couplings had been undone and the train was ready to move to the other end of the platform and be coupled up to the guard's van. This would be bad news for the jazzmen.

Joanne brought out a glass of pink champagne for Simon Jacoby and a pint of special for Charlie. She gave Simon a big kiss.

"For being such a wonderful man!" she said.

As she returned to the restaurant, she saw Raynes – and cut him dead.

Tom was busy congratulating the driver and the fireman.

"A splendid day. A wonderful achievement. We've looked forward to it for so long."

Simon looked at the main dials in the cab.

"She coped magnificently. Brian Williamson's done a brilliant job – against all the odds. She'll be an enormous asset for years to come."

Raynes watched the water sleeve being removed; the little train moved forward and the points were changed. *Lady E* was now ready to reverse down the track behind the carriages. But she was in no hurry. She too was having a welcome break.

As he watched the manoeuvres, he was suddenly conscious of Lydia standing beside him with a sparkling glass of champagne.

"A gift to the Trojan Horse," she said. "I think you deserve this."

Raynes smiled.

"Is this a poisoned chalice?"

"No. It is a small thank you for what you have done for both Joanne and myself. She finds it impossible to say anything to you; but I am speaking on her behalf.

"You have rescued us from a very embarrassing situation which has gone on for far too long. I suppose we could have gone to the police – but there is always a danger of these things backfiring. We didn't want the past to catch up with us. It seemed easier to pay up."

"She's been using Derek's private papers."

"I know. Derek liked to dig up the dirt on people. He liked to discover their Achilles heels. Then he had some power over you. He liked to tease people – and bend them to his will. He really didn't need to bother. Most women would have done anything for him. She used his private documents to bully other people. Where did you find them?"

Raynes lied happily: "In the castle tower. That was his private security box. It was just a question of finding the key."

Lydia said: "We knew we could have gone to the police and she might have been arrested. But what would that have done to her mother?"

Lydia seemed to be friendly – but Raynes was still cautious.

"Would you be kind enough to take a sip of this champagne?"

Lydia drank enough to assure him that it was safe to drink. And she also bent forward and gave the Inspector a generous kiss.

"Just to show you how grateful we are. Would you like to come inside and have some refreshments?"

"A cheese omelette?"

"No. We have a much more expensive menu today. Canapés, truffles, *pate de foie gras* . . . Only the very best for her Ladyship!"

Raynes produced the ticket Brian had given him.

" I already have a ticket. And I have paid my £150."

Lydia looked mystified.

"I don't know how you managed to get that. We've done our best to prevent the riff-raff from getting anywhere near the bar! But I daresay you are an exception."

Raynes happily followed her into the restaurant. Since he was not going back to the official lunch, he stuffed himself with the eats; but avoided any more drink.

He noticed that Lydia's lipstick was implanted on his glass. Vital evidence if he should keel over. But perhaps she was now a reformed character. He would like to think so.

Whilst the special guests were making their way back to their carriages – and the jazzmen were picking up their instruments – Raynes returned to his car and fastened his safety belt. He set off on his long run to meet Emily's partner-in-crime.

It should give both of them a nasty jolt.

35: On Guard!

Raynes was ushered into the visitors' room at Swansea prison. Marc was brought over to his table. He was wearing a bright blue pullover and grey trousers.

He looked suspicious.

"Who are you?"

"I am Richard Raynes. I'm one of the helpers on the Railway. I have been staying at the home of your girlfriend and her mother at No 14 Chapel Road."

"So why have you come to see me?"

"I need some information."

"About what?"

"Derek Barclay."

"He's dead."

"I believe you used to work for him?"

"Not for long. He was on my back all the time. I couldn't do anything right. He really bugged me. I worked with him for four days – but that was enough."

"A harsh taskmaster?"

Marc sighed.

"It might have been better if he'd told me what to do before I started. But he didn't. All he did was pick on me."

"Did he pay you for those four days?"

Marc looked surprised at the question.

"Actually, he paid me for the whole week. But he said I didn't deserve it." He added: "I don't have any happy memories about him."

Raynes nodded pleasantly – as if he agreed.

"Well," he said, "since last Christmas, people have begun to wonder whether his death was an accident – or whether he was murdered. I'm sure it won't matter to you either way. But I want to know if you have any better memories of Sunday July 10, last year?"

Marc smiled politely.

"None at all."

"You weren't burning down any holiday cottages that night?"

"Certainly not!"

It wasn't a lie. But Raynes detected a slight ambivalence in the reply. He looked at the young man thoughtfully.

"I'm surprised you remember nothing. Emily has a very clear memory of what you were doing . . ."

Marc waited to hear what his girlfriend had said.

" . . . She said that you spent the evening together in your flat overlooking the upper station at Abernirvana."

"That's true."

"Was that all you were doing?"

Marc's unease at the question showed that he had something to hide. It was worth digging a little further.

"That's all I'm telling you!"

"How did she get home?"

"I gave her a lift in my car."

"And what time did she arrive home?"

"About midnight. Her mother's very strict about that."

"And where did you go after that?"

"Home."

"Not to the station yard?"

A look of panic appeared in Marc's eyes.

"Are you a policeman?"

"A Detective-Inspector."

"I don't talk to people like you."

"I know. But I want your help."

"My help?"

Marc looked at him in disbelief.

Raynes laid his cards on the table.

"Derek Barclay was killed that night. He died in the station yard. Somehow, he got his two legs chopped off. If you were near the station yard late that night, you may have seen something – or someone."

Marc said nothing.

"Some people have been kind enough to say that you might have had a grudge against Derek."

"I didn't kill him!"

Raynes looked the young man straight in the eye.

"I believe you. But I still think you saw something that Sunday night which might give us a clue to Derek's death. I'm not interested in your burning down people's holiday homes – although I'm told you've done quite a few of them. I'm not here to accuse you of anything. I'm not here to force a confession. I would just like to know if there was anything you saw whilst you were driving down from Abernirvana to Pwddldwc – or on your return journey – which might have caught your eye – or looked suspicious."

Marc was silent.

Raynes decided to offer some inducement.

"If you were able to help me, I might be able to get you out of this place more quickly."

Marc sneered at him.

"You wouldn't do anything for me! A copper? Help me? No way!"

Raynes said: "I'm not working for the Welsh police. I'm doing this for the Railway. They have asked me to find out whether it was an accident or a murder. And the people on the Railway want to find out who did it. Even Emily wants the truth to come out."

"She's never said that before!"

"Well," said Raynes, "I've found her extremely helpful. She's provided me with the Railway's membership list for last year. A duty rota of all the staff who were working on the weekend when Derek died. She got me the coroner's report and several newspaper cuttings. She also gave me a photograph of a dinner dance where most of the suspects were taking part. She said who they were. I paid her £225 for all the information she gave me. And I'm prepared to give her another £300 if you help me."

Raynes reached into his inner pocket and produced Emily's letter written on scented note-paper.

"She also sent me that."

Marc read the letter.

"She has helped me. Can you? I don't care if you burnt down another cottage that night . . ."

Marc clearly battled inside himself as to whether he should speak to his visitor. He had nothing to lose on this one. He might be stuck in jail for his full sentence. If there was a chance of getting out earlier, it was worth taking.

But, on the other hand, he didn't like this man. He didn't trust him. He was using him to provide evidence against another person, who would probably end up in Swansea prison. Who might find out who had grassed on him. There could be unpleasant consequences. So far, he had kept his nose clean. Caused no trouble. He might soon be going to an open prison.

Almost ten minutes passed before he spoke.

Raynes waited patiently. He knew the longer he remained silent, the more the pressure would be on Marc to say something. He could understand his fears and anxiety.

Marc decided to say a little bit more.

"We were together that night. We hadn't been burning any cottages that night; but we had burgled a house about twenty miles up the coast. We often give a cottage the once-over before we burn it. To see if there's any valuables, any cash, any jewellery worth taking. Sometimes, we sell the stuff at a car boot sale, Other times, we take it to a dealer. We sell the stuff before the owners even know their house has been burgled." He looked at Raynes. "That's no secret. I admitted that in court. But after that, we went back to my place . We had a fish supper, a roll in the hay and then I took her back to her mam . . ."

This was the part Raynes was interested in.

"You left Abernirvana at what time?"

"About five past twelve."

"And you reached Pwddldwc about ten minutes later?"

"Yes."

"And what did you see?"

"I saw someone driving Derek's van up to Caercraig."

"You saw it?"

"And the driver." Marc looked pleased that he had kept the inspector waiting so long for this trivial piece of information.

"Did you know who the driver was?"

"I didn't. But Emily did. She knew exactly who it was. She couldn't think why he was driving it. She didn't even know Derek had been down that weekend. No one had seen him or his van. Of course, at that moment, we didn't know anything about the murder. It was the next Saturday before it appeared in the paper."

"Did the person see you?"

"I don't think so. I don't think anyone would have recognized my car."

"And where exactly did you see it?"

"Just as you turn up that lane which leads to the station."

"And to Castle Farm?"

"Yes."

"And who did she say the person was?"

A loud voice said: "Time's up!"

Raynes looked at the clock.

Yes, it was six minutes past four. The prison authorities had been generous to the visitors. Those extra minutes had been a great help.

He stood up.

"Thank you, Marc. You have been most helpful. I wonder

if you could just give me the name of the van driver before I go."

But Emily's boyfriend was unwilling to offer the Inspector any more help.

"I'm not going to tell you who it was. I'm not going to grass on another human being. If she wants your filthy money, she can tell you herself! You're getting nothing more from me!"

36: Bush Telegraph

As Raynes got out of his Rover in the car park at the back of the *Railway Inn*, he found himself face to face with Emily Williams, whose eyes were blazing with anger and who fell on him like an avenging angel.

She battered him with her fists.

"You double-crossing bastard!"

He grabbed hold of her wrists and pushed her away.

"You have deceived me!"

"Not at all."

The Inspector wondered if she had discovered the theft of her bank books.

"You have been to see Marc!"

"Yes, I have been to Swansea. I am very glad you told me where he was. He was the last piece in my jigsaw."

"You never told me you were going!"

"You never asked. I imagined that you would be very busy on the Railway, what with *Lady Ermintrude* making her maiden voyage and selling books and postcards to all her admirers." He smiled pleasantly. "If you had asked, we could both have gone down to Swansea together. It would have been a great pleasure to see both of you behind bars!"

The black button eyes suddenly became cold and hard.

"I hope you are not accusing me of anything, Mr Raynes?"

Raynes looked thoughtful.

"As a matter of fact, I am. I think you were heavily

involved in your boyfriend's criminal activities. I think you profited from the stolen goods. I think your political views have caused you to break the laws of this country. I think you have been very lucky not to be jailed. Mr Hayward must have pulled some very powerful strings on your behalf. I think that if the full truth were known – as it is to a number of people – you would not be going to Grasshallows. You would be joining your fellow conspirator in jail."

This was a fairly strong indictment.

It did not make the slightest impact on Miss Williams.

"You accused Marc of killing Derek Barclay!"

"As a matter of fact, I didn't. I asked him if he had seen anything on his journey from Abernirvana to Pwddldwc, when he was taking you home on the Sunday night."

"You asked him if he had been in the station yard?"

"I did. But I also said that I didn't believe he had killed anyone. I asked him if he could help me – as you have done."

"Me?"

Emily looked amazed that Raynes should think she would ever help an English policeman.

Raynes reminded her. "You sent me the list of members. The duty rotas. The photograph of all those people at the dinner dance. You gave me their names. I am sure a lot of the information was provided by Mr Hayward; but the letter was posted in Wales. You sent me a bill for £225. Have you forgotten that?"

Emily had not forgotten anything.

Raynes added: "I showed Marc your letter to prove that you were helping me . . ."

"My letter?"

Raynes was curious.

"Didn't he tell you that he had read the letter?"

"No, he didn't!"

Raynes smiled.

"Lovers shouldn't hide secrets from each other."

"He's not my lover!"

Raynes raised his eyebrows.

"Marc said that you had a very cosy evening together in his flat in Abernirvana on the Sunday night. He said that you had eaten a fish supper and had a roll in the hay before he took you home."

Raynes watched Emily absorb these details. The tremor of fury on her lips suggested that Marc had erred badly in giving the Inspector any information.

Raynes added: "You left Abernirvana at five past twelve."

"I know when we left."

She sounded bitter.

Raynes decided to add to her discomfort.

"Marc admitted that the two of you had been burgling a cottage that night. A place about twenty miles away. He said the two of you often gave a cottage a once-over before you torched it." He paused. "Marc said: 'we' . . . not 'I' . . . And then he said that you sold the goods before people even knew their property had been stolen."

Emily was silent.

Raynes decided to add the additional information he had obtained from her bank books and her blue notebook.

"He told me that you divided the spoils between you. Each of you took half. You were saving up to go to University – and you needed the money."

Raynes smiled.

"So Marc was very helpful."

Emily stared straight into the Inspector's eyes.

"Is that all he said?"

Raynes smiled.

"Good heavens, no! He said that when you were somewhere near Caercraig, you saw Derek's van – probably being driven up to the Castle car park. He didn't recognize the van – but he said that you did. He didn't recognize the driver – but again he said you did. And it wasn't Derek Barclay!"

Emily's face was now a white mask.

It looked as if the bush telegraph had failed to convey the full story.

Emily could not believe that Marc had blabbed. They had

agreed that they would say nothing about that night. And they never had. How could this wretched policeman have wormed out all these details?

"How did you find out about all this?"

"I offered him £300 . . ."

Emily breathed vindictively – like a bull preparing to charge at a matador.

" . . . but he refused. He told me that he wouldn't take my filthy money."

Emily breathed a sigh of relief.

But it was too soon.

Raynes said: "Marc told me that you would confirm his story."

That was not true; but Emily would not notice his delicate lie after so much damning evidence had already been revealed.

Raynes put on a look of polite interest.

"So, do you confirm his story?"

"I confirm nothing."

Raynes sensed that she was about to turn on her heel and go. He said: "Perhaps you could answer one or two questions – which have nothing to do with Derek Barclay or his murder . . .?"

Emily looked sullen and unhelpful.

" . . . Was it you who phoned Tom Hayward and told him I was back in Pwddldwc?"

Emily weighed up the pros and cons of answering that question. But she could see no personal disadvantage in replying to it.

"Yes. I was thinking that he should know you were here."

Raynes nodded appreciatively.

"And was it you who phoned the *Railway Inn* – on my first night at your house – to tell them that I was a policeman acting under cover?"

Emily felt quite proud to answer that one. It would show how much she despised this *saesneg*. In fact, all *saesnegs* . . .

"Yes," she said, "I told them."

"Not one person in particular?"

Emily immediately sensed danger.

"No. I spoke to Anna."

"But were you not trying to protect someone?"

"I am not answering that question."

Her lips were thin and quivering.

"You already have. Anna has already told me that you phoned . . ."

Raynes gave Emily a hard look.

"And there is one other question I would like you to answer. Did you telephone David Cadwaller and tell him that I was staying in the *Railway Inn*?"

Emily said nothing.

"You know what happened here last night? How Sir David tried to kill me? With a shotgun?"

Emily looked at the Inspector with complete contempt.

"I know exactly what happened last night. People have been talking about it all day. They are all very sorry that Sir David has been arrested. And they are all very sorry that he did not succeed in killing you!"

Raynes looked at the Welsh girl with a tinge of sadness.

"Do you really hate me that much?"

"You should never have come back to the village. You were warned. Tom told you to keep away. But you were pig-headed. You wanted to destroy our community . . . You want to destroy the Railway . . .! Yes, it would have been better if Sir David had shot you."

Raynes had little hesitation in hitting back equally hard.

"But you did tell him?"

Hatred blazed out in Emily's eyes.

"Yes, I did."

Raynes said quietly: "Sir David was guilty of attempted murder, which would be a crime even in an independent Wales. When he goes on trial, you will be charged with being an accessory to that crime. Because you told him I was there – and encouraged him to try and kill me.

"The reason you did this was to protect the person who

killed Derek Barclay. Yes? You hoped that if I was kept away from the village – or was killed by Sir David – that person would escape justice. And when that person goes down, I can tell you this. You will go down with them!"

Emily Williams felt like spitting in the Inspector's face; but she controlled herself. With some dignity, she walked out of the car park and up Chapel Road. But when she got back inside her house – and threw herself on her bed – she wept. Tears of anger and frustration – that all her efforts had been in vain. And that wretched, hateful policeman would win.

37: Hot Mail

On Sunday morning, Arlene Jacoby drove the luxurious BMW up to the front entrance of Pwddldwc station. Simon was already in his blue dungarees and black T shirt – ready for a full day's work on *Lady Ermintrude*.

"Bit of an anti-climax after yesterday?" she said.

"There are bound to be plenty of people here today. She got a good write up in the Press."

"Is Charlie doing all right?"

"He's very energetic and enthusiastic. But he hasn't got Tom's charm or wit. I miss that."

Simon sprang out of the car.

"Don't forget your lunch basket!"

"Did you put in a bottle of wine?"

"Champagne! You deserve the best."

Arlene drove the car down to the parking spaces on the seafront. She would work for three hours in the tea room before going off for lunch with James.

Normally, their car would have been parked at the back of the *Railway Inn* but this perk had been surrendered when they moved to the hotel down the coast.

However, Arlene reckoned the inconvenience was worth it. Joanne would soon cast her eyes on someone else and it would be safe to return.

Arlene got out of the car and walked back along the seafront. There was a figure standing at the corner. It was that dreadful policeman, Mr Raynes, who was now sleeping in their room and washing his vile bourgeois body in their jacuzzi. She had no doubt he was wanting to speak to her. Should she ignore him – and just walk on? Better to be polite . . .

"Good morning, Mr Raynes."

"Good morning, Mrs Jacoby. May I have a private word with you?"

"If you must."

"I think you may find it to your advantage."

"I doubt it."

Raynes shrugged his shoulders.

"As you know, I have been investigating the death of Mr Barclay . . ."

" . . . And almost getting yourself killed!"

She laughed.

(If he had been shot, she would have cheered.)

"I'm afraid it's an occupational hazard for us policemen." He smiled ruefully. "However, in the course of my investigations, I have discovered that you are being blackmailed by a rather unscrupulous young woman – and are paying her £100 per month."

Mrs Jacoby put on one of her superior, aristocratic looks.

"I'm afraid you must know more than I do. I'm not aware of paying out any money to anyone. And even if I were, I wouldn't admit it to you."

"Perhaps your husband is paying the money?"

"My husband would never submit to blackmail. He would always prosecute."

That was all she was going to say.

But her denials did not ring true.

"Well," said the Inspector, " I don't think there could be two people called Arlene Jacoby. Your name is quite clearly printed in Miss Williams' bank statement."

Silence greeted this remark.

Raynes said: "I would like to bring an end to this unpleasantness."

"How?"

"You may be interested to know that, beside the bank statement, I also found a pack of letters, written on pale lemon-coloured paper. I have not read them; but the writing is similar to your entries in the visitors' book at the *Railway Inn*."

"So you are hoping to blackmail me as well?"

"Certainly not. I would like to hand over the letters to their rightful owner as soon as possible."

"Why didn't you bring them with you?"

"I have them in my car. The station tea room is not exactly the ideal place to hand over private documents."

Mrs Jacoby shrugged her shoulders,

"Well, bring your car down here."

Raynes looked to his left. There was his red Rover 400. "I have them here," he said. "Providing you are willing to accept them?"

Mrs Jacoby said nothing. She looked up and down the sea-front. No witnesses.

"O.K."

Raynes opened the door of his Rover and, from under the front seat, he drew out a white package. He handed it over.

Arlene looked down at the despised policeman.

"I can't think how you got them."

"Don't bother asking. Just check if I'm right."

Arlene opened the package. She saw the lemon-coloured sheets of paper. Her flowing handwriting, her appalling spelling and her pathetic attempts to appear naughty but nice. She remembered writing to Derek with youthful passion as a besotted teenager. Tears ran down her cheeks as she remembered the girl she had once been. So impetuous and trusting.

She looked at the dates on the first letter and the last. They seemed to be all there. It was amazing to see how many she had written.

Raynes said: "Would you like to put them in your car?"

"I would like to burn them!"

"Well, they're yours to burn."

They walked back to the BMW. Mrs Jacoby hid the package under the black slip mat in the back of the car. No one would see them there. She locked the door and breathed a huge sigh of relief. Simon was safe. She was safe.

"Derek Barclay kept your letters. He refused to hand them back – even though you threatened to take direct action against him – just two or three weeks before he died."

Mrs Jacoby raised her eyebrows.

"Are you accusing me of killing him?"

Her gratitude to the Inspector evaporated like a summer's mist. She looked cold and hard.

"No," said Raynes. "But I'm sure the thought must have crossed your mind. Only the thought of Simon's career held you back. Am I right?"

"I'm not saying anything."

"Derek did not keep your letters at home. He kept them down here on the Railway. Last July, they were hidden in the castle tower. When he died, you may have thought of approaching his wife, Virginia, but she wouldn't have known where they were."

Mrs Jacoby reacted very strongly.

"I should never have approached that wretched woman. That guttersnipe. She accused my husband of murdering Derek. She accused him of covering up the truth. I've received a whole string of anonymous letters, but I know who sent them. She even accused me of having affairs!"

"With Mr Thompson?"

Her gaze was withering in its intensity.

"I think everyone knows our relationship is 100% platonic – on both sides. Mr Thompson is a man of great honesty and integrity. He is a dear friend whom I have cared for since his wife died. Our common interests are good food and local gossip. We enjoy both."

"Does he know about the letters?"

"James knows nothing about my private life!"

Arlene was not a good liar.

"Well," said Raynes, "your private life doesn't interest me. What interests me is how Miss Emily Williams got hold of the keys of the castle. How she managed to find the letters; and why she decided to blackmail you."

Mrs Jacoby looked a little more forthcoming.

"She needs the money to help her through university. I was willing to help her."

Raynes raised his eyebrows.

"A hundred a month?"

"Peanuts!"

"But she didn't hand over the letters, did she?"

"She said that she would hand them over when she went off to university."

"Did you believe her?"

"Not entirely," Arlene admitted. "She was very much under the influence of that evil creature . . ."

" . . . Marc?"

"Yes, Marc. I'd forgotten his name. I'm sure he'd have told her to keep them."

"And if that had happened?"

"If it had gone beyond September, I'd have gone and spoken to her mother. If she had been unable to help me, only then would I have gone to the police."

"Not P.C. Roberts?"

Arlene raised her eyes heavenwards.

"Not that dolt! God forbid! We do have friends in the police . . . At least, Simon does. But I would have preferred to avoid that."

Raynes smiled more confidently.

"Well, your worries are over. – and you didn't need to bring in the heavies."

Mrs Jacoby vouchsafed a thin smile.

"Well, thank you, Mr Raynes, for taking the trouble to find and return them."

It was all the thanks he would receive.

38: Morning Glory

James Thompson usually washed his car on a Sunday morning before going to lunch with Arlene. He always waited till the chapel folk were safely in their pews, so that they would not see him "working on the Sabbath". Although he did not share their antediluvian views, he did not wish to cause offence. After all, most of them were long-standing customers.

He was looking forward to seeing Arlene. She had been on the phone fifteen minutes earlier with some good news. The much-despised Mr Raynes had done some good at last. He had found the embarrassing letters she had written to Derek Barclay and given them back to her. She was so relieved. The sword of Demosthenes – or was it Damocles? – had been lifted from above her head – and she was so happy. She would tell him the whole story when she picked him up at 12.30pm.

Her news cheered up the vet as his hosed down his splendid 3.5 litre Land Rover, built like a tank, bearing the proud badge of the RCVS – the Royal College of Veterinary Surgeons. It would hold its own against the flashy panzers of the *nouveau riche*.

He had reached the wheel hubs when he suddenly realized that he was not alone. That wretched policeman had crept up on him unawares.

He smiled – a professional smile.

"You survived, Mr Raynes?"

"Thanks to the courage of Marion Davies."

"She's a very fine woman."

"And so is Lady Margaret."

"Indeed. This should give her a much-needed break. She needs it." He looked at the Inspector. "I think you said two years?"

"There's always the possibility he will get bail. Being a rich man, he should be able to pull a few strings."

Mr Thompson switched off his hose.

"The devil looks after his own."

Raynes looked thoughtfully at the vet.

"You don't like Sir David?"

"No. But I'm in a very difficult position. He is my best customer – by a long chalk. Over forty per cent of my income comes from looking after his flocks and herds. I try not to offend him in any way."

He looked at the Inspector.

"But you went in with both feet!"

Raynes said: "I had no alternative. When you are faced with almost certain death, you go for the jugular. I was very surprised that no one had investigated the disappearance of that child. I can understand why P.C. Roberts wouldn't have dared to say anything. But surely other people must have had serious anxieties?"

Mr Thompson shrugged his shoulders.

"Sir David is a paranoid psychotic. He spends his life attacking people. He can't bear opposition of any sort. The moment you started asking questions, you would immediately be put on his hit list. And there's no telling what he would do."

Raynes nodded.

"Lady Margaret came to see me yesterday morning. Mainly to apologize for what had happened the night before. But she said she was sure the child had been killed. Father Morris thinks it was buried in the lake beside Abernirvana."

"It wouldn't surprise me."

Raynes gave the vet a long, searching look.

"Do you have any information which might indicate the possibility of murder?"

Mr Thompson decided that this was the moment to offer the Inspector some hospitality. They couldn't spend the entire morning standing out in the driveway.

"Would you like to come in for a drink?"

They went into the kitchen and Raynes accepted a Carlsberg. Not that he really wanted anything to drink. He had had an excellent breakfast and could still taste the coffee. But there was every chance the vet could fill him in on some of the details . . . so he was prepared to be sociable. He sat silently whilst Mr Thompson poured himself a generous gin and tonic.

"You were asking if I had any evidence?"

"Yes."

"Well, I probably shouldn't tell you this, but Sir David did ask me for a couple of capsules of morphine to put away 'the little bugger'. It could have been for an animal; but, thinking about it later, it could have been used to get rid of the child."

"You didn't administer it yourself?"

"Good heavens, no!" The vet took a swig of his gin and tonic. "He probably shot him. He shoots most things – as you know. But I did wonder – later – whether he might have used it for other things."

He smiled disarmingly.

Raynes did not smile. He was sure that he had been told a lie. Perhaps more than one. Would Thompson the vet ever refuse his best customer?

He said: "Margaret also told me that her husband wanted to kill Derek Barclay. He spoke about it many times in the months before Derek died."

Mr Thompson nodded.

"He spoke about it continuously. It was an obsession with him. I told him that since he would be the most obvious suspect, the police would be on his doorstep right away."

He took another sip.

"I told him there were plenty of other people who wanted to kill Derek. Why not leave it to them?"

"Because of all his affairs?"

"Yes. He just couldn't stop himself. Even though he had a lovely wife – a very attractive girl – he continued to go for everybody else's wives and girlfriends. It was a clear case of satyriasis . . . Ifor definitely wanted to kill him – after what he did to Marion. But Ifor was only capable of showing his true feelings when he was drunk.

But, in that condition, he was in no fit state to mount an attack. But there were plenty of others."

Raynes looked thoughtful.

"I should think it must have crossed Simon Jacoby's mind . . ."

The vet looked surprised.

"Simon would never have done a thing like that – even when he was sorely provoked. He had to put up with constant complaints about Derek. But all the ladies stuck up for him. And he was doing so much good work for the Railway that you couldn't really get rid of him."

"But Derek's affair with Arlene might have affected Simon's career prospects?"

"The affair was over long before Arlene met Simon."

"Yes. But Derek still had the letters she sent to him. If those letters had been given to the Press, I'm sure Simon's chances of becoming a judge would have been severely dented. He would have been a laughing stock amongst his peers."

Mr Thompson looked more confident.

"But you've found the letters and given them back to her. She's just phoned me and told me. She's delighted."

Raynes quickly pricked the balloon.

"But did she tell you that she's been blackmailed for quite some time?"

Mr Thompson looked shocked. His face went white.

"No, she didn't."

Raynes believed him.

"She and Simon have paid out quite a lot of money."

"How dreadful! Who would do a thing like that?"

Raynes raised his eyebrows.

"Someone you know quite well."

Mr Thompson stared at him.

"You heard what Marion said on Friday night. 'That blackmailing little bitch from Chapel Road'. Miss Emily Williams. Your employee. Don't tell me you didn't know what she's been up to."

The vet was silent.

"She's been blackmailing Arlene for almost a year. You ask her how much she's had to pay. It may surprise you."

"But how did she get hold of Derek's papers? Did his wife give them to her?"

"No. I believe they were hidden in the castle at Caercraig. When Derek died, Emily took charge of all his private papers. You see, she had the keys to the castle!"

The vet continued to look deeply distressed.

"But why should she blackmail anyone?"

"She needs money for the university."

"Her mother would be horrified."

Raynes looked at the vet.

"How much are you paying her each week?"

"£25. But she earns that. She's been working here for two or three years. I've never had any cause to complain. She works hard." He paused. "But I think she's changed since she met Marc. He must have put her up to it. You probably know he's in jail . . ."

Raynes nodded.

"I visited him yesterday."

"He's a nasty piece of work."

"He is."

There was a silence in the kitchen as Raynes waited to see if the vet was going to say anything more. He wasn't. So, with some reluctance, Raynes moved on – into more dangerous territory.

"I'm surprised you didn't know more about Emily's extra-curricular activities."

"I had no idea. Arlene never said."

"Arlene wasn't her only victim. From what I have seen, you have been paying her fifty pounds a week in addition to the £25 she earns. You've already paid out more than £2000. That's quite a large amount of money."

There was a desperate look in Mr Thompson's eyes – and his voice was reduced to a whisper.

"How did you know about that?"

"I've been examining her bank accounts."

"Did she show them to you?"

"No," said Raynes. "But her mother did. As you said, Mrs

Williams was deeply worried about where all this money was coming from. Fortunately, she also found a little blue notebook, containing a list of all the people whom she was blackmailing – including you and Arlene – and we were able to match the names to the sums paid. Mrs Williams has asked me to try and put things right. It can't go on."

The fact that the Inspector knew all about the payments completely floored the vet. He pushed his glass away. He put his hands to his head and groaned. He never realized that Inspector Raynes had lied to him. His account sounded both straightforward and reasonable. Mrs Williams would naturally be distressed.

Mr Thompson pulled himself together.

"Mr Raynes," he said. "Will you please go. I need to have time to think about all this. What I am going to say to Mrs Williams? It's been a terrible shock."

The Inspector had a helpful look on his face.

"I'm sure it has. But it can hardly have come as a surprise. You've been paying her for forty-eight weeks. And Arlene has been paying for the same length of time. Either you were paying her for sex . . ."

Mr Thompson reacted violently.

"I have never touched her!"

"You've led a blameless life?"

"I have. I've never touched any woman since Catherine died."

Raynes said: "I believe you. But there must have been some other reason why you paid out so much money. Did Derek Barclay know something about you – something which could have caused you deep embarrassment?"

Mr Thompson objected strongly to this suggestion:

"Derek Barclay had nothing on me!"

The Inspector looked thoughtful

"But perhaps you had something on him?"

"Mr Raynes, stop playing games with me! Tell me what you know."

The Inspector hesitated – before revealing his hand.

"I appreciate," he said, "that this is a very difficult matter to raise. But Virginia Barclay told me that her husband had an affair with your wife, Catherine, many years ago. This must have been very hurtful to you – as it was to the others. Are there any letters . . . any photographs . . .?"

Mr Thompson drew a deep breath.

"There are no photographs and no letters. But, as you say, there are many bitter memories. Catherine and I befriended Virginia and Derek before they got married. They stayed with us most weekends. I had no idea anything had happened between her and Derek. She never said. My wife and I were completely devoted to each other. I nursed her right through her last illness. We couldn't have been closer."

"How did you find out?"

"She confessed. Just a few days before she died. Clearly, it had been troubling her. She wanted to be honest with me. It would have been better if she had said nothing. But she felt she had to tell me . . ."

Tears poured down the vet's cheeks.

Raynes said: "Did you forgive her?"

"Of course."

"But you never forgave him?"

"No." He sighed deeply. "As you say, it happened a long time ago. He had moved on – to Marion and Lady Margaret. He probably had an affair with Emily Williams . . . I shouldn't be surprised."

"Were you glad to hear he had died?"

"I must confess I was. I felt that justice had been done."

There was another silence. And Raynes was glad of it. He was wondering how much this man could take. But since he had now begun to speak, the Inspector felt inclined to push his luck a little bit further.

He said quietly: "It was justice in which you had a hand."

Mr Thompson looked at him sharply.

"It was an accident!"

Raynes shook his head sadly.

"If it was an accident, why are you being forced to pay £50

a week? Emily must have some proof that you were involved in Derek's death. In fact, I know she has. I think that you took justice into your hands and she is now holding a gun to your head. And because you know you are guilty, you are paying up. Not for sex – but for silence – to protect your secret."

The vet seemed to have recovered his nerve.

"Mr Raynes, this conversation must go no further. I cannot answer any more of your questions. I certainly do not accept any suggestion that I was involved in Derek Barclay's death. I must consult a lawyer."

"I think it would be inadvisable to bring in anyone else."

"Well, I'm certainly not saying anything more to you. You are a police officer."

Raynes said: "That is true. But I am not a member of the Welsh constabulary. I have no powers to arrest you – or charge you. This case has already gone through the proper legal channels. The coroner's court has decided that it was an accident. I am not going to take any steps to overturn that verdict."

"Well, why are you here?"

"Just to find out the truth. Tom Hayward invited me over to Pwddldwc to spend a weekend on the Railway. But that was not his real reason for inviting me. He wanted to put an end to Virginia Barclay upsetting all the visitors by saying that a member of the Railway had murdered her husband. I was asked to decide one way or the other.

"Given the facts of the case, I had no doubt that it was murder. Virginia had every reason to criticize the coroner's verdict. I told her I would do my very best to find out what had happened.

"Once I met the members of the Railway, I realized I had opened a particularly nasty can of worms. And the wickedness is not just confined to the Railway people.

"The locals seem just as bad. I have had to deal with theft, fraud, adultery, alcoholism and violence. Poison letters are being circulated and people are subject to blackmail. There has also been a massive cover-up with regard to Lady

Margaret's son. Many people have tried to prevent me completing my investigation. I have been threatened with knives and guns. As you yourself are witness.

"If I am answerable to anyone, it is to Mr Hayward who commissioned me to discover the truth. I also think Virginia deserves an honest explanation of what happened in the railway yard that night. But she does necessarily need to know the name of the murderer. Beyond that, I will not go.

"I think, Mr Thompson, that speaking to me may be your safest option."

39: Venienti Occurite Morbo

Mr Thompson looked at the Inspector. The light of battle had returned to his eyes.

"So you think I am a murderer, Mr Raynes? But have you any proof? Nothing but a name in a blue notebook and £2000 generously given to a schoolgirl, hoping to go to university."

Raynes welcomed the challenge. The opportunity to put his cards on the table and demonstrate the undeniable truth that the vet had killed Derek Barclay in the station yard.

He began quietly; "When I first heard about you, it was as a man with a great compassion for animals. Your care for Dolly was noted by everyone. You thought nothing about going out late at night to care for sick and dying animals. Indeed, your alibi for the night of July 10 last year was that you were with David Cadwaller looking after Princess.

"When I challenged you on the accuracy of that alibi, you were able to produce immediate written proof from your business files. You were out for three nights in a row caring for this particular animal, which would suggest to most people that you had no other thought on your mind. However, even at 10.00pm, the night is still young.

"During those three nights, Derek Barclay was believed to be in Pwddldwc. His wife thought he was here; but no one saw either him or his van. And yet, on the Monday morning, his van was seen in the car park at Caercraig and his body was lying unnoticed in the station yard.

"This was Derek's last weekend in Pwddldwc. He was about to go on holiday with his wife and family. I am sure that had he been in the village that weekend, he would have dropped in to the *Railway Inn* and had a pint. The fact that he didn't made me think that he was tied up, drugged up – or otherwise rendered incapable of moving. My thoughts naturally turned to the two people who dispense drugs – you and Dr Campbell.

"Most of my speculation about Derek's whereabouts centred on two farms. Penbass and Castle Farm. It would be easy to hide Derek's van in some outhouse. No one would see it there.

"Ifor had every reason to hate Derek because of his frequent adultery with his wife. Usually, he drowned his sorrows in drink. But perhaps, at last, one dark night, the worm turned and Ifor struck back?

"When I heard about Sir David, I thought I was on firmer ground. Here was a man who had a violent dislike for Mr Barclay. He had already attacked his van and slashed his tyres. Sir David was quite open about his desire to kill him. But on the night in question he had an alibi. You. This made me wonder if you had done the murder together.

"But then you told me that you had discouraged Sir David from doing anything nasty and had suggested that other people might have their own plans for getting rid of him. Perhaps you had your own plan? But what would be your motive? Your wife's relationship with Derek happened quite a long time ago. Her confession was known only to the two of you. There was no honour to be defended. Why should you want to kill Mr Barclay now?

"I think that you would agree that Sir David was the most obvious suspect. He had a very strong motive. His wife's affair was bad enough. But to discover that she had produced an illegitimate child was a deep humiliation for a proud man. The fact that, for four or five years, the child was passed off as his son and heir was almost unbearable.

"We know what he did to his wife. Beating her so brutally that she ended up in a private nursing home for three weeks. His anger was also visited upon the child – possibly adopted – more probably killed. It may be that you did give him those capsules of morphine . . ."

"I did not."

"If the child's body is found, we shall discover the truth."

Raynes' casual remark hit the vet hard. He had not thought of the body being exhumed and examined. The Inspector watched his reaction with interest. He had been sure the man was lying.

"So now we move to the station yard and a man with two legs severed beneath the knees. He has died of heart failure, loss of blood or shock. Shock is the least probable cause of death because Derek was heavily sedated. But much of the evidence that he had been sedated would have been lost as the blood drained out of his legs into the ballast beneath.

"This is not your usual sort of murder! I wondered if this sort of death had ever happened before. I asked my colleague in Grasshallows to look up police records and see what he could find. Almost immediately, he discovered that a Mr Philip Packer had died on a stretch of railway line at the entrance to the Box tunnel. His head and one arm were chopped off. I am told that Mrs Packer has often talked about her husband's death, secure in the knowledge that she had a cast-iron alibi.

"Sitting in your favourite corner seat in the *Railway Inn*, you would no doubt have heard the story related several times. The germ of an idea was planted in your mind. A drugged body, a stretch of railway line and a dismembered corpse. Difficult to prove that it was more than an accident – and yet the circumstances are deeply suspicious. No fingerprints, no rope attached to the body; very little of the drug left in the system. Five days of exposure to the elements; the rapid decomposition of the body – and there is very little evidence to go on . . ."

"You admit that?"

"I do."

Thompson the vet poured himself another gin and tonic.

Raynes continued: "Now Derek's death did look like an inside job – done by one of the Railway staff. Someone who could drive the diesel loco. Someone who had access to the keys. Just two or three people at the most. Which is why some people have pointed the finger at Brian Williamson or Father Morris.

"The diesel would have to be moved out of its siding. The points are manually controlled – so no problem there. The diesel was coupled to just one coach – because there were no grisly remains on the wheels of the other two carriages. That coach was uncoupled and towed about twenty yards down the track. The body was placed on the line. The coach was shunted back – over the legs. The diesel was driven back to its siding. The job was done in less than ten minutes.

"Now, of course, a tractor could perform the same task. And so could a 3.5 litre Land Rover." Raynes smiled. "I noticed that Sir David has one or two high-powered Land Rovers. They seem to be his favourite form of transport. And you, of course, have a similar model parked outside your front door.

"The empty whisky bottle – free of all fingerprints – was left beside the track. A clear suggestion that Derek had been drinking that evening. Under the influence of drink, he had either fallen beneath the carriages or committed suicide. He had consumed some whisky – or someone had poured it down his throat; and the rest had been poured over his clothes.

"This was not a very good idea, because Derek Barclay did not drink whisky. His favourite tipple was lager – as you should have known. His wife's suspicions were aroused when she heard about the whisky. A glass or two was possible; but not a whole bottle. That was the first clear sign of foul play.

"When was the job done? It could have been done at about 8.00pm; before you went off to see Princess. But I think that was unlikely. Quite a few people were still around at that time of night. You might have been seen. It is far more likely to have been done when you returned from Castle Farm. All the Railway staff would have long since gone and most of the locals were now tucked up in their beds. That would suggest some time after 11.00pm.

"Derek Barclay was lying, heavily sedated, somewhere in this house. Perhaps in the room where you do your operations? Where you cremate the bodies? Nobody would be in here over the weekend. Derek was perhaps wrapped up in a thick sleeping bag. He could be dragged quickly out of the house and into the back of the Land Rover. It would take only a couple of minutes to reach the station gates.

"And there was no problem getting in! You had Derek's keys. One might speculate how they got into Emily's hands. I would guess that they were lying somewhere in the surgery. She saw them; she recognized them; she took them. I suspect that it was then that she started to blackmail you."

The vet suddenly looked very uncomfortable. He had been sitting back, listening to Raynes' exposition, with a superior smile on his lips. But that look had gone. Mention of the keys had caught him off his guard.

"Once you were inside the station yard, you were fairly safe. Your Land Rover could easily cross the railway lines. You have a massive tow bar. There would be no problem coupling and uncoupling the coaches. Derek would have been unloaded and laid across the track so that his legs overhung the right-hand rail. His ankles would be neatly tied to the left-hand line with some bandages or tapes – or something that would not leave any mark on his flesh.

"With Derek lying slightly downhill, it would have been quite easy to pour whisky into his mouth. If you poured too much in, you might have choked him. Perhaps you did? The rest was poured indiscriminately over his clothes and the empty bottle was left close to his left hand. Perhaps originally his fingers clutched the bottle.

"You got back in the Land Rover and started your powerful engine. You pushed the ten ton coach back down the line and over his legs. You recoupled the carriages. And the unpleasant job was done. You looked under the carriage to make sure that the lower legs had been cut off. They had moved a few inches – but so had the body. Derek's blood was now draining out. When his heart stopped, it would be reduced to a dribble. You removed the tapes or bandages holding the ankles and threw them into the back of your car. You drove out of the station gates, leaving Derek to decompose. You knew it would be four or five days before his body would be found.

"I would imagine that when you returned home, you burnt your gloves, the sleeping bag, and all the tapes or bandages in your cremation furnace.

"There remained Derek's van. It was still hidden in your garage – or perhaps somewhere on the sea-front. It must not be seen – or it would give the game away. It needed to be moved to some place where Derek might have slept overnight. The castle was the obvious choice. Only a few hundred yards from Castle Farm! If suspicions were to arise, they would point to Sir David Cadwaller – not you.

"So, some time after midnight, you drove Derek's van up to the station car park at Caercraig. You locked the van and walked home. It was a beautiful, starry night . . ."

Raynes paused to see how James Thompson was reacting. He had paid very close attention to the Inspector's narrative. He had shown a professional interest in the details – almost as if he was checking off the points one by one, noting any errors.

He smiled at the Inspector.

"Is that it?"

"Almost."

With a more confident voice, he said: "I don't think you have been able to provide any proof that I murdered Derek. You have painted a very interesting picture. I am sure the murderer did many of the things you have suggested. But there is nothing to prove it was me. Do you honestly think that I would risk my life, my job, my place in this community – just to get rid of that worthless man? I am quite sure Ifor

Davies, Archie Campbell, Graham Naylor, Brian Williamson – and even Simon Jacoby – could have organized that same scenario which you have described. If I had wanted to kill him, I can assure you that I would have killed him many years ago. Why should I wait till now?"

Raynes said: "When did Catherine die?"

"Two years ago."

"In 1988. And she made her confession shortly before she died?"

The vet was silent.

There would have been no reason to kill Derek many years before.

Raynes said: "I think this murder was planned very carefully. Over the space of a year. It was designed to look like an accident – or a suicide. The victim was completely unprepared. He wasn't expecting an attack. You invited him back to your house for a meal. You poisoned his drink – or his food."

Mr Thompson laughed.

"Is that why you haven't touched your Carlsberg? Are you frightened I might bump you off?"

Raynes eyed him coldly.

"You can't be too careful round here. One attempt on my life was quite enough. Anyway, I've left a couple of notes to say where I was going. Just in case."

Mr Thompson shook his head.

"You're paranoid!"

"Not at all. Just plain common sense."

If he was face to face with a cold-blooded killer, he could not afford to make a single mistake. This man was cornered. Anything might happen.

Raynes laid his final card on the table.

"There is just one more piece to go into the jigsaw. When you were driving Derek's van up to Caercraig, you were seen turning into the lane leading up to the castle. You were turning off the Pwddldwc to Abernirvana road. Marc was taking Emily home and they were in his car when they saw you.

Marc did not know who you were; but Emily did. He did not recognize Derek's van; but Emily did. Their headlights caught you for a few seconds. But it was enough.

"At that moment, they did not know why you were driving Derek's van. But the discovery of the body in the station yard explained everything. She knew – they knew – that you had been involved in Derek's death."

Raynes shrugged his shoulders.

"That's it."

Mr Thompson said nothing – but he seemed to be breathing a little more heavily than before. And he seemed to be thinking. Raynes watched him like a hawk. In a second, he could be in a fight for his life.

But the vet was not seeking a fight. He was wondering how to get out of this disastrous situation. Could anything be salvaged from the wreckage? Could the Inspector be trusted to speak only to Tom Hayward? Mr Thompson knew that he could trust Tom to be discreet. He would never say or do anything that might harm the Railway or the village.

He looked up.

"I'm in your hands."

"Indeed you are. But I shall keep my promise. I'm not going to report you to the police. I'm not going to ask the coroner to re-open the inquest. I'm not going to prevent you continuing your valuable work in this community on which hundreds of lives depend. Animal lives.

"I am going to ask the Welsh police to investigate the whereabouts of Timothy Cadwaller, Derek's illegitimate child. I think we should find out what has happened to him. I think all the excitement about Sir David's trial will provide an effective cover for anything you have done."

"What about Emily?"

"Well, you know her better than I do. I think she is very fond of you. Very protective. When I came to see you on Thursday night, she was very shocked. I now understand why. But her first instinct was to protect you. I think that is a good omen.

"I would suggest that you keep paying her £50 a week. It is a small price for freedom. It will keep her happy. She will need a lot of financial help over the next three years. Once she has got her degree, she will probably leave Wales for good – as her sisters have done.

"If she ever threatens to say anything, you could remind her that she could go to jail for all the things she has done. She has the keys which she pinched from the surgery. She knew that you were involved in Derek's death, but she did not report what she knew. She has committed blackmail on the grand scale and she was involved in the burning and looting of several holiday homes. I think she will realize the wisdom of keeping her mouth shut. As a Welsh girl, she is naturally full of guile!"

"There speaks a *saesneg*!"

Raynes stood up.

He smiled.

"Did I miss anything?"

Thompson the vet looked up.

"It was chloroform – not poison. Old-fashioned methods often work best. It was followed by a much diluted shot of Xylazine hydrochloride repeated every three hours. And it was not a sleeping bag but a horse blanket that was used to transport him.

"You were right about the Land Rover and the van. But I would have preferred to get away with it. I'm sorry about that. I'm not sorry about anything else. I have no regrets for what I did. I still cannot forget what he did to my beloved Catherine and the guilt she must have endured all those years."

Raynes nodded.

"Revenge is a dish best served cold."

"Ice-cold."

Raynes moved towards the door. He would feel safer out in the fresh air. He wanted to get out of he house before Arlene arrived to take James out to lunch. He had been watching the clock, and she would be here some time in the next fifteen minutes.

The vet followed him out into the driveway.

Something seemed to be troubling him.

Raynes asked: "Have you got something else on your mind?"

"I have."

Mr Thompson adjusted the wing mirror on his Land Rover. He looked at the Inspector.

"Have you sent in your report to the Welsh police?"

"It's drafted; but not sent."

"I think I may be able to help you."

Raynes was surprised.

"In what way?"

The vet stared into the distance.

"I think you said that Margaret's child, Timothy, was buried in Lake Nirvana . . ."

"It is a possibility."

Mr Thompson shook his head.

"No. He is buried in the castle at Caercraig."

"Really?"

"His body was buried in the ruins of the castle tower . . . Derek found the box containing his remains when he started restoring it. He re-buried the body in a more secure location, and he told Sir David what he had found . . . and what he had done."

"No wonder Sir David hated him!"

"Yes. But in the same conversation, he told him that he was not Timothy's father. I don't know whether Sir David believed him. Probably not. Derek told him that he had signed an affidavit telling the police where Timothy's body could be found. If anything happened to him, that affidavit would go straight to the police.

"I knew nothing about any of this until after Derek had died. The only person who knew anything about it was Emily. Perhaps, for safety's sake, he placed the document in her care. And when Derek had his 'accident', she immediately grabbed his keys and made for the castle tower. I didn't know anything about the blackmailing material Derek had accumulated over the years. But she knew. He must have told her about it. And, of course, she made the most of it. And continues to do so."

"So where is the document now?

Raynes posed as an innocent abroad. There had been no sign of the affidavit in the two box files.

"I have it. She was terrified that Sir David would find out – so she gave it to me."

"Is it filed in the surgery?"

"No. I wouldn't leave it there. My secretary might find it. No, it's hidden in this car. In a lockfast safety box. I was keeping it in case I was accused. I think it would provide sufficient motive for Sir David killing Derek."

"Indeed."

The vet looked Raynes in the face.

"I think you should have this document. I think you should send it with your report to the Welsh police. They may decide to dig up the castle. This document will show them where to look."

Raynes said: "If you give me the affidavit, I shall send one copy to the police and one to Lady Margaret. I think she ought to know what has happened to her child."

"She was too afraid to ask."

"And Derek never told her?"

"He didn't want to hurt her. At least, that's what he told Emily. Of course, he could have been lying . . ."

Raynes said provocatively: "So he died of an overdose of morphine?"

The vet frowned.

"The child may have been sedated – he probably was – but the bullet is still lodged in the child's brain. I haven't seen it; but that's what the document says. I shall get it for you."

Mr Thompson opened the rear door of his car and unlocked a steel drawer built in under the back seat.

Raynes was still frightened that Mr Thompson might draw out a pistol instead of an affidavit. But the vet only extracted two sheets of paper, and then locked the drawer.

"I keep my special injections in there. It's safer."

Raynes quickly skimmed through the document. He read it twice.

He looked at the vet.

"Thank you. This will be a great help. I will send this with my report to the Welsh police. I think that this will ensure that Sir David serves many years in jail. Can you make sure that Timothy's grave remains untouched?"

"Emily will see to that."

Out of the corner of his eye, Raynes saw the large BMW turning into the street.

Arlene Jacoby would not want to see him.

"Do you have a back gate?"

Mr Thompson pointed to the left.

"The tradesman's entrance is over there."

40: No Whistle-blowers Here!

The Inspector returned to the *Railway Inn* and packed his case. He descended to the front hallway where Anna had already drawn up his bill.

"So, Mr Raynes, you are leaving us?"

"My work is done."

"You are not staying for lunch?"

"I thought the restaurant and bar were closed till 7.00pm on Sundays?"

"We were given special dispensation this weekend for *Lady Ermintrude*."

"Otherwise I might have stopped off at the castle for a couple of ice creams."

Anna laughed.

"Remember the cameras!"

"Ah, yes. The ever-present eye."

"Besides, if you had gone up there today, you'd have found Bob doing his stuff. Not quite so romantic!" Her eyes twinkled mischievously. "Whereas, after lunch, I was thinking of trying on my new red bikini. Would that have encouraged you to stay a little longer?"

Raynes smiled.

"I think it probably would. Especially if Bob was well out of the way." He looked at the steady flow of customers making their way into the restaurant and the public bar. "But surely you are far too busy?"

Anna came down to earth and handed him the bill. "I suppose we are." She adjusted the gold hoops in her ears. "And what would Marion say?"

"She got there first!"

Anna chuckled.

"Actually, we tossed up for you in the kitchen. And she won!"

"Is that how it was?"

"You men have no idea!"

Anna watched the Inspector signing his cheque.

"So you have found what you were looking for?"

"I have identified the murderer – and spoken to him."

"Will you be reporting him to the police?"

"No. I see no point in re-opening old wounds."

"James will be very relieved to hear that."

Raynes looked at Anna.

"You knew who the murderer was?"

"Of course we knew; but none of us would have said a word. He's a lovely man. What would Pwddldwc do without him? Who would look after all the animals?"

"Do you know why he killed Derek?"

Anna nodded sadly.

"I had James weeping in my arms the night Catherine told him what she'd been doing with Derek. Till then, he knew nothing about it. It was a terrible blow."

"He took his time in getting his revenge."

"I think he wanted to do it properly. To make sure it looked like an accident. It was Mrs Packer who gave him the idea."

"He didn't show much mercy."

"He had a lot of anger. The desire for revenge burned extremely brightly."

"What did he say when the body was found?"

"'One less bastard!'"

"Did you share his view?"

"Certainly not! I was very fond of Derek. He was one of my exes. He got me this job." She smiled. "He saw me in and out of my bikini. It was a bit smaller in those days. Didn't have to stuff it all in!" She laughed sadly. "And he was a regular customer – in season; out of season. He played darts with Bob. Got on well with him. And, of course, he did so much for the Railway. His death really hurt."

"But you didn't say anything?"

"No one said anything!" She looked at the Inspector. "I'm sure I've said it to you before; but trade is all important in this part of Wales. All we've got is the Railway. Without it, this place would be dead. Bad publicity – murder – would do us all terrible damage. It's better to say there's been an unfortunate accident. That's soon forgotten. But murders – never!"

Anna looked at Raynes, wondering how much more she could say.

"That's why people disliked you so much. Because you brought it all back. Listening to that wretched woman in the tea room. Asking all those questions. Simon told Tom to make sure you never set foot in the village ever again. He was very angry.

"But then, on Thursday, back you came. It gave us all a really nasty shock. And Sir David could have killed you. I did warn you . . ."

"You did. And I was very lucky to escape. But I have now found the answers to all my questions."

"Was there more than one question?"

Raynes looked at Anna.

"A great deal more. Who was the person sending poison pen letters? Who was blackmailing whom? How many holiday homes were burnt down? Was Marc the only person involved? Why did it take so long to restore *Lady Ermintrude*? Was the Appeal money embezzled? What happened to

Margaret Cadwaller's son? Who was his father?"

"You got an answer to all those questions?"

"Yes. In just three days," Raynes said proudly. "Not bad going. But of course I knew what I was looking for when I came back. And Father Morris was a great help."

"He didn't know about James."

"No. He thought it was Simon Jacoby."

Anna looked thoughtful.

"It could have been . . ."

"But it wasn't." Raynes said firmly.

"No. And you managed to get all the answers."

Raynes sighed.

"Things would have been a lot easier if I had not had to contend with that little bitch in Chapel Road. She tried to trip me up at every turn. She has a finger in so many pies."

"Marion dealt with her most effectively."

"She did. But I didn't realize how dangerous she was."

"It'll be a lot better for everyone when she goes off to university . . ."

"In Grasshallows!" said Raynes.

"Of course!" Anna laughed. "That's where you live! I would say your troubles have only just begun! But if you need to escape, come back to Pwddldwc. You'll always get a warm welcome down here."

41: Tunnel Vision

When Detective-Constable Carlisle arrived at Grasshallows Police Station on Monday morning, Raynes was already at his desk.

"All done?"

"Yes. The police have arrested a man."

"For Derek's murder?"

"No. For attempting to murder me!"

Carlisle laughed.

"You enjoy living dangerously."

"This was 'edge of the cliff' stuff."

He told Carlisle what had happened in the hallway of the *Railway Inn*.

"A bed-warming pan?"

"A solid copper antique – with a long wooden handle. My guardian angel hit him so hard she could have killed him. They've told her she may be charged with assault."

"But now he's behind bars?"

"Just temporarily. Once his lawyers get to work, he'll soon be out on bail."

"Then he'll be back on your trail?"

"I hope not. I've put in a report charging him with child murder. That was about two or three years ago. When I made the charges, there were about thirty witnesses present. No one knows exactly what happened to the child. But I have been told that his body is buried at the castle. If it turns out to be him, then Sir David will go to jail for quite a long while."

"That's Derek's child?"

"We thought it was Derek's child but it now appears that he may have been fathered by someone else. I think the real father was Virginia Barclay's new boyfriend . . ."

"The driver of the Jaguar?"

"Yes."

"Does he know he was the father?"

"Probably not. But he might have been quite a good choice. Rich; upper crust; heir to the Greenaway millions."

Carlisle looked at the two box files sitting on Raynes' desk.

"So what are you doing now?"

"Tidying up. I'm having all this stuff photocopied. It's evidence against a blackmailer."

"A blackmailer?"

"Yes, we've had the lot. Adultery, pornographic photos, fraud. Poison pen letters, accusations of embezzlement, blackmail. Not to mention Mrs Packer killing off her husband. It's been a most exciting case."

"Has the murderer been arrested?"

"No."

Carlisle was surprised.

Raynes said: "I quite liked the guy. And as you know, I have no jurisdiction in Wales. The case is closed. The coroner has given his verdict. I'm going to hand over the facts of this case to Tom Hayward – and let him decide what to do."

Carlisle shook his head in amazement.

"It's most unlike you – not to follow the thing through."

Raynes smiled grimly.

"Mr Hayward's going to face some nasty shocks. I want to see what he thinks we should do."

"Will you need me?"

"Of course I shall need you. I must have full notes of what is said." Raynes looked around the office. "We shall need quite a lot of coffee – and some hot milk. I think our distinguished guest prefers latte." The Inspector looked towards the main office. "Perhaps you could ask one of the grateful dead to rustle up a packet of chocolate biscuits. I should like to appear welcoming."

Carlisle laughed.

"Poor chap! He doesn't know what he's in for."

"No," said Raynes, "But he got me into this mess. So he must accept the consequences."

* * * *

The distinguished publisher of the *Grasshallows Echo* appeared twenty minutes later. By then, all the photocopying had been done and there was a strong smell of good coffee pervading the office.

Raynes stood up.

"Good morning, Tom."

"Good morning, Inspector."

Mr Hayward had learnt to treat any such signs of bonhomie from the Inspector with great suspicion.

Coffee was poured out and Raynes moved his chair out into the centre of the room, so that it looked like a casual conversation. As it might have been, had not Carlisle been checking his pencils before sitting down to take notes.

"This is Detective-Constable Carlisle."

"We've met before."

Since there seemed to be no willingness to engage in small talk, Raynes plunged straight in.

"I've found your murderer."

"I'm very glad to hear it."

"It's not perhaps the person you suspected . . ."

"It never is."

" . . . Mr James Thompson – the vet."

"Really?"

That did surprise him.

"Have you notified the local police?"

"No. I'm leaving the decision to you."

Whilst Mr Hayward was digesting this unpleasant piece of information, Raynes briefly outlined the case:

"Virginia Barclay gave us a list of some of the ladies her husband had associated with down in Puddleduck. Not a complete list. Not an up-to-date list. But an interesting collection of female talent – including the unforgettable Ariel Stevenson!

"Amongst that list of delectable young ladies was Catherine Thompson. That name did not immediately register with me – although on my first evening with Mrs Williams, she did mention that Catherine Thompson was one of those who died because the cancer treatment she received came too little and too late.

"It seems that Mr Thompson had no knowledge of his wife's affair with Derek Barclay. He and his wife had befriended the young couple – before their marriage. But Derek abused that kindness. It might have passed unnoticed but – before she died – Catherine decided to confess to her husband."

"A great mistake."

"He forgave her; but he did not forgive Derek. A deep anger burned within him. Once Catherine had died, he decided that he must get his revenge." Raynes paused. "Catherine died about two years ago . . .?"

"Yes. About that."

"He had heard from many other people about Derek's affairs. He had probably looked on them with amused detachment. But, once it had impacted upon his own family, he began to think about the damage Derek had done to so many people's lives. He and Marion had had a great time – but what about Ifor? He was a broken man. Derek's affair with Arlene had led to guilt and fear. Margaret Cadwaller's illegitimate child had been passed off as Sir David's heir. The child might have been killed, but Sir David's anger remained at fever pitch.

"James Thompson told the landowner not to do anything rash. But whatever advice he tendered to Sir David, he decided to get rid of Derek himself. He decided – as many have done before – to commit the perfect murder.

"Sitting in the corner seat in the bar, smoking his aromatic tobacco, he listened to Joyce Packer telling how she had got rid of her husband. Like me, Mr Thompson had no doubt that Joyce was guilty of her husband's murder; but she had the perfect alibi and a friend willing to commit perjury on her behalf.

"He decided that he would also stage an accident – this time in the station yard. It would happen on a Sunday night when all the volunteers had gone home. There would be no one around for the next four or five days which would ensure that, by the time the body was found, it would have begun to decompose – possibly removing vital evidence.

"It was a particularly cruel murder, which shows how much hatred and anger Mr Thompson felt for Derek. He did not rush to kill him. He waited till the man delivered himself into his hands . . . A Friday night when he had nowhere to stay. He invited him to supper. I thought he might have put something nasty into his food or drink, but James told me he had used good, old-fashioned chloroform.

"Once he had got Derek out cold, he injected him with repeated doses of Xylazine hydrochloride, a substance he used to sedate sick animals. A few extra grams could easily be accounted for in his records, which were scrupulously maintained.

"It was fortunate that he acted when he did, because he was able to provide for himself an excellent alibi. He was looking after one of Sir David's prize cows on Friday night, Saturday night, and Sunday night. It also provided an excellent alibi for the farmer, who had been threatening to kill Derek for the past two years. One alibi – two suspects – both neatly covered.

"It was on the Sunday night, when he got home from Castle Farm, that the murder plan was put into operation. James wrapped Derek's body in a horse blanket and transported it down to the station yard. Using his powerful Land Rover, he moved the carriages back and forward, which cut off Derek's legs and left him to bleed to death. The whisky bottle was left to suggest a drunken accident; but all the other evidence was taken away. Mr Thompson believed he had committed the perfect murder."

Mr Hayward was anxious to make sure Inspector Raynes had got the right man. He asked: "Did James tell you all this?"

"He added a few details."

"But he didn't plead guilty?"

"No. The evidence came later."

"And what was that?"

"Well, like all murderers, he made a few mistakes. His first error was to get rid of Derek's van which had been hidden in his garage. He decided to move it to the station car park at Caercraig. But as he turned off the main road, he was seen by Emily and Marc who were on their way back to Pwddldwc. They couldn't think why the vet should be driving Derek's van. But once the body was found, Emily realized what must have happened. She also recognized Derek's keys lying in the surgery whilst she was doing her daily cleaning job."

"She knew?"

"I told you she knew. But she didn't say anything. Like most people in the village, she had a great affection for the vet. He was a pillar of the community and she felt sorry for him after the death of his wife."

"She should have reported what she had seen."

"Indeed she should. But as I told you in the dining room in the *Railway Inn* on Friday night, she was blackmailing the murderer at the rate of £50 a week. He has now paid Emily £2000 to keep her mouth shut."

"Good God!"

"She was a vital witness on the night of the murder; but said nothing. She found Derek's keys; but did not hand them in to the police. She used the keys to obtain Derek Barclay's stash of letters and photographs, which he had hidden in the castle tower. With that material, she has blackmailed Arlene Jacoby, Archie Campbell, Father Morris, Lydia Naylor and Joanne Kennedy – and many others. She has used Derek's death to her own advantage and, in the process, feathered her nest. She is now worth over £8000."

Raynes sat back in his chair to see how Mr Hayward would react to all this.

His face was blank and his mouth was hanging open. Raynes could see that he had two gold teeth. The man was staring at the carpet as if he was in a trance. He could not believe all that he was hearing. At the beginning, he had thought James Thompson was the villain of the piece; but now it appeared that Emily was equally guilty of perverting the course of justice and could face a long jail sentence.

All he could say was: "What am I going to say to Mrs Williams?"

Raynes thought that this was probably the least of Mr Hayward's problems.

Before proceeding to the next part of his *denouement*, the Inspector remembered his duties as a host. "More coffee?" he said.

But Mr Hayward made no reply. He probably didn't even hear the question.

Raynes poured out a second cup for both of them and gave Carlisle the chance to catch up.

Eventually, the publisher picked up his coffee and drank

about half a cup.

Raynes decided it was time to continue.

He said: "I expect you were wondering why Emily and Marc were travelling back to Pwddldwc so late at night . . ."

Tom was not wondering about them at all; but he was soon to be told.

" . . . They had not been burning down a cottage that night; but they had been to a holiday home twenty miles up the coast, where they had stolen cash, jewellery and antiques, which they sold at a car boot sale on Saturday 16 July . . ."

Mr Hayward looked horrified.

"Who told you this?"

"Marc."

"He's in jail!"

"I went to see him on Saturday afternoon in Swansea prison."

"You shouldn't believe anything he says!"

"Well," said Raynes apologetically, "I asked Emily to deny it, but she didn't."

"You've spoken to her?"

"She attacked me physically in the carpark at the back of the *Railway Inn* on Saturday afternoon."

Mr Hayward looked like a cornered animal.

Raynes added to his misery: "I have checked up on her bank statements and other sources of information . . . " He indicated the box files on his desk. "And they show in the utmost detail what she and Marc received from each burglary. She has received about £2000 from theft and £6000 from blackmail. I thought you would like to see the evidence . . ."

Mr Hayward continued to look appalled.

"How did you get this information?"

" . . . without any further questions!"

The harsh authority of the Inspector's words crushed any thought of protest.

He drew the box files towards him and took out the bank statements.

"Please look at these. You will notice the weekly earnings

from Mr Thompson – £25 a week. They stop in August 1989 when Marc was arrested. From then on, she used that money to pay for her bus fares to Swansea . . ."

He waited till Mr Hayward had had time to see the pattern of payments.

" . . . You will also see the £50 entries each week from Mr Thompson; the monthly payments of £100 from Arlene Jacoby and Father Morris. And the smaller sums going in at regular intervals." He pointed to a particular payment of £10.

"That's what she's getting from the Methodist minister!"

"Good God! This is terrible!"

"It is all blackmail money. If you turn back to the statements from June 1987 to June 1989, you will see large but irregular sums coming in every few months. These represent the proceeds from goods stolen and then sold. This is an immense amount of money for a schoolgirl to have accumulated in her account."

Raynes waited for the message to sink in.

"You will notice that, a short while after the money is received, it is transferred to her savings account. Her purpose was to keep her current account quite small – and avoid any awkward questions."

After Mr Hayward had had time to look through the savings book, Raynes passed over the blue notebook which recorded the totals received from the dealers and the car boot sales all neatly divided between M and E; and then the list of blackmail victims – with their names and monthly contributions.

The publisher realized that these documents must have come from Emily's home in Chapel Road. But he could not believe that the Inspector would have broken into the house and stolen them. Someone else must have taken them and given them to him. Raynes had told James Thompson that he had had the help of Mrs Williams – but that would not wash with Tom. Let him wonder who it was.

Before Mr Hayward decided to ask any more questions, Raynes said firmly:

"I have returned the love letters to Arlene Jacoby, photographs to Father Morris, incriminating documents to Joanne Kennedy and Lydia Naylor. I would appreciate your help in contacting the other blackmail victims so that we can get all the incriminating material back to them as soon as possible. I would also appreciate your advice on how we should deal with Emily Williams and James Thompson!"

Detective-Constable Carlisle drew a neat line under his notes and waited to see how Mr Hayward would respond.

There was a long silence whilst he continued to stare at the contents of the blue notebook with its damning evidence. He then went back to the current account statements and compared the figures with those in the savings book. Emily's guilt could not be clearer.

Tom was conscious that Inspector Raynes was waiting for an answer. But, understandably, he felt completely crushed by what he had seen. He had never expected to see such devastating proof of wickedness in a person he had cherished from childhood. He was totally incapable of seeing a way out. All he could think of was Mrs Williams' impending distress. Her tears. Her sorrow. How could he ever go back and stay in their house? They would never want to see him again.

To break the silence, Raynes said: "If you have no ideas, may I make a few suggestions? I think we should insist that Emily pays back all the blackmail money she has received – from everyone except Mr Thompson. That evidence will be needed if there is a trial. So that money will stay in her account.

"I feel that she may as well keep all the proceeds of the burglaries – since that case has already been dealt with. Marc has received his cut and paid the price – for the two of them. That money could be used for her expenses at university. It will make her a very rich student.

"I would suggest that she makes the withdrawals from her savings bank under your supervision. You must retain the bank book till all the victims have been repaid. You can return her current account, bank book and statements. It will give you an opportunity to discuss other issues with her. Does that seem a reasonable solution?"

Tom seemed relieved. There was a way out after all.

Raynes continued: "There is no reason why her mother should know anything about this. You can return the box files. I shall put all the blackmail material into sealed envelopes. You will write to all the victims and explain that the material will be sent back to them – and all their money repaid. You will not mention that the police have been involved. But, when I get the cheques, I will send them with the sealed envelopes to the victims. And no more will be said."

Inspector Raynes felt that he was doing a great deal more for Emily Williams than she deserved. He would get no thanks from her. She would continue to hate him. But it would help Tom to continue his personal support for the family.

"Is that fair?"

"Very fair."

"There will be no publicity. No public embarrassment. No need to employ a lawyer. No expense. But a lot depends on how you handle it. But please make it clear to Miss Williams that she must co-operate in every detail . . . Or . . . the whole lot will be sent to the Welsh police. Everything has been photocopied and I shall write a very full report of all that has happened. She must understand what will happen if she does not cooperate – to the last detail."

Tom said: "I think she will."

"Blackmail is a horrible business."

"It is. But I don't think she'll be very pleased."

"No," said Raynes. "But she will know that you have her best interests at heart."

Tom seemed to have recovered his composure.

"And what about Mr Thompson?"

"Well," said Raynes, "that is perhaps easier to deal with. What is to be gained by re-opening the case and over-turning the coroner's verdict? One man goes to jail. A man, who in every other way, plays a valued and respected part in the life of the local community. A large number of people – mostly farmers – depend on him. Who would replace him?

"Mr Thompson's life has been one of great integrity and dedication. He has not chased after other women. He nursed his dying wife with enormous care and devotion. These things cannot be ignored. He was deeply upset by his wife's confession. Totally shattered. I can understand his anger and his desire for revenge.

"There is no direct evidence linking the murder to the vet – and the circumstantial evidence would cause deep distress to other people." He paused. "I am thinking of Mrs Williams. There are several other people in the village who have already guessed that Mr Thompson killed Derek Barclay. They have said nothing – and will remain silent. I would like to leave it that way."

Raynes looked at Tom Hayward.

"You asked me to find out whether it was a murder or an accident. The commission came from you. I have told Mr Thompson that I would report my findings to you. This I have done. I think you should go to the vet and talk things through with him. I think, in this case, we should let sleeping dogs lie." He smiled.

"Suitably anaesthetized, of course!"

42: *The Last Victim*

And that should have been the end of the story! Raynes thought it was. Tom Hayward desperately hoped it was. But human beings have an unpredictable way of upsetting the applecart and bringing ruin upon themselves and their neighbours.

Mr Hayward did what he was told and went back to Pwddldwc to speak to Thompson the vet. He returned the almost empty box files to Emily and informed her that if she did not repay the blackmail money, the Inspector would send the full details of her criminal activities to the Welsh police. After a long and bitter argument, she had acquiesced. Cheques had been signed and the sealed envelopes returned to the victims. The whole process had gone smoothly – and no one was any the wiser. Mrs Williams remained completely in the dark. So far, so good!

The bad news was that, on the Friday morning, Sir David's lawyers succeeded in getting him released on bail. The angry landowner was allowed to return to Castle Farm whilst further investigations were made into the fate of the missing child.

Following the receipt of the affidavit from Inspector Raynes, Margaret Cadwaller phoned Nigel Greenaway to tell him that the missing child was almost certainly his. She felt that she should warn him that the police might once again appear on his doorstep.

The news had a curious effect on Nigel. Although he dreaded another visit from Inspector Raynes, he felt a great surge of pride that he should have fathered a son. He and his wife had been married for almost twenty years – but they were childless.

His paternal joy was soon turned to dust when Lady Margaret told him that the police suspected that Sir David had killed the child and buried him in the castle at Caercraig.

This made Nigel extremely angry. Almost immediately, he came over to Pwddldwc to comfort Margaret and see whether there was any hope of finding the child's body.

It was whilst he was staying in Castle Farm that Sir David was released from prison. There was no warning that he was on his way. He walked into his kitchen to find a man in a camel-coloured dressing gown, drinking a cup of coffee and reading the *Financial Times*. Sir David did not wait to hear any explanation or excuses. He immediately went for his guns. But they had been confiscated by the police.

Except for one!

Lady Margaret had hidden a shotgun and a box of ammunition. She had not intended to use it; but she felt that she might need some protection when her husband returned home. Sir David's anger built up to its usual fever pitch. And when he did not find his guns, he attacked Nigel Greenaway with a pitchfork. Lady Margaret handed the shotgun to Nigel.

On Friday afternoon, Anna Patterson phoned Inspector Raynes to let him know that Nigel Greenaway had shot Sir David Cadwaller in his front sitting room at Castle Farm at 10.45 that morning. Nigel had now been arrested and charged with manslaughter. The writ he had issued against the Railway had been withdrawn. And P.C. Roberts had tried to give "his friend" the kiss of life, not realizing that he was dead!

This was now the chief talking point in the village – whilst the murderer and the blackmailer walked free.

Raynes asked how all this had affected the Railway. She was delighted to say: "The Puddleduck is fine and the new locomotive is proving a great success."

But there was even better news. As a thank-offering for the death of her husband, Lady Margaret had offered to pay the entire bill for *Lady E*. Dr Campbell was ecstatic – even without the help of any drugs. And Kathleen Williamson was so grateful for her generosity that she had agreed to continue as Secretary of the Railway Preservation Society.

The Inspector phoned Mr Hayward but he had already been told. Presumably by Emily. He asked how all this had affected Virginia Barclay. Tom said: "She is weeping her heart out in Wolverhampton!"

Raynes said: "Tell her that it was Sir David who killed her husband!"

Mr Hayward was shocked at the suggestion.

"But he didn't . . ."

Raynes said: "Dead men tell no tales!"

Detective-Constable Carlisle was amused by the Inspector's callous advice. At least Virginia would have someone to blame. Someone who could not answer back! Another cover-up. He hoped Tom Hayward would accept his advice.

Rather mischievously, he asked Raynes: "Who do you think will be playing with Derek's train set – now that Nigel has been arrested?"

Raynes looked at the picture of Lydia Naylor which was

now framed and had pride of place on his desk.

"Well," he said, " I can assure you of one thing. It won't be me!"